NOT CONSTANTINOPLE

NOT
CONSTANTINOPLE

A NOVEL

NICHOLAS BREDIE

DZANC
BOOKS

**DZANC
BOOKS**

5220 Dexter Ann Arbor Rd.
Ann Arbor, MI 48103
www.dzancbooks.org

Library of Congress Cataloging-in-Publication Data

Names: Bredie, Nicholas, author.
Title: Not Constantinople : a novel / Nicholas Bredie.
Description: First edition. | Ann Arbor, MI : Dzanc Books, 2017.
Identifiers: LCCN 2016038921 (print) | LCCN 2016055288 (ebook) | ISBN
   9781941088753 | ISBN 9781945814099
Subjects: LCSH: Americans--Turkey--Istanbul--Fiction. | City and town
   life--Turkey--Istanbul--Fiction. | Change (Psychology)--Fiction. |
   Istanbul (Turkey)--Fiction. | Domestic fiction. | Psychological fiction.
Classification: LCC PS3602.R4335 N68 2017 (print) | LCC PS3602.R4335 (ebook)
   | DDC 813/.6--dc23
LC record available at https://lccn.loc.gov/2016038921

First US edition: June 2017
Interior design by Michelle Dotter

Printed in the United States of America

10   9   8   7   6   5   4   3   2   1

For Nora

From the first, Istanbul had given him the impression of a town where, with the night, horror creeps out of the stones. It seemed to him a town the centuries had so drenched in blood and violence that, when daylight went out, the ghosts of its dead were its only population.

—Ian Fleming, *From Russia With Love*

These differing attitudes toward the act of conversion help to explain how more Christians turn'd Turk than vice versa—but the question "why?" remains unanswered. One Captain Hamilton explained the motive which induced some Renegadoes to stay on in Barbary: "They are tempted to forsake their God for the love of Turkish women, who are generally very beautiful."

—Peter Lamborn Wilson, *Pirate Utopias: Moorish Corsairs & European Renegadoes*

SPRING

ONE.

FRED CALLED THE POLICE twice. The strangers in the apartment just stared as he dialed. When Fred tried to explain in English, the police hung up. The second time, he tried saying "There are strangers in our apartment" in Turkish. After conferring with one another, the police said yes, there are. It wasn't the first time his phrasebook had failed him. Only later did he learn that the word he used simply described those "not from here."

The people in the apartment seemed relaxed. They had not been caught in the middle of anything. Virginia and Fred, with their sacks of smuggled care-package goods, were the ones stealing in from the darkened hallway. There were three strangers. The man had rosy puckering lips surrounded by a dark goatee. The woman and her infant came in from the kitchen. The whole place smelled of cabbage, and all the lights were on. The man stood doughily, unthreatening as Fred slammed the receiver on the vintage rotary phone. Their few Turkish friends loved that phone. As children they had used the same model to dial up fairy tales, read slowly to them by a famous actress at thousands of lira a minute. It had been a phone company scam to run up their parents' bill. Knowing that now, they were nostalgic for it all the same.

Virginia's hand found the neck of the Jack Daniel's protruding from one of the sacks. Wielding the square bottle like a mace, she demanded that the strangers remove themselves. She was like the one animatron in a wax museum, sloshing the liquor in small but sincere strokes while everyone else froze.

"Isn't that, like, an eighty-dollar bottle?" the man said, unperturbed. "Are you sure you want to waste it on me?"

"No," Fred blurted. He knew just how much he missed home: less than the eighty dollars it took to buy the Jack at the local shop, but more than seeing his smuggled bottle smashed to deliver a less than lethal blow. He muttered something weakly outraged like, "There's plenty of cheap Turkish wine in the house to kick your ass with." But an impasse had clearly settled, in the same way that stale air settled in the apartment's central corridor.

Dropping the phrasebook, Fred walked to the kitchen and took the middle knife from the magnet strip. It was not the largest knife they had, but for being neither precise nor forceful it was underused and still sharp. Returning, he said, "What the fuck do you want?"

The knife was loose in his hand, as he'd heard it ought to be when you really meant something by it.

"Er," the man said with an air of cautious self-assurance, "this is our apartment."

Fred and Virginia had floated home that evening a half-inch above the winding, broken pavements that lead to their building. They'd had one of those perfect City days. Their friend Jake was passing through, laid over on the way to work with refugees in "the real Middle East." They'd taken a brisk ferry ride across the Strait to Asia, where they'd sat eating grilled fish and drinking aniseed liquor, gazing back at the dome and spire silhouette of the City's ancient heart. From there, you could imagine the City as it had been, a place of such wealth and maritime power that distant Vikings simply referred to it as "the important city." The three of them did their best to ignore the triad of skyscrapers that loomed just in the background, by the airport.

They'd traveled back across with a nice buzz. On their way to Jake's hotel to pick up the suitcase-worth of American comforts he'd brought, they stopped off at a gallery opening on Independence Avenue. Independence Avenue ran along the spine of the promontory that defined the City's old, but not ancient, quarter. It ran a half-mile starting from the Hilton and Ceylan InterContinental hotels of the Watering Square. It ended at the underground funicular that took passengers down to the banks of the inlet and the pontoon bridge across to the ancient heart. Virtually the whole length of the Avenue was fronted by decrepit nineteenth-century arcades. They were like dusty layer cakes left in a shuttered cake shop. Though in decline, each was still a hive of activity, concealing behind its façade cobblers, watch menders, shipping companies, dealers in black-market cigarettes, shops full of clothing fallen off the back of the truck, gypsy-themed dance halls, movie palaces, and, in at least two cases, churches. The brothels and beer bars were kept to the alleys just off the Avenue, and further down were the old neighborhoods, among them High Field where Fred and Virginia lived. There were also the few galleries, mostly frequented by foreigners and Nightmakers, a class of Turkish hipsters who'd picked up a taste for urban decay in Berlin.

The show featured photos taken by a notable French performance artist. Visiting the City, she'd become fascinated by one of its modern myths: that, though the City was comprised of two peninsulas set in the water like Sistine fingers, there were people in the sprawling suburbs who had never seen the sea—migrants from the rural East who'd come to work in the vast textile mills that lined the transcontinental highway. The artist claimed to have tracked some of these people down. They lived in the infamous "built-overnight" slums that spilled off hillsides into dusty gullies. She described her process as being like Ulysses' final journey, where he is condemned to travel far enough from home that his oar is mistaken for a dowser's wand. She then piled these folk into a rented van and drove them the half hour from their homes to the water's edge.

Fred and Jake were openly skeptical—these people had to know there was water all around them. What were the chances they never took a bus to see for themselves? But Virginia thought there was something there, in the way, say, an elderly man was pictured with his eyes closed against the hazy blue open sky. Couldn't they see there was a breeze in his mustache that seemed both a surprise and a relief? The men said perhaps they hadn't had enough aniseed liquor to make it out.

They'd gone back to Jake's hotel room, where he loaded them up with black beans and Mexican hot sauce and organic almond butter and vanilla extract and, most importantly, tax-free liquor. "Happy Valentines Day," he had said, though that was a few days past. It felt more like Christmas, the one they'd just missed because their new Turkish employers didn't believe in it. Christmas Day they'd both been holding class, College Writing in English, for their Turkish pupils up at the Castle.

Needless to say, on their way home Fred and Virginia had been thinking about an apple with almond butter and a nightcap, and not the bizarre facet of Turkish property law that had come up months

ago when they signed their lease. Their landlord was a British journalist named Marvin, with a boarding-school haircut and a tendency
for digressions. His new Turkish wife had poured the tulip glasses of
tea and neatly presented each of them with a cookie. "Now the thing
is," Marvin had said, "there are laws about foreigners buying property
here in the neighborhoods in the old part of the City. Just like there
are laws against foreigners buying antiques. You have to understand it
from the Turkish perspective. They've been burned before—foreigners making off with valuable things, the Elgin Marbles and so forth.
Those belonged to the Turks at the time, though I think the Greeks
would be sore to admit it. Regardless we have them now, and possession is nine-tenths as we say. But as for this place, in order to buy it,
I had to have a Turkish proxy. An old man. He was sanctioned by the
government to buy here, so I gave him the money to buy it. As far as
I know, he and the money went back to the village in the east where
his family had first come from. He's likely dead. I haven't heard from
him in three years. When the laws change, we have the documents to
prove we own the flat. But in the meantime, keep all the bills in his
name. Everyone does this."

Fred and Virginia had been so new they didn't even expect the
cookies to be salty. Of course they'd signed the lease, accepting this as
normal. They did ask why the neighborhood was called High Field.
Marvin didn't really know.

"Maybe it was once where the fields began? Honestly, the names
don't necessarily make sense. No one knows why Friday Gully is
named Friday. The neighborhood just north of here was called Horse
Stables—that is, until the Greeks were driven out, then they changed
the name to Good Riddance. That one makes sense."

———

"You don't really own this apartment," Fred said with none of the conviction he wanted. The knife felt insincere, its plastic handle sweaty in his hand.

"No, we really do." The man was smiling.

Clearly Virginia had remembered the lease signing too. She now clutched the Jack Daniel's bottle like she was going to take a drink.

"It was just a proxy thing," Fred said slowly, working through possibilities. "Just because only people from here have the right to own property here, for now. Doesn't mean you really *own it* own it."

The man spat, "The people who live here aren't from here, and they sure as hell don't have any rights to these buildings. Squatters from the east. They can't even heat these places, keep the plaster on the walls or glass in the windows. They just live here because the generals that stole it from us told them they could. So don't talk to us about *own it* own it."

Things didn't always add up in the City. The apartment was right in its center, a stone's throw from the ramshackle grandeur of the Orient Express hotels. But most of their non-foreign neighbors spent their days scrounging firewood or trading old pots and carpet scraps with the rag and bone man like it was the post-apocalypse.

The man's mouth naturally settled back into a smile. None of the sarcasm of his statement remained on his face. The woman came forward. She was fishlike, all cheeks with a thin, drawn mouth and dark hair held back with a hair band. She had a kind of afflicted prettiness, Fred thought, with curves evident beneath her grey sweat suit. With her free hand, she presented Virginia with a few delicate sheets of paper.

"That's the deed," the man said. "A copy."

Virginia held the pages to the light as if they were inked in lemon juice. "A bunch of Arabic," she concluded.

"It's Ottoman," the woman corrected. The child squirmed in her arms. Giving the man a look, she receded into the room that had served as Virginia's studio.

"What are we supposed to do with this?" Virginia asked.

"There's a translation on the third page. It says that Nikolas Tourvpoulos owns unit five in the World Apartments. This is unit five, and I am Nikolas Tourvpoulos, the third."

"The apartment belongs to a British journalist, Marvin Cooke. He bought it from some Turkish guy years ago, and we rent it from him. The lease is somewhere, in Turkish and English. Maybe your uncle sold it and just didn't tell you." Fred was as powerless and as self righteous as an old woman in the Social Security office. "Whatever. This is our apartment, and we'd really appreciate it if you left."

"I'm sorry," the man said. "I'm sorry for Marvin Cooke and for whatever money he gave to the squatter he found here. Guy's probably gone back to where he came from, some godforsaken hamlet just this side of the desert. Probably bought the whole town up with Marvin Cooke's English pounds. That's the world we live in. When I take this deed down to the General Directorate of Foundations, it will all be sorted out and we'll have our home back. In the meantime, you can stay here as our guests."

"We pay rent," Virginia snapped. The guy might have been unflappable, but he was between Virginia and the private relief of her paints.

"Well, I suggest you stop paying," the man said, "until we get this sorted out. If you could get me in touch with your landlord?"

"He's in Burma," Virginia cut in, "on assignment, with his wife. No phone, probably no email. They aren't supposed to be there."

"They aren't the only people who aren't where they're supposed to be," the man said heavy with irony. "Anyway, we've set up in this room, and it's all we need for now. We'll stay out of your way. And unlike the people who drove my dad's family out of this place, we'll give you plenty of time to find somewhere else. But you might want to keep your ear out, if you know what I mean."

He almost bowed, maybe just bobbed his head, still smiling. He shut the door to the studio behind him. A solid floor-to-ceiling wooden door with an ornate handle, in style the same as separated all rooms of the apartment from the central hallway, and the same that separated the apartment from the building's shopworn stairwell. They were one of the things Fred and Virginia most liked about the apartment. The doors had been sanded to their original pine, and when open they gave the place a great sense of airiness and light. When closed, they could be locked. It was an apartment in the Ottoman style: a windowless central space for the public, and vast spaces fit for a harem behind closed doors. The bolt on Virginia's studio door turned from the inside.

When they came home from work most days, the hour of jostling through the metro and the minibuses behind them, Virginia would strip entirely: dropping sacks of unmarked student work and empty Tupperware, then stepping out of whatever modest dress she'd spent the day teaching in. She'd stand there a minute, and it was as if the tattoos on her back reclaimed their color. Then she'd slip into her studio for an hour or two before dinner, emerging enrobed and careless. Fred found himself besotted with her each time this happened. For all they sneered and struggled with their job, they kept it apart from their home life. The doglegging alleyways of their High Field neighborhood, its antique fruit stands and obscure wine houses couldn't have been more different than the Castle where they taught, with majestic view across a parking lot bejeweled by new Audis to the

Black Sea beyond. To travel between these opposite ends of the City was to travel through time and wealth.

Virginia looked at Fred. They were in the hallway, their hallway, with their American joys lying inert at their feet. Fred wondered if it was worth calling their friends April and Ata to get the cops over and the invaders expelled. But he had a gut-twisting feel for how it might go: he and Virginia unarmed against a deed they couldn't read, their landlord beyond reach. They could go to the consulate, but that might embroil them in a legal dispute. Fred hadn't even registered their presence here with the authorities and the local cops or filed the appropriate tax forms. The stifling small offices of the bureaucracy with their ironically cloudless blue walls, it was too much for him. He hadn't left his own well-tamed country to play by rules abroad. They would just have to figure this out on their own. It might be as simple as changing the locks when the strangers stepped out.

Virginia was welling up. In the fluorescence of the hall light, the one they never turned on, her eyes turned to mirrors.

"It's okay, baby," Fred said. "It's no worse than when we had bedbugs."

Virginia shook her head. "It's not that," she said. "It's just that we have to go to work tomorrow." She sucked in a little sob, catching it and shuddering. Fred shuddered too, in spite of himself.

TWO.

EARLY ON, THEY HAD relished their walk to the Castle bus stop. Setting out from their door down Throat-Cutter Lane, they'd greet the majestic stray dogs that made their home there. The dogs were sad-eyed and strong jawed and took expansive naps. Fred and Virginia would then cut down a staircase, the lovers' staircase, that had an improbable stereo speaker improbably playing Latin music. It had been mounted in an abandoned doorway by the owner of the tea garden below so his young customers would feel comfortable making out there. Coming home in the evenings, they had to tread between necking kids with eyes shut tight as dreamers. The City was a good place to be young. Everyone tasted of smoke and tea. The Ministry of Public Health had worked to keep pornography illegal, so sex ideation remained exciting. Fred envied their innocence. Virginia envied their seemingly limitless time. Ascending the steps through the couples, they knew they were home. Descending them, the music fading into the neighborhood's drone of cars and construction, was more like certain classical myths with unhappy endings.

The tea garden backed onto a teal-green mosque, a squat, practical one with a Koranic LED ticker and halogen lights ringing a minaret topped with what looked like a large tin funnel. But for what it lacked in grandeur it made up for in its muezzin. When they first moved into the apartment, his call to prayer would halt them. They'd be preparing dinner or talking work, even fucking, and they'd stop to heed the call. It was more of a croon, which set it apart from the City's many shrill ululators. It was like he was singing just for you. His voice carried something of the taste of cardamom. Even as he joined the daily cacophony of their lives, he could still take them by surprise. Work mornings they would skirt around his minaret, down past the ablution spigots, to the market street. On Sundays this was where produce vendors hawked the fruit that hadn't made it off the shelves the previous week, alongside socks, underwear, and other practicalities. It was a popular destination for the neighborhood's migrant poor, who came in the early morning, and its bohemian expatriates, who preferred the early afternoon.

Maybe because of this long sleepwalk down to Cupboard-Stream Lane; they always seemed to forget something. Mornings came on them in fits: the sound of some too-large truck trying to thread through Throat-Cutter, its copilot screaming for the driver to "come come come" as close as possible to their building; the nasty caw of a gull on their windowsill; or some half-cooked dream about the earthquake, their whole hillside sluicing into the inlet below. By the time the alarm began its frantic between-stations hiss, they were un-asleep. But they never really awoke until the bus reached the Castle. It was then they would realize what they'd left behind: lunch, money, student work, running shoes.

That morning, the bus had already passed the Watering Square with its patriotic statue in pink marble, descended by the Full Garden Palace, ascended again along Pirate's Boulevard, passed through the financial district, traveled the length of the strait along Big Stream Road, and was beginning to climb the final hill. The final hill, which at the last ice age's end held back the rising strait. The final hill, which was eventually breached by the strait, fattened by glacier melt, flooding the lake beyond and lapping up the prehistoric human cities that had developed beside it. Including the one belonging to Noah, who had his boat ready to float on the newly formed Black Sea. So it is true that the City was born when history began, the completion of the strait giving the City the topography that has defined it and will define it until the Black Sea empties in the opposite direction and God destroys the world with fire. Fittingly, the ascent was the longest part of the journey, a series of labored switchbacks around shanties, speculative apartment developments, and livestock.

They were passing a hunched man shoeing a horse when Virginia realized she hadn't brought her pumps.

"Just teach in your running shoes." They were dressed for the gym, an extended morning run their stress-reducing requirement. Run in the morning, wine at night. The regularities of a life subtended by a weekday, workaday foreignness.

"You don't know what those girls are like," Virginia said. "Do you think I wear heels because I enjoy them? They protect me from the scorn of the surgically altered. Running shoes? They'll never take me seriously again."

Fred and Virginia arrived the previous autumn, which meant nose bandages. At first they thought it was the result of some sort of endemic violence, but they eventually surmised that so many, boys and girls, couldn't have been punched in the face at the same time. It was a case of mass rhinoplasty. Virginia asked April, their friend and colleague, why the kids didn't get their noses done the summer before, showing up with faces already perfected. The bandages proved they could afford a good nose, April explained, that it wasn't just a freak of nature. They'd laughed about it at the time, but the same scrutiny applied to them. Fred traded his flannels for oxfords, and Virginia taught in dresses once reserved for Thanksgiving and Christmas.

It bought them a little credibility, but now it was nearly spring, mating season. The outdoor pool had opened. The weather wasn't warm enough to swim, but the cabanas were a revolving door of tentatively exposed girl-flesh during peak daylight hours. The parking lot, which rolled down the hill from the pool, was a drive-in theater for boys with new-model German convertibles. And the classrooms became opportunities to "get to know you better." It was only through an exhausting mix of humor, sex appeal, authoritarianism, and American cache that Fred and Virginia managed to impart something like an education to the Castle kids. And it was only because they were both from working people that they bothered trying.

The bus reached the Castle gates. The Castle itself was on the opposite slope from the main road, so no casual passersby could behold the campus. It was the only university in the world with two non-emergency helipads.

"April doesn't teach when I do." Virginia found her resolve. "We can trade off."

"Or you could teach barefoot." Fred said

"You know, you are really not helping."

"I wasn't being serious."

"Some things are serious. Having people living in your apartment is serious," she hissed.

It was the first they'd mentioned it since the night before. Their morning ritual had been the same, except for Fred putting their few valuables in the bedroom and locking it.

"I'm going to write Marvin first thing. I'm sure he's got a friend or a lawyer or something. Get them out legitimately." Fred was keeping his voice down. He didn't want their colleagues on the bus to know what was going on. Like all expatriates, their colleagues sustained themselves on four things: travel, booze, gossip, and Schadenfreude.

The bus door swung open and they descended into the cool, pine-scented world of the Castle.

The office next to Fred's belonged to the university's sole classicist. A survivor of a string of similar positions from the Gulf to Egypt, he referred to the Castle as "the camp." He'd openly joke about the medical school offering scholarships to twins and having a fifty percent graduation rate. He said this in such a well-formed Oxford accent, from behind such lake-blue eyes, that administrators would laugh and agree. He lived in a boarding hotel for transvestites, saving to buy a place in the south, where he could put his accent to work giving tours.

"Adrian," Fred tapped on the doorframe, "can I ask you about something?"

"So long as it has nothing to do with teaching." Fred shook his head. "Okay, but step in, I want a cigarette with my tea."

Opening his window, Adrian motioned for Fred to towel the door. Outside, the kids lolled in packs, smoking their own cigarettes.

"I can't smoke out there. I'm afraid they'll smell the homosexual on me and rip me apart like the Bacchae."

Fred had run into Adrian and his "roommate" in the Monopoly shop that sold booze in their neighborhood. Adrian had put up a bit of pretense about saving money by bunking up, but the relationship was clear. Fred wondered if he was the only one at the Castle who knew.

"Have you ever heard about, uh, people moving into other people's places when those people are away?"

"Of course." Adrian didn't skip a drag.

"Really?"

"Happened to some archeologist friends of mine. They were in the east at a dig site for some time, and returned to the City to find two families living in their flat. Took them years to get rid of them."

"Years?"

"The laws protect squatters. That's how the government developed this City on the cheap. The 'built-overnight' slums. If you can prove you lived in a place for a short period, a weekend even, the owner has to take you to court. And you can stay in the place until it's proven you don't belong there. About half the people in the city took advantage of this law to stake out some little hillside near the factories. Some took up in abandoned places too, after the Greeks and all were driven off. And some, like the ones my friends were stuck with, must have gotten a decent law school education. But it was my friend's fault. They went ahead and did this stupid thing, having some local buy their place for them to skirt the neighborhood protection laws. That meant they had to go through a Byzantine, pardon the pun, process to prove they actually owned the property."

Adrian sipped his tea as Fred's heart sank.

"Wait," Adrian said, "is this happening to you?"

Fred didn't nod, but he found Adrian's cigarette smoke had turned acrid. Out the window, the pine trees were caught in a gale off the sea.

"But you're renters. Let the owner sort this out." Adrian reached out the window and flicked the butt toward a gaggle of undergraduates. "Move your stuff out. I can get you a room at the hotel for cheap, until you find a new place."

"This kind of thing really happens here?" was all Fred could say.

Adrian nodded. "Pretty much anything you can imagine happening has happened here. Along with some things you can't."

Climbing from the breath-damp Watering Square Metro station, Fred and Virginia hit a wall of cops. Ordinarily they would hump their various bags of books and gym clothes down Independence Avenue and then take a hard right down into their neighborhood. Independence Avenue was one of the City's only walking streets, if walking could be defined as a contact sport played between gaggles of youth strutting in European athletic brands and cowled old ladies dragging their broods past the ice cream parlors. But this evening it moonlighted in its other role, a forum for the wronged, of which there were many in the City. They were on the other side of the police's plastic shields, chanting and waving placards. Fred was dimly aware the Turkish Air Force had bombed people in the east of the country. A few papers had dared assert the victims were cigarette smugglers, rather than Kurdish militants as the government claimed. Most days, life in the City was essentially the same commercial cycle of work, food, sleep, and play Fred and Virginia knew from the States. Moments like this, it became clear they were in another country. There weren't F-16s bombing Mexican-Americans on the border of Arizona back home, at least not yet.

The cops seemed relaxed, content to let the aggrieved fill the Avenue with their chants and bodies.

"Maybe we should ask one or two of them to come home with us," Virginia said. "Let them sort out what's going on."

Fred sized up a sample cop. He was a hungry-looking kid, tooled up in a suit of black plastic armor. Perhaps he'd relish the chance to bash the Greek's head with his nightstick, throw him down the worn marble staircase. The kid certainly wouldn't appeal to the Greek's respect for the rule of law.

"Just kidding," Virginia said a bit hopelessly. "But you know, there's nothing in the lease about sharing the place with Greeks. We could just find another place."

"Something in between," Fred said. "Give it a month. Things are different here."

They took the long way home.

THREE.

"THAT'S TOUGH," APRIL MUSED, ignoring the fishermen staring at her red hair. "The first few times you feel really guilty and obliged. After all, these people have flown across the world to see you. You take them all the way down to the historic peninsula, the ancient part, and walk the sites with them. Show them the weeping pillar in the Holy Wisdom and tell them how they can try and make a wish. Then take them out to one of those expensive multi-course fish dinners where they can drink as much aniseed liquor as they can handle. And they do, because they don't know what it feels like the next morning. You do too, because you're proud to be here. After the first few visitors, you lose your taste for tourism. But they keep coming, taking extra long showers and eating all your bananas, milling about because they haven't read the goddamn guidebook and are waiting for you to tell them what to do. The worst is when they get into your care-package supply. I had one guest make herself five peanut butter sandwiches so she would have something handy for her days of sightseeing. She 'just didn't know' you can't get peanut butter here. Well, you can, but it's this expensive oily mess imported from Holland. Tastes nothing like the real stuff from home."

Virginia was walking the Strait with April. It was a tradition they were trying to start on Sunday afternoons. April would take the Coast Road bus down from her neighborhood of Therapy to the Cradle Stone neighborhood—so named, Fred had told Virginia, for a Byzantine church built to house a stone manger rumored to have sheltered the baby Jesus. Virginia could walk from High Field; it was about ten minutes across the Watering Square if you cut through the vast campus of the State Radio and Television offices. They met at the end of the Pirate's Boulevard. Once the mooring place of the Ottoman corsairs, the only pirates left were in its "bookshops," where photocopies of any text and DVD-Rs of any movie could be purchased for slightly above the cost of production.

"But really," April continued, "you could lose someone in that apartment of yours. I don't have much sympathy. You know how hard it is to carve wood in your living room? Even if you vacuum, the floors start to look like one of those corner bars in Wicker Park or Ukrainian Village."

"Can't you carve outside? You have two terraces." Virginia was surprised by her own relief at being misunderstood. It was like April was clearing up some local custom she had yet to understand. Or some part of expatriate life that was annoying but you got used to. She and Fred hadn't even lived in the City long enough to have friends overstay their welcome. Jake had been the first, and only visited because he worked in the region. Some of their closest friends had only just begun to noncommittally inquire about how long they could stay, should they decide to invest in costly transoceanic air tickets. Virginia was reconsidering her standard answer: as long as you like. In their current situation, maybe it would be best if no one came to visit.

April had suggested these walks because Virginia must have questions. They had been in art school together in Chicago, though April was a few years older. They'd dated the same guy, though mercifully not at the same time. This fact made Virginia a little wary when April reached out and encouraged her and Fred to apply for jobs at the Castle. April had already been working there for three years and found herself on the hiring committee. At that time, Fred and Virginia were feeling more starving and less artists. Even in Providence, Rhode Island, with the lowest rents on the Eastern seaboard, they ate some variety of beans for dinner five nights a week.

Fred immediately took to the idea of "money and adventure." He was only vaguely aware they were being drawn across by a jet stream of hot money, capital fleeing financial instruments that had suddenly become mere houses. Virginia was a little more cautious, perhaps because the boy they both dated had implied April was impulsive. Eventually she wrote it off because April was a redhead and had broken up with him. As had Virginia after a couple months, though she was a brunette so who knows how things were explained to the next girl. Anyway, here she was, half a year after taking the job, walking with April toward the Middle Village, where the palaces fell away and they could walk along the water's edge.

At the Middle Village, which was really only about a third of the way up the Strait, they took a brief detour to a tiny shop that specialized in authentic motorcycle paraphernalia.

"You can get copies of this stuff anywhere," April explained. "The City is full of fakes—fake Fendi bags, fake soccer jerseys, fake Harley-Davidson belt buckles. You'll know you finally belong here when you seek out the real thing."

Virginia ran her fingers over Indian-fringe vests and engineer boots as April negotiated in broken Turkish over a jackknife in the display case. The knife was for Ata. April was his old lady. He was not the leader of the motorcycle gang "Poison's Greatest Hits," but he did run the garage where the gang hung out. He was a Turk, born in Bulgaria. Virginia had heard the story of how they met. April told it like the whole episode was shot with Vaseline on the lens: some rainy day at a beachside pension; Ata in the midst of a solitary quest to bike the craggy, Roman-era byways along the White Sea. The Turks called it the White Sea, having first encountered the Black Sea. Everyone else called it the "middle of the world," but the Turks had come from far enough away to know this wasn't the case.

April was trying to get away from her first year at the Castle, when she'd lived up on the campus. All she knew of the City then was what she'd read in books and what she heard in the screams of wild dogs and baby owls. Suddenly she was his Roxelana, the famous Ukrainian queen of Suleiman's harem. Her out-of-place pallor and red hair transformed into assets. They made a striking pair astride Ata's bike, him with his dark, Khan-like mane and beard, her like a Titian painting in black leather. And through this, April was reborn a native, one of the City's own.

She unfolded a couple large bills as the clerk carefully placed the precious, authentic knife in its leather holster. Virginia couldn't help but think of the famous dagger housed in the Cannonball Palace, its uncut emeralds, fist-sized, not unlike April's eyes in color.

Up the Strait from the Middle Village was the first bridge. The span was no greater than the George Washington, but there was something charming in the idea that the bridge tied together East and West. That Asia was just over there, if you could wait out the traffic. April was going on about a bike trip she and Ata were planning. They would weave through the cars on the bridge and then the open road tracing the eddies of the Black Sea all the way to the mythical towers of Trebizond, a place so famous the Turks could not change its name. It was going to be a scouting mission for Ata, since the city had been the western terminus of the Silk Road after Baghdad was destroyed for the first time. Ata's life ambition was to ride the length of the route, through the ancestral homeland of all Turks to the four ancient capitals of China.

Virginia was letting her mind wander a bit. Not that she didn't like being reminded of the historical currents that ran through this part of the world, alongside its earthquake faults. But it didn't quite capture her imagination like it did for others, Fred especially. There were times when Fred could step into it like a giant soap bubble, one that sealed him up from the City's grit and gave everything a nice rainbow patina. She wished she could join him in there sometimes, but what kind of painter would she be if she trained herself to overlook what was actually there for ideas of what was once there.

They'd made it to the Albanian Village, about halfway up, and April was talking about the famous white strawberries that once grew on the hillsides there. Only three years ago, you could still find them in some markets, but she had ceased to see them. It was some sort of sign. Virginia interrupted. She thought she would bring up the Greeks again. It was the kind of question that an expert in the City could answer. One that desperately needed an answer. But instead, as they walked past the rows of old men tending their fishing rods, she asked, "Do you think this place is home?"

April's face was the kind that loved being animated. Caught in thought unexpectedly, it turned jowly and tired. Finally she said, "My family moved around a lot."

"But you think you'll be here awhile? Sort of settle down? We make enough money."

"It's not bad, is it? You know Ata lives in kind. People used to bring him food and beer to fix their bikes. The first time I gave him fifty bucks to buy groceries, all he came back with was steaks, cheeses, and bottles of Goldmine aniseed liquor. I had to send him back for vegetables."

"But do you ever think you're going to feel at home here? I mean, you have Ata, I imagine that opens a lot of doors."

"Yeah, he's great. We have a lot of traveling to do. And even though they slave us up at the Castle, being here has been great for my work. I'm completing a new piece every five, six months."

"That's good."

There must have been some ambiguity in Virginia's tone because April immediately added, "Woodcarving is a lot more labor intensive than painting. Painting you can always add, woodcarving you can only take away."

Virginia didn't press the point any further. In the distance, she could see the two castles built by Mehmet the Conqueror. Designed to control the Strait before his siege of the City, they were called the "Throat-closers." The Turks made wine from a grape of the same name, wine Virginia had learned to avoid. It was Mehmet who said, "I will conquer this City, or it will conquer me." Fred liked that quote. He liked saying it before starting to grade a stack of essays.

They had made it to Baby, wealth's center of gravity along the Strait. It was a steep hillside over the water stacked with mansions and terraced nightclubs. The rumor was that Castle kids would come here on weekends and drop a thousand dollars a night trying to reenact scenes they had seen in hip-hop videos.

"You know," April said, "these all used to be Greek villages. Fishing villages. You wonder if they knew what they had before they left. It's like the Indians who traded Manhattan for beads."

"I'm pretty sure they were kicked out," Virginia said absentmindedly. They'd been walking almost two hours and the winds out of the north were picking up. Early spring was pretty warm in the City, except along the Strait, where nothing impeded the cold air blown from the steppe across the Black Sea. This far up, the fishermen tended braziers as they waited for their lines to show life.

April grunted. "Maybe. Nothing's particularly straightforward when it comes to this place—I'm sure you've picked that up by now. You'll have to ask Ata about how the Bulgarian government tried to change his name. I love the history, mostly because I didn't have to live it."

"We do."

And so she laid it all out for April, the Greeks and their strange deed, their missing landlord, Adrian's grim prognostications about their legal options. The fact that the people were in her studio as they spoke, and though she was grateful to have a studio for the first time in her life, she didn't so much care about the studio as the people who were in her home, and maybe had a right to be there. If they had a right to be there, she didn't want to be there. And if they had no right to be there, she wanted them out.

April walked on for a bit, showing no particular shock. "I feel like I've heard of something similar happening." The cliffs were casting long shadows. Their goal was eventually to walk all the way to Therapy, three-quarters the length of the Strait. A full twelve miles. But the days were still too short and they had only ever made it to the second bridge. The waterway took a sharp left here, so even as they walked along it they looked straight at the Asian shore, right at an expansive fish establishment, windows at the water's edge. Virginia felt the eyes of the diners on her and April, wondering at these lost female specimens hoofing their way along the opposite bank among the hunched fishermen.

"There is a simple way of dealing with this," April said. It was like she had downed a bottle of white wine, that combination of sugar urgency and lubricated clarity. "We're going to take you two to Bulgaria with us. We're planning on going this weekend, we've borrowed a car. Once the Greeks get comfortable with the idea of you being gone, they'll wander out. For groceries or something. The point is, they won't be thinking about it, and once they are out of the apartment, two of the members of Poison's Greatest Hits will just go up and change the locks."

"Really." Virginia was grateful, but not entirely convinced.

"Yeah, they hang out just up the street anyway, at the Purple Wave. They sing karaoke there. They'd be happy to take care of this for Ata and his friends. We won't even have to tell them it involves Greeks."

"Well," Virginia said, thinking about the long bus ride home to her occupied apartment, "we have wanted to get out of town."

FOUR.

THEY'D FINALLY FREED THEMSELVES of the City. Driving the little borrowed car, Ata told them all that the City would end after the next hill. Eventually this was true, but by the time it happened he'd tired of telling them it would. When the City was founded, it encompassed seven hills. And for fifteen thousand years, seven was enough. Now the City covered countless hills, hanging its concrete apartments in pastel layers overtop one another. The hills' names went from familiar to abstract, from Steep Hill and Breezy Hill near the city center to Agreement Hill, Ownership Hill, and Contract Hill. On the furthest, nameless hills, the buildings were slapdash, the slums built overnight.

"I did that once too," Ata said. "For this family in the Paper House district. I just said, hop on the back of my motorcycle and I'll take you to the sea." The four of them had agreed not to discuss the Greek situation, since it was being taken care of. So Virginia described the exhibit they'd gone to with Jake.

"Did they take you up on it?" Fred asked.

"The father did. He brought a plastic bottle of seawater home, poked pinholes in the cap and sprayed his wife and children with it. He explained this was what the sea was like."

"Jesus," Virginia said.

"The father must have believed they'd never get there themselves. He was just trying to share. You shouldn't judge," April cut in. This was her adopted culture they were talking about. The car fell silent. Way out past the airport, Fred suggested they tell the one about Virginia mistakenly touching a mufti she thought was their muezzin. But they'd all heard that one before. Virginia suggested Fred read from his spec script, but he lied and said he'd forgotten his notebook.

There wasn't much between where the City ended and Bulgaria began, just flat, arable land. Fred and Virginia had lived within the City's density for seven straight months, long enough that this landscape struck them as strange.

"If you think this is strange," April said, "wait until we get to Bulgaria. It's not just strange, it's the opposite."

They arrived at the border crossing just as the evening mist had begun to seep out from the forests. As Ata negotiated with the customs agent, April, Virginia, and Fred examined the agent's proudest interceptions. A woman stuffed into a bus bench seat. Kilos of heroin between a Lada's console and firewall. A man who'd lined his pants with bacon. All trying to travel from Bulgaria into Turkey.

"What kind of punishment do you get for bacon smuggling?" Fred asked.

"Flogging, probably. Have you tried getting bacon in the City? It's easier to get pot, and cheaper," April said.

"I never ate much pork before. I think I've forgotten what it tastes like."

"Bulgaria will remind you. It's like reopening an old wound."

Ata interrupted. The agent needed to interview April and Virginia, to make sure they were not trafficked women.

"He thinks you're a pimp?" April asked.

"Isn't I?"

"You mean 'aren't I,' and no, you're not."

"The agent is worried you are trying to bring your earnings back to Bulgaria. Turks don't mind foreign women coming to work, but they won't let them take their money out of the country."

"It's like the harem," April explained.

"No, baby. It's like the Hotel California." Ata grinned, exposing the gap where an incisor had been knocked out. Ata had been part of the student movement in the City before the last successful coup. He'd been studying law, but the blow convinced him to follow other pursuits.

Having confirmed the girls were in the business of educating the children of the country's elite, not fleeing its brothels, the border agent was happy to let them drive off into the encroaching mist. At the first hamlet, the first tavern, Ata equipped them with six liters of beer, pork skewers, shepherd's salads, and a trim bottle of red wine for the ladies. It was opaque like the night sea.

"Is it okay to do this?" Virginia asked after a long pull on the bottle. The road had become rockier, the pines thicker, and the fog more densely reflective of the headlamps. Ata's speed remained constant.

"As long as Ata doesn't get into the plum brandy," April said.

"Not until breakfast, baby." Ata smiled.

Fred was the one who felt like the baby, sucking on his beer, knees akimbo, letting himself be driven into the night.

At breakfast in the Bulgarian pensione, April and Virginia bowled their yogurt and muesli. They established themselves in a worn corner booth and sat like they had when they were back in art school together: lithe, serious, talking work.

Ata and Fred lingered over the buffet. It was a spectrum of pink: soft bologna, bloodied ham, speckled dry sausage, gloss bacon. Ata piled his plate with strips of pure white, slipping one in his mouth, past his friendly muttonchops.

"Of all the bacons, this is my favorite," he said. "Try one with a little paprika."

Fred popped it in his mouth. No real taste, just a feeling of heaviness. It was like a stick of pork Trident.

"Don't chew it," Ata said. "Just let it dissolve under your tongue."

"This is pork fat."

"Yes, preserved in the cold, packed in the snow and ice at the beginning of the winter. I was afraid we came too late for it. It's best to have this in the morning, with some plum brandy from my father's supply. Then you can drink all day if you wish."

The fat had begun to melt, tallowing its way down Fred's throat. Before long, everything from teeth to gullet was coated. "How about that plum brandy?" he croaked.

Ata produced a flask. Washing the sliver of fat down, there was no burn, just the waft of fruit spirits and relief. Fred plated some of the other pork products.

"You know, April is really happy you two decided to move to the City. I'm really happy too. I think you're the kind of people who will find the magic of the place, isn't it?"

"Thanks, man," Fred said. Magic would be nice, but they were still trying to find a decent, drinkable bottle of Turkish wine. Familiar bottles were prohibitively expensive, taxed for being both foreign and "profane." Stuff you might pick up at a gas station back home could run as high as fifty dollars. Booze was worse. Buying Turkish wine, taxed only for being "profane," they kept getting bottles made from a mix of "ox-eye" and "throat-closer" grapes.

Getting to the booth, Virginia asked why every other diner had a twist of red and white thread pinned to his or her clothing. It was a small thing, the kind of thing Virginia noticed. A glass that had been moved, a frame made crooked: these were the things that caught her bird-like attention.

"It's a talisman against the uncertainty of spring. You never know with spring. Like a newborn, so many ways it could die," Ata explained.

"Then we ought to get some ourselves," Virginia said.

They spent the day, talismans affixed to coats, wandering the ruins of the City of Midday. It had once occupied a little island, less than a mile square, set just offshore in the Black Sea. In its heyday, it had been a grain port, exporting wheat to the City, where, as in ancient Rome, bread was a citizen's right. They walked over the hollowed-out shells of Byzantine churches while in the background, looming over them, were the wall of condos that made up Sunny Beach, a summer resort for Russians. At this time of year, they were as abandoned as the ruins, though not nearly as picturesque.

"If you save up a little over the next few years, we could all go in on a place here," April suggested. "They're not that expensive."

"For walls and a roof you pay extra, isn't it" Ata snaked a heavy motorcycle jacketed arm around her as they stepped through a de-molished nave.

"We're actually trying to put away most of one salary, for a place back in the States," Virginia said matter-of-factly. She then paused, wondering if this was the first time this plan, which she and Fred had only discussed in the broadest of dream strokes, had been spoken of as a reality.

"Back in the States!" Ata scoffed. "What's back in the States? I've had your hot sauce. My grandmother makes one ten times as hot. It takes the chrome off a tailpipe, isn't it. What would New York be after four earthquakes and a thousand years? Nothing, isn't it. Name one thing you have in the States that you can't have here."

"Pilates," April said, shaking off Ata's arm. "I've been all over the City trying to find a place to do Pilates."

"Pilates, what is Pilates?"

"It's like yoga," Virginia began to explain, "but sort of more therapeutic."

"April doesn't need more therapeutic. We live in the place the Greeks called Therapia. The air is therapeutic."

"Ata thinks everything is therapeutic. Playing guitar is therapeutic, goat's head soup is therapeutic, drinking all night at the motorcycle garage is therapeutic."

"It is baby, it is. You just need to relax."

"Sometimes I wouldn't mind doing something really therapeutic, like Pilates."

"Pilates." Ata looked at them. "Do you do Pilates?"

Virginia nodded. Fred shook his head.

"You know, in Bulgaria they mean the opposite. Shake for yes, nod for no. I think it's the only country in the world like that," April said.

"The only country in the world where the women don't waste time with Pilates," Ata grunted.

———

They had dinner in a beached pirate ship. It was the restaurant at-
tached to one of the resorts, so it was off-season empty. The waitress,
in jeans and an eye patch, put all three colors of wine she had on the
table. All were sweet and cold, served in bottles that could have been
taken from "The Sorcerer's Apprentice." They drank the pink one,
and when it ran out, they mixed the red and white. Ata and Fred had
roast pig, gelatinous in its own fat. The girls flaked the breadcrumbs
off their fish fillet. The wine had taken hold, so it didn't much matter.
Ata was telling stories of the Bulgarian countryside. He recalled how,
the night Communism ended, his mother took all the banknotes
from under the mattress and threw them in the fire. She could walk
into the woods and find bags full of mushrooms. If you can do that,
who needs a government?

A few toasts to anarchy and the wine was finished. The topic
slipped toward work. The Castle was owned by the country's largest
holding company, whose interests had always intersected with the
army's. The confluence of the two cultures seemed to bring out the
worst of both in the students. They were at once savvy consumers
and mutinous conscripts. They expected their teachers to do their
work for them, just as they expected their mothers to drive up to the
dorms and make their beds. There was plenty to gripe about, but Ata
saved them.

"You are in another country. All that will still be there for you
when you get back." The tide lapped out quietly.

Ata took them to the old Communist Party headquarters, now
just a "party headquarters." The exterior was glass and concrete, the
cold international style that promised grain and justice for all. The
neoclassical public hearing rooms had been hollowed out for gaming
tables and the basement had been transformed into the Jokers Club.

"That's where the hookers are," Ata explained. "They turned the big processing area into a lounge and then use the cells for..." April was giving him a wide look of disbelief, so he stopped.

They found themselves in the bar set in the top-floor offices of the secret police. The décor was Miami Vice: black polka-dot wallpaper, cocaine white leather sofas. It was called the Umbrella Lounge, after the stockpile of poison-tipped umbrellas found there. The cocktails were made with real American liquor. Virginia took a few tentative sips, her knees folded up onto the booth. Fred was so enjoying his renewed relationship with Jack Daniel's, he almost didn't notice the telltale slump set into her slim shoulders. Or maybe he chose to ignore it.

"April, maybe we can go back to the hotel?" Virginia asked softly.

April was clutching at Ata's motorcycle jacket. Having drunk off all the frustrations of breadwinning, she saw him for the adventure she fell in love with. The man who took her on the back of his motorcycle up into the heathery hillsides, who built her a fire and sang to her in the sad language of nomads. You could read all of this in the green of her eyes.

Virginia tapped on Fred's shoulder. "You need to take me home," she said. She would have a hangover tomorrow, one of those that would settle in her lean frame like a low-pressure zone. It would be a hard drive back to the City, and he felt for her. He wanted to hold her cheek, perfect as a shell. Maybe let her hair out of its tight bun, let his hand come to rest on her ass. Fred went for his billfold tentatively, giving Ata plenty of time to stop him.

"April," Ata said, "take Virginia to the soup restaurant, put her and yourself to bed."

"Baby, you and I can stay together."

"No, my soul, be a good friend to Virginia."

Three years is a long time in a cultural life. When Fred first talked to April about moving to the City, she waxed poetic about the great convenience of having groceries delivered. You didn't even have to come downstairs if the order was small enough, just lower a basket from a window and the grocer would do the rest. Fred only later discovered that this wasn't a service, but how the men of the City kept their wives from walking the public streets. April obeyed like a good woman of the City.

The girls gone, they had another round and discussed Ata's plans to ride the Silk Road. They talked a lot about the carburetor settings, something Fred knew nothing about. Finishing their drinks, Ata suggested they visit the Jokers Club.

"I don't think I could do that," Fred said. "I feel like Virginia would smell it on me."

"Bulgarians don't smell. If you get one that smells, she's Romanian."

"All the same, I just don't think I can."

They had another drink. A greasy guy in a white tux emerged, and microphone to lips did a Bulgarian Toni Curtis. The whiskey turned sweet in Fred's mouth, a sure sign he'd had too much.

"Do you like living in the City?" Ata asked.

"The bread is salty and the steps are steep."

Ata looked puzzled. "You don't like the bread? I'll take you to the best bakery, they have an old stone oven, more than a hundred years old."

Fred wondered why the hell he'd dropped a quote from *Purgatorio* except that he was a dickish drunk with a pricy education. He tried again, sincerely. "The language is impenetrable. When we first arrived, we could only go out for twenty minutes at a time. We spent the rest watching American TV reruns. The apartment has helped. Virginia has space to paint."

"Painting is good, therapeutic. April used to sculpt wood, but now she just stresses about her job."

"It's not a good job, but the money is good," Fred said, crunching an ice cube.

"You're good at not talking about it."

Fred nodded, then shook his head. The wallpaper swam out of focus, but might have even if he were sober.

"Come, let's go to the Jokers. It is a better bar for men. We can just talk, with each other or with the girls. Their English is better than mine even." Ata was already on his feet, unsteady.

Fred shook his head, worsening the spin.

"Here that means yes," Ata laughed.

The Jokers Club was black on black. The lint and dandruff caught on the girls' spandex shone bright in the blacklight. So did the plaque on their teeth, Fred thought. In the center of the lounge was an enormous black gloss table cut in the shape of a grand piano. On the piano bench, a half-dressed girl was diligently pecking a version of "Stairway to Heaven" on the built-in Casio keyboard. A cocktail waitress moved through the room, her silver tray lined with sweating vodkas.

Ata sat Fred down. "Those two look nice," he said. One was an hourglass redhead, a version of April only younger or more dimly lit. The other was cherubic, her glasses the only straight lines on her body. She was in the stool next to Fred faster than his eyes could track, her arms up adjusting the chopsticks in her hair. The buttons of her blouse strained, showing lace and flesh.

"He's just here to talk," Ata said, signaling for vodkas. "C'mon, you're an English teacher. Teach her something."

The April lookalike giggled, downed her vodka, and ordered another. The one next to Fred seemed crestfallen. Annoyance was high in Fred's throat. He'd just wanted to have a few more drinks. Whiskey in this quantity was taking him back to a time untainted by being a foreigner. He had almost forgotten the whole thing with the Greeks. Now he was sitting at a fake piano table next to a sulking, plump prostitute. She drew little streams on the table with the vodka perspiration.

"It's not you…" Fred glanced up at the girl. "I'm just visiting, with my wife."

The girl looked around in a panic, as if to confirm that no wife had entered the Jokers Club.

"Ata," Fred decided to ignore her, "why were the Greeks run out of the City?"

"They fed the street dogs poison. So did the Armenians and the Jews. The dogs came to the city with the Turks, and only when the last one is gone will the Turks leave."

"The Turks are dogs, dirty dirty dogs," the plump prostitute said. Fred wasn't sure whether this was a come-on or she really meant it. But she must have, because she added something in Bulgarian and a knife flicked open in Ata's hand. The April lookalike shrieked and tossed her vodka all over Fred. This got him out of his seat just at the same time as Ata. And though it had been fifteen years since his last game as a defensive end, Fred managed to come between Ata and his second stuck pig of the night.

———

Ata got them two beers to go. They walked along the beach back to the hotel. The condos loomed above them like a concrete wave threatening to break over the sea.

"They changed my name," Ata finally said.

"What?"

"When I was eight, they came to my family and told them my name was Stephen and I was a Christian, since all Bulgarians are Christians. I'd go to a school where I'd learn in Bulgarian how the Bulgarians were a great people who drove the filthy Turks from their land. And if I came home to my parents to speak Turkish, they'd have to send us all to camps in the north to learn what it meant to be Bulgarian, far from the land given to us when we rode with the third sultan of the empire and the lords of the horizons." Ata swung his arms wide, releasing an arc of beer like a sudsy scimitar.

"What did your parents do?"

"What they had to do. They named me Ata, you know: the first, the father, the source, the horse. No government was going to change that to meaningless Stephen. So they took me to where I'd be safe, with my own people, isn't it?"

Fred looked out over the sea. The moon hung just above it and reflected like the pearl set in a drowned man's eye. It felt mild for February, perhaps the talisman was working. Or perhaps it was the vodka.

"That was 1984." Ata had cooled off a bit. "I always think I'll come back here and things will be different. But things are never different. Tell that to those Greeks hiding in your apartment, if they try and get back in after the locks are changed."

When they finished their beers, they cast them into the sea. The friendly sea, so friendly it will empty itself out. It pours itself down the Strait that runs through the City, which the Turks call the Throat and the Greeks called the Ox-ford. Sometime before the world ends, the sea will have given its last drop, the Throat will be parched, and the two sides of the City will be reunited. This figures somewhere among the kaleidoscopic dooms of the City, prescribed since before its foundation. So Fred thought as he made his way to sleep.

FIVE.

[Scene: Nick Adams' apartment. Certain elements should seem familiar, reminiscent of a certain sitcom from the nineties. The camera centers on a worn-out teal couch. Off to the right are a pair of stools at a breakfast counter, the galley kitchen behind them. Between is the door to the exterior. Certain aspects should be changed to indicate that this apartment is in the City: a heavy tin tea table sits in front of the couch; over in the kitchen, a classic Turkish stacked kettle, sort of like a Russian samovar, is visible beside a poster advertising romantic moonlit nights along the inlet; on the breakfast counter, an array of large-format duty-free boozes. From beyond the windows, the occasional yells in Turkish from street vendors or rag and bone men. The light carries that sepia melancholy that comes from the unique combination of sea air and coal smoke.

Nick Adams has big jowls for his age, a Teen Wolf haircut, and could pass for dashing if he wore anything other than big box store T-shirts and jeans. He is pouring two whiskies into tulip-shaped tea glasses. Jake Barnes is rounder, softer the way alcohol shapes certain men as they age.]

Nick: So I turn around to figure out what this guy's about—he's been following us since we passed the mosque, talking all the way.

Jake: And he's wearing the whole getup?

Nick: Yeah, the thawb, the little pillbox hat, the scraggly beard. The guy could make a fortune playing Terrorist #2 for Hollywood.

Jake: And Catherine Barkley thought he was the muezzin?

Nick: In her defense, it was about time for the call to prayer, and that muezzin is the best. No annoying ululations or anything. He's the Frank Sinatra of muezzin. A real crooner, like he's singing just for you. And he's nothing if not on time. It's dusk and boom, he's serenading your living room. Beats the hell out of church bells. This other guy was heading toward the mosque in a distinctly White Rabbit fashion. Late for an important date, you know what I mean. It was a logical conclusion after a few drinks.

Jake: But this guy wasn't him.

Nick: No sirrie bob. And Catherine, being Catherine, goes up to him and tells him, in English, that she loves his singing. I think she even touched his sleeve. After that, he stopped heading for the mosque and started following us. Following us and saying something. So I turn around to figure out what's going on, and as I look into his massively dilated pupils, I realize he's speaking English.

Jake: That's convenient.

Nick: He's saying, "Do you have sex?"

Jake: Jesus, that's awkward. Are you guys?

Nick: (Ignoring him) And so we're there with Osama bin Watching You and Catherine is asking me what the guy is saying, if he's saying something about her or the singing. I'm holding a bottle of wine in a plastic grocery bag, hoping to take her back here. So I say the first thing that comes into my head: She's my sister.

Jake: How'd Catherine take that?

Nick: I think she would have been more flattered if I'd said, "I wish," or "After several heartfelt conversations and candlelit dinners." But I was a coward. I dragged her down the street and the guy didn't chase us. It's probably hard in one of those long skirts. But he got on his little Nokia phone. I told Catherine we should come here and hole up. We were just up the block, I mean it was a golden opportunity. But I guess she was a little miffed by the whole sister thing and suggested we go sit in a bar on that evil little tourist trap, French Street. Something about how it was the only place in the City we would actually blend in. [Nick comes over to the teal couch and sits.]

Jake: I'm sure it had nothing to do with the state of this apartment.

Nick: [Ignoring him] Anyway, I think he followed us all the way to French Street, took one look at the gigantic pastel papier-mâché tulips and the throngs of drunk Australians with their Russian hookers, and moved on. But I expect to dine out on this encounter with radical Islam for years to come. It plays right into what most people back home think happens here every day. To honor! [This is the typical Turkish toast. Nick and Jake raise their little tea glasses of whiskey and drink.]

Jake: To knowing when to run away. Oh, and it's not French Street anymore. They changed the name to Algeria Street.

Nick: Doesn't have the same ring to it.

Jake: The ministers did it. Apparently the French made some stink about how the Turks should acknowledge the Armenian genocide—how it was the first ethnic cleansing of the twentieth century and set the tone for everyone else, the Germans, Soviets, etc. The ministers changed the name to remind the French of their own history of inequity, though I don't think anyone in France much cares that a staircase lined with hookah and hooker bars in Istanbul no longer bears their national imprimatur. Do you get a lot of noise off it at night?

Nick: Weekends until three a.m. Worse are all the cabs idling to whisk the drunk Australians back to the tourist hotels. It's like I have my head in the oven from Friday night to Sunday morning.

Jake: And there's still mold?

Nick: This is Istanbul.

Jake: And there's still water coming in from the upstairs neighbor's shower?

Nick: Gotta keep the mold damp.

[Jake stands up and goes to refill the tea glasses. He goes for what looks like a whiskey bottle]

Nick: Switch to aniseed liquor. I'm not going out of town for a while.

Jake: [With aplomb] I may be able to give you a reason to celebrate. I think I found you a new apartment. It's a two-bedroom off a charming alleyway in the High Field. Nice old Ottoman feel to it, but just redone. The building has a courtyard; it even has a linden tree. It's a winner, just the kind of place that begs for a lady's touch.

Nick: I assume you know I don't live in this apartment for aesthetic reasons.

Jake: That's the best part. It's cheap. Maybe half what you pay now.

Nick: So what's wrong with it?

Jake: It's got Greeks.

[Reyhann busts in. He's got his motorcycle jacket on. The message it sends is "the Fonz." He cruises right past Jake to the fridge, where he cracks a beer, rinses his mouth out with it, spits in the sink, and then backs onto one of the stools.]

Reyhann: Hey, hey, just had to wash the bugs out of my teeth, isn't it?

Nick: Aren't you just coming from next door?

Reyhann: Yes, but tonight the gang is going to the Purple Wave Lounge to sing karaoke and I don't want anyone to see bugs in my teeth.

Jake: [Itching at the possibility of another whiskey] It's got Greeks. Apparently they just turned up one day saying the place was theirs. That it belonged to their family.

Reyhann: [Reminiscing] I remember when my neighborhood used to have Greeks. They were at the grocer, the fishmonger, and the sweet shop. It wasn't bad having them, just a kind of buzzing when they talked to one another. But somewhere along the line we managed to get rid of them, isn't it?

Nick: So this place has roommates. I mean, there are other people living there.

Jake: Not exactly. They're just sort of around. The owner says they mostly come out at night when everyone is asleep. You find some traces of them in the morning. Bits of cabbage. There might also be some odor from their cooking.

Nick: Well, I guess I like moussaka.

[SCENE: Nick sits with Brett Ashley in a café booth, again familiar but with Turkish accents: the classic boncuk, or blue eye, gazes out benevolently between them. There is the requisite print of the Father of Turks examining the defenses of Gallipoli with his tall fur hat and pipe. Brett looks like Courtney Love if Courtney Love worked a telephone switchboard. They are drinking beer and nibbling at the cocktail nuts between them]

Nick: So what do you think?

Brett: I think Jake wants in my pants.

Nick: I mean about the apartment, with the Greeks?

Brett: But the thing about Jake is, he's lazy. He was with that ratty specimen of Turkish femininity for over a year because she cooked him stuffed peppers and kept his glass full. I always figured we'd see the last of her when her cigarette finally ignited that aquanet sculpture atop her head. But like the rest of them, she had her fun and then settled down with one of her own. You should really get in on that while you live here.

Nick: What, exactly.

Brett: The locals. You spend all your time chasing Catherine Barkley just to take her back to the States. Like some wayward caveman, single-minded in clubbing and recouping a mate. Let a little Istanbul magic in while you're here. Money and adventure.

Nick: You would know.

Brett: Tut. I've always walked away before they had their fill. I know how to keep a man interested.

Nick: But what do you think about the apartment? I've had roommates before, and this sounds much better. You don't have to hassle them to pay their half of the utilities.

Brett: I'll say this for the Greeks, they know how to make cheese. This Turkish stuff that they call feta is like what feta would be if you made it out of melted Saran Wrap. That unnatural sheen it has, the way it clings to your teeth. It's funny, talking about it, I miss the real thing. It's like you're fine with this dildo, maybe you even convince yourself you like it more because it has one of those little stimulating bunny rabbits, and then, suddenly, only the thing itself will do.

Nick: Feta cheese?

Brett: [With innuendo] I really miss it.

———

[Scene: Nick's apartment. Nick enters in a hurry. Jake and Reyhann are at the breakfast nook playing backgammon and drinking beer. Reyhann is winning easily.]

    Nick: The apartment with the Greeks, I want it.

    Jake: Funny you mention it, because I was thinking...

    Reyhann: Capote! [This means he's won, in Turkish.]

    Jake: That was in cold blood.

    Nick: I want the apartment with the Greeks.

    Jake: Well, I was thinking.

    Nick: What?

    Jake: That I might take the apartment with the Greeks. I went over there and, you know, you'd hardly know there were Greeks in it, there's so much light.

    Nick: You offered it to me! Look where I'm living. [Reyhann is at the fridge opening another beer.] Look what I'm living with.

    Jake: Okay, well you should at least look at it. You may not like it.

    Nick: I know I'm going to like it.

    Jake: Well, just look at it. We'll look at it together. I'm pretty sure I saw some mold when I was there. And the water pressure in the shower is just terrible.

    Nick: Still sounds better than this place.

    Jake: Okay, okay, let's go over there now. I have the keys. But think about it: you'd have some other nationality lurking about all hours.

    Nick: [Eyeballs toward Reyhann]

    Jake: I see your point.

    [They leave with Reyhann, beer in hand, in tow.]

———

[SCENE: The other apartment. It's beautiful and light, with large ornate doors that have been stripped and sanded to a fresh pine. Jake is showing Catherine Barkley around, calling her attention to various imperfections: the sink is too small, the baseboards don't match up in places, some indiscriminate black stuff he claims is mouse droppings. A viewer might think Catherine Barkley works as a telephone operator. Nick is wandering around alone. Cue to Nick in the hallway.]

Nick: These interesting ceilings. Sort of arches made of brick.

Jake: [From off camera] The landlord said they are good in an earthquake.

Nick: Why good in an earthquake? The strength of the arch?

Jake: [Entering the hallway with Catherine] No, the bricks hit you in the head, and you don't have to worry about what happens after the earthquake. [He opens a door. Behind it is a Greek man. This is obvious, perhaps because of his mustache, perhaps because he is eating a gyro. Nick quickly closes the door on the man, but not before Catherine sees him].

Catherine: Who was that?

Nick: Nothing, a workman. Eating a kabob.

Jake: I'd say that was a gyro.

Nick: What's the difference.

[On cue, Reyhann busts in the front door]

Reyhann: Kabob is best. It's the original, isn't it? The Greeks just copy. They copy kabob, they copy baklava, they copy coffee, they copy aniseed liquor, they copy white cheese. None are as good as Turkish originals.

Catherine: Who is this?

Nick: My neighbor, from my old apartment. He drops in, like people do here.

Catherine: I can't say I like the idea of sharing my intimate space with foreigners.

Nick: But don't you want to feel the Istanbul Magic.

Catherine: I do, and I do out in the Turku bars. But at home I just want to feel home.

Jake: Sounds reasonable to me.

Nick: Sounds like something out of the Junior Orientalist League. The way I see it, you should open yourself up to the City in full, let it change you.

Catherine: You can't get away from yourself by moving from one place to another. [With that, she exits]

Jake: You going to go after her?

Nick: In a minute. It's such a beautiful apartment. So much light, so cheap, so many culinary opportunities. Feta. I can't imagine living anywhere else.

SIX.

FRED AND VIRGINIA WERE among the first to the cartoonist's party. Partially because the cartoonist's studio was just a few jagged blocks away, and partially because they were out of the house more now. Things hadn't been resolved by Poison's Greatest Hits. They came home from their trip to more strange foods in their refrigerator. Virginia's studio supplies had been moved into a narrow unused room. Before, Virginia and Fred had jokingly called the room "The Cage," after the section in the ancient palace where the sultans kept their deranged siblings. But the room had also been a sort of promise of the future unspoken between them, a place you could put a dog or a baby. The easel only fit flush against the wall, and there was no window. Virginia went in there on occasion, but never for more than a few minutes.

Coming home from work, they would spend an hour quietly in the kitchen listening for sounds of the occupiers. Often there were none, and they relaxed. Sometimes there'd be noise or light coming from under the studio door. This kept them quiet, or more often turned them away. They'd drop their work things and trek up the hill to the café owned by a famous photographer. It was a nice spot, full of nostalgic items from the years when the City was small and sad.

The photographer had made a career of photographing the City at its most careworn, scenes from twenty years ago that seemed from the past century. The place was popular among those who liked to remember the City before: before the factories, before the financial district, before the migrants and the endless horizon of slums. Fred and Virginia set up in a corner booth and quietly read or typed or ate a plate of dumplings, waiting for bedtime. Every once in a while, Fred would crack a joke about leaving home only to leave home. Virginia would smile.

"Only six more months will I have to live with that interception. Six months, two weeks, and three days." The cartoonist gave Fred a pat on the back and Virginia the traditional cheek kisses to welcome them to the party at his studio. Fred had met him a month or so ago, at a different party: the neighborhood Super Bowl party, a midnight-to-five-a.m. event for true believers only. The cartoonist had lived in Pittsburgh with his wife and had been wearing his terrible towel across his shoulders like a squirt of mustard. The party was held by a guy from Alabama who did contract work in Iraq. It was open to all who walked in the door of his spartan crash pad. Apparently he did this every year, as a public service.

In the second quarter, Ben Roethlisberger threw an interception to Green Bay, who returned a forty-yard touchdown. The game was over, Fred told the cartoonist. Fred had grown up with the Washington Redskins, and so knew something about football games being over. But the cartoonist had hope, beer, and no day job. He stayed until sunup to see the Steelers lose 31–25. Since then, the cartoonist had called Fred occasionally to talk football. It was something he couldn't get anywhere else.

The cartoonist's studio was in a suite shared by a few cartoonists. The City's newspapers were each owned by holding companies with established political allegiances, or the government itself. So cartoons became one of the only sources for unvarnished opinion. The cartoonist drew a strip called "The Wolfman." The Wolfman was a character very much like the cartoonist himself: a political dude who traveled the City's dives getting in deep conversations about the day's issues, usually with big-eyed, big-titted girls. It could be said that the cartoonist's wife was long-suffering, and it could be said that she had her reservations about the cartoonist's studio, which had a few damp couches, a small refrigerator, and an entrance off the public street. She was unpacking finger sandwiches in the corner.

Virginia asked if the cartoonist had heard about the attack on the gallery opening a week ago. He had. The Gallery Nein had opened an exhibit called "Tin Gods." It was an exhibit of statues depicting the country's military heroes, from the City's conqueror to the Father of Turks, emitting various bodily fluids. Hearing about this, a group of aging toughs took a break from another night of tea and backgammon at the local conservative party offices and kicked the shit out of a handful of foreigners and Nightmakers who were sloshing wine in plastic cups out front. The liberal papers said it was an attack on free speech, not first on the country's list of inalienable rights. The conservative papers said the gallery-goers were drunks in a neighborhood of working-class families. The cartoonist thought it was good for everyone involved. The conservatives could point to the moral degradation caused by foreigners, the artists could feel like they really got their point across. "No such thing as bad publicity." he smirked, trademark Wolfman. "I learned that in America."

His wife's gaze was on them, so the cartoonist turned his attention to Fred, taking him over to the beer fridge. Left to presumably join the wife at the refreshments, Virginia opted to play DJ with the cartoonist's music selection instead.

Fred found himself, a couple of drinks in, sitting with the cartoonist and another cartoonist friend of his.

"Umut here just got out of jail," the cartoonist said.

"For what?"

"He did a cartoon of the prime minister's wife. She wasn't wearing a headscarf."

"You can get thrown in jail for that?"

"A headscarf wasn't all she wasn't wearing. And not wearing wasn't all she wasn't doing," Umut said. He spoke English like a valley girl.

"He did three months for libel," the cartoonist said.

"Have you ever been to jail?" Fred asked, sucking in his law-abiding beer gut.

"Yeah, I did six months for aiding the terrorists. I had the Wolfman talk to this crispy girl from the east. He tells her she should speak her own language, because it is the language of love."

"Crispy?" Fred asked.

"Like hot and fresh. We call them crispy here. I thought we got that from America?" Umut added. He was slowly assembling a joint.

"They put you in jail for that, saying that Kurdish is the language of love?"

"Well," the cartoonist smiled, "I sort of said that in my time as part of the gendarme out East, I fucked a lot of crispy girls and they made better lovers than the peacocks of this City. More naturally they do it, isn't it? They said I was advocating the gendarme abandon their posts against the terrorists."

"It was good times out East," Umut said. "Remember when we intercepted all that hash?"

"And you ate it to keep that prick colonel from finding it."

"I thought I'd be like fucked up for my whole life." Umut already had big eyes, and he opened them comically wide.

They started joking between themselves in Turkish, the cartoonist doing impressions of the blitzed-out Umut, Umut doing impressions of the prick colonel. Fred began gathering himself up to seek out another beer and Virginia. The couch was deep with age and use.

"Wait," the cartoonist said, "you haven't told us about the Castle." He flicked open a Zippo lighter and lit it by running it across his jeans. Fred almost laughed at this throwback.

"What's there to know? It pays our bills. It's fucking far away."

"C'mon." The cartoonist took the joint from Umut and handed it to Fred. "Everybody knows the place is just full of the best chicks money can buy. I mean, oiled-up weekends in the south followed by milk baths and colon flushes and face poison. All wrapped up in imported panties for the City's little princes. It's gotta drive you insane, them sitting in your classes crossing and uncrossing their legs." Thus spake the Wolfman.

Rather than answer, Fred took the joint and tried to conjure up the hottest student he could remember. From the whirlwind of hair extensions and eyeliner, he was vaguely proud that he couldn't pinpoint one particular student who raised his pulse. The pot's dull hum flooded in, and the whole thing struck him as absurd even as he wondered what it would be like to pull the tights off an under-twenty ass bent across his office desk.

"What he wants to know, like are they crispy or are they peacocks?" Umut pinched the joint away from Fred's frozen hand.

"I don't think they know how to fart," Fred managed to say.

The cartoonists looked at each other, then Umut spat the joint from his mouth in an eruptive cackle. The cartoonist joined, throwing in a coyote howl or two that Fred figured was professional affect.

"Fucking peacocks," he said. "So many feathers you can never find the damn hole."

Fred was getting too caught up in the details: on one hand a plate of KFC, on the other a live peacock. Greasy, glistening, warm but dead in your hand or a little puff of a nasty, hard-to-catch thing. Was that all there was to it, and isn't it the male peacocks with the feathers? His eyes locked on the yellow slinkys of Virginia's leg warmers through the forest of jeans.

Sensing Fred's renewed distance, the cartoonists fell back into their native tongue. Fred excused himself with some muttered thanks for the high. He made for the rough location of the leg warmers by way of the beer fridge.

Virginia was cornered by a bearded man, but in a good way. She had the cool edge of a windowsill to rest on, and the man held a bottle of red wine in his left hand with which he kept Virginia filled. The man, in a sailorish cable knit sweater, was a painter. He was telling Virginia about the gallery show of his work in the stylish Baby neighborhood. Ten pictures in a sunny little spot by the water was how he described it. He stood to make some serious money. In fact, the party was for him; he was the guest of honor. Virginia didn't mind that he was playing himself to the hilt. She didn't even much mind that he thought it was "interesting" that she was a painter too. He had saved her from the cartoonist's wife, whose half-English conversational forays revolved around Pittsburgh and jealousy. Virginia didn't know much about either.

Fred had sidled up next to the painter. He looked unkempt and oversized in comparison, with a six-month-old haircut and a T-shirt hammocking his soft middle. He had a beer between two fingers like a cigarette. He was high, which struck Virginia as cute. *Let's see how he does*, she thought, adjusting her perch on the sill.

"The thing about painting in this City," the painter was saying, "is that everyone believes you need to capture grandiose beauty and melancholy. In the art academies, if you paint a white mosque, someone comes over and tells you to put a yellow wash on it. I don't do that. If I see a white mosque, I paint a white mosque."

"Where do you go to see a white mosque here?" Fred butted in.

"Well, you could start with The Calm Ones Mosque in the ancient cemetery across the Strait. They finished it a year ago. It's like the Sydney Opera House of mosques. I did a series on it, nestling it in a thicket of tombstones from the era of the conquest. You know the ones, stuck crooked in the ground, topped with different turbans. I'd say it looks like the Wizard of Oz."

Fred scowled a bit.

"We should visit," Virginia said to him. "We don't get out of this part of town much, except to go to work."

"You work together?"

"We live together," Fred said flatly.

True, but Virginia felt a little peed on.

"You teach English?" The artist kept his commanding position, arm braced on the wall next to Virginia's window.

"Writing," Fred corrected. He swigged his beer, balancing it on the back of his palm in case anyone was watching. The studio was nearly full. A woman with a pixie haircut reached through the three of them to open the window by Virginia. The air had that damp bone-chill of the City's nights, but it was quickly lost in the cloud of body warmth and cigarette smoke from the studio.

"Writing in English?"

"Yes." Fred felt out of shape. His high was entering the phase of dull comfort. In his youth, it would be time to go get a burger with chili and Cheese Whiz.

"You're married?"

Virginia shook her head. Fred glared at her. Virginia was a terrible liar, and she prided herself on it.

The painter sipped his wine. *Is it true you people find foreign women irresistible*, Fred thought to ask. No, better to save that one. Who cared if he couldn't resist Virginia; only the inverse concerned Fred.

"So," the painter said, "what was it that drew you to the City?"

"The money," Fred answered.

Virginia didn't contradict him.

"It must be nice to make money teaching something you're born with."

"You weren't born a painter?"

"I studied painting."

"I studied English, literature."

Fred knew how this would end. Virginia was never going to go home with the artist. But she wanted to see him play his hand. He'd played it badly, maybe because he was high. He should have swept her off her feet. Instead he was going punch for punch.

"I like English literature," the painter said. "Jack London especially."

"Dogs and the cold," Fred said. "There's a lot to like." Even being sincere, he came off as an ass.

From the crowd, a guy approached. Fred hoped it would be the cartoonist, coming to pull them back into the mix. Instead it was another darkish, handsome type. He was wearing the same sweater as the painter.

"This is my brother," the painter explained.

"Does your mother still dress you two?" Fred spat.

Virginia giggled. Fred watched her clavicles as they rustled, like they were caught in a breeze. He was that breeze.

The painter was flummoxed. He and his brother talked their language in a clipped fashion. Virginia was off the windowsill. "I've got to pee," she said. Passing Fred, she pinched his butt. Fred watched her pencil skirt weave into the party's crowd.

"I wish I knew English well enough to do that," the painter said.

"Take my class." Fred didn't turn around. He felt suddenly exhausted. In front of him was a room full of people making a go of it, here in the cultural capital of their culture. And here was he, pedaling his birth language in the name of some kind of adventure. Was he as special, as different as he sometimes felt, or was he just someone who couldn't make it at home? Maybe the pot had just shifted into that reflective, self-pitying phase. His beer was empty. He should go find Virginia.

They caught up with the cartoonist just as he was getting too drunk to speak English. His wife must have left, because his arm had slid around the waist of a short girl. In the half light, she was all cleavage and liquid eyeliner.

"Nil here is a, a what, a housing person. A fair housing person, who works for fair housing. And she and her organization are throwing a huge huge party out in the Water Tower district to raise money for the gypsies. The government's kicking them out, going to put up condos. Kicking out the gypsies, well I guess all the rest of the world's already done that. We've let them stay two thousand years! But the gypsies know how to party, and Nil knows how to party, so it's going to be a great party." He gave her a squeeze and asked her something in Turkish. From the back of her cigarette pack, she pulled two cards and handed them to Fred with a conspirator's smile.

"Two tickets," the cartoonist explained. "It's in a month, on a Saturday."

"We'll be there," Fred said, "but we've got to get going now."

"Okay," the cartoonist said. "You know where to find me. Six months!"

The narrow streets had filled with the haze of soft coal. It smelled halfway between tar and death. Virginia took Fred's arm as they worked their way home over the cobblestones.

"In college, I read all these Dickens novels," Fred said, "and I never once wondered what they smelled like. But now I know."

Virginia laughed, even though it didn't make much sense. "You were cute tonight, all defensive."

"I know I've got a good thing." Fred shrugged. He was afraid he didn't sound totally convinced.

"Let's not go home."

"You want to go to a bar or something?"

"A hotel, just somewhere we'd really be alone."

They continued in the general direction of their apartment. Street-lights in the neighborhood had been strung between the close-leaning apartment buildings and shone like spotlights on the timeworn stones.

They passed through one where a pair of dogs tore at some bit of carrion, little links of spine glistening like Tic-Tacs. Fred was about to say, "Well we could cross the boulevard and stay at the Big London Orient Express Hotel." It was the only authentic hotel in the area. The Hilton, the Marble Sea: these were inordinately expensive and sterile, their rates driven up by business travelers. They frequented the London Hotel bar, with all its antique travel trunks and birdcages strewn about like a shipwreck beach. But the rooms were really for the girls who worked the bar, nervous Russian bottle blondes who pretended to read airplane seat-pocket magazines in the corner booths. Jake said he'd stayed there once and the fucking in the next room had kept him up all night. The thought of fake moans brought saliva to his mouth unexpectedly. It wasn't the romantic gesture she had in mind, and there was no halfway point for his desire to meet hers. He kept quiet until they reached the door to their building.

"I guess not, then," Virginia said.

Fred took his keys out of his pocket

"I wish you'd say something."

"There are only like five hours until dawn. Why don't we save it for sometime we can really enjoy it?" He meant it. He had a reserve of gallantry somewhere that could embrace intimacy and clean sheets. But in this moment he'd misplaced it.

"Whatever." Virginia walked in. The automated light clicked on to the gaunt foyer. "I would really enjoy sometime going back to it being just us."

SEVEN.

IT WAS FRED'S LEAST favorite time in the semester. Mandatory individual conferences. MICs. Each of his students was required to appear in his windowless office, ostensibly to discuss his advice on how they could improve the essay they had written for his class. The real purpose was to confront plagiarists. MICs were exhausting. He would do nearly twenty in a day, rushing the good kids in and out the door, describing their shitty grammar and diction as "non-standard" and suggesting small changes. Unsystematic flourishes really, which only someone still in love with language would consider to be corrections. But it was those little errors he corrected that proved the papers to be the genuine article. Let a thousand flowers bloom. It was the perfect papers, with every participle in the right place, that had surely been written by some senior at Ohio State hustling a little cash.

Fred knew because he and his college friends had written essays for prep-school kids for drug money. They called it "The English Majors' Widows and Orphans Fund" and rationalized the whole thing as being sort of like private tutoring except more lucrative and without the constant explaining. They had even made bumper stickers that read, "My Kid Is an Honor Student because His Papers Were Written at Union College" and put them up around town. In a small font, there was a business email for new clients. If he knew then that he'd be on the other side of the table in a few years, he wouldn't have done it for any money. Well, maybe not *any* money, but not inconsistent money that quickly went up in smoke.

When the plagiarist student arrived for his or her MIC, the process began. The Castle had a tortured policy when it came to dealing with cheaters. It couldn't let them thrive, especially since most were quite brazen. Yet it couldn't do without them. They were the children of the generals, used to having things done for them by housekeepers, cooks, tutors, and their mothers. They were paying full fare, and if someone was finally going to step forward and have the other half of the library filled with books, it was going to be one of their parents.

Oguzhan was one such case, entering tentatively. He had signed up for the last meeting of the day, hoping to slip by unnoticed. Unfortunately, he was a huge kid, obviously English illiterate, who spent class periods staring at his smartphone and practicing his signature. He'd handed in a perfect essay, full of invectives against the denigration of women.

"Have a seat, Oguzhan." Fred was pretending to examine some finer point of the kid's essay so he wouldn't have to meet his eyes. He could tell the kid was in fight or flight, and if Fred was to get anywhere he'd have to lull him into a false sense of security. The goal was to extract a confession. A confession which would no doubt be lost in a drawer after a semester, but nevertheless a confession that proved Fred was doing his job and that the university wasn't simply printing diplomas for cash.

"So," Fred said, "I really liked your essay."

A craven grin filled the kid's face, the desired effect.

Fred continued, "But I was a little confused at this part." He pointed out a particularly well-written paragraph about how "the media hampers women's advancement by either sexualizing them or critiquing them for taking on masculine characteristics."

Oguzhan gazed at the paper and Fred watched him sound out the unfamiliar words. "It's about the womens," he concluded.

"Yes, but what about them?"

"They are sexy sometimes, it's a problem."

Fred pointed to the word "hampers." "What do you mean by 'hampers,' here."

He could feel the kid's unease. "I'm tired," Oguzhan said. "My head hurts."

"I'm just asking you what you meant. You wrote it, after all?"

"Yes, I wrote. Just now my head hurts, I can't tell you."

"But maybe you had a little help, you know, with the words. Words like hampers."

"No. No. No help. I wrote." Even though there were no consequences, the real cheats never confessed. If they confessed, they would have to rewrite the paper, which probably meant paying someone to write a believably bad paper and accepting the believably bad grade they rightly deserved. But they were never disciplined, let alone suspended.

Fred skipped ahead in his script. "Look, Oguzhan, it's clear to me you had help writing this paper. If you'd just write out on this form that you had help writing this paper, you can rewrite it."

"I wrote. Why would I rewrite? These are my words."

"Then what does hampers mean?"

"My head hurts."

"Hampers?" Fred was thinking of the dirty laundry that was accumulating. Last time he was going to do the wash, the machine was full of the other people's stuff. Opening the door, a massively cupped lace bra tumbled out. He left things where they were, embarrassed.

"This is my essay. I wrote."

"Well, I know you didn't, and I'm going to send it to the disciplinary committee with my evidence you didn't write it."

This was the threat that often turned them. But sometimes they were either too smart or too stupid to believe Fred would go through the bureaucratic nightmare involved in pursuing a plagiarism case.

Oguzhan's bottom lip went fat. Fred did his best to maintain a friendly but aggressive posture. He hadn't drawn this one out as much as usual. He was tired. Outside his office door, the halogen lights of the hallway promised only the long ride to the halved apartment.

"I wrote."

Fred could hear the seconds click on Oguzhan's watch, some kind of expensive oyster perpetual timepiece, self-wound tight from living on an arm that was, Fred imagined, always giving him satisfaction: smoking, eating, masturbating. He was a little afraid of the rage he felt forming behind his ears. Oguzhan's initial waft of cologne was giving way to rancid BO. Some of the wealthiest kids didn't bathe in the cold months. Their parents still had a deep-seated fear of drafts.

"Oguzhan, the choice is simple. Just write that you had help with your essay and nothing bad will happen. If you don't, it could turn out badly for you."

"I wrote."

The kid had sad, over-weaned eyes. They weren't malicious, as much as Fred wished they were.

"I wrote."

And this was the problem. Fred could never know for sure. Oguzhan might have written the paper, just as monkeys might type out

Dickens. Or he might have been like Fred's own little brother, who sent all his college papers home to their mother to be polished. Fred had to ask himself, did he believe Oguzhan didn't write the paper because he had real evidence, or just because of the dimness in the kid's eyes? Silly as it sounded, he actually lost sleep over these situations.

"Look, Oguzhan, all you have to do is say you didn't write it and we can move on. You can rewrite it, totally forgiven."

"But if I rewrite myself, there will be more mistakes and I'll get a lower grade."

"You'll get the grade you deserve." Fred tried to make this sound kind, since the kid seemed to have almost confessed.

"I'm not taking a low grade. This is the fourth time I take this course."

An impasse. Fred would have to make good on his threats, a whole day's worth of work gathering a case against this kid, talking to his other teachers and the administration. A whole day Fred could be doing something else, taking home the same money.

"Oguzhan, how much did you pay for this paper?"

"Pay? I wrote."

"Seriously, Oguzhan, how much did this paper cost?"

"I'm not telling you. If I tell you, then I have to rewrite, pay again, not pass the course and pay again for next semester. I pay too much."

Fred was going to press him for exact figures, but he felt pity for the kid. He was getting shaken down on all sides. He could take a decade to graduate and spend enough on his bachelor's to get his name on a building. Probably put his paper-writers' kids through college too. "Okay, Oguzhan. You can go."

"I can go?"

"You'll hear from the discipline committee." But the kid was out the door. Fast, for a child that size.

Fred left the office with all the papers strewn about on the floor behind his desk. There'd be a minute tomorrow to sort them out, and he hoped to have the inclination to do it then. It was nearly 5:30, when the convoy of faculty buses left the Castle to various corners of the city. The rush of adults, burdened with computer bags and precarious stacks of grading, always struck Fred as an evacuation.

Adrian was just locking up his own office as Fred started for the bus.

"You know what those wretched interrogations you do remind me of?"

Fred shrugged. It was policy to keep the office door open during MICs, so if a dean walked by they'd appreciate the bustle and busyness. The side effect was a whole hallway of chattering punctuated by pleas of innocence. He figured Adrian hadn't picked up on his questions about the economics of cheating.

"There's a letter from Pliny the Younger about the persecution of early Christians. He basically writes Rome and says, here's how I'm treating them: If they confess, I tell them to step on a cross, drink a toast to the Emperor, and they can go home. If they don't confess, I torture them a little until they do, or I'm satisfied they are innocent. If they won't step on the cross, I feed them to the lions. Rome writes back saying, sounds good to us. Then Pliny writes back saying, the problem is they won't step on the cross, so I'm going to need to rotate in some new hungry lions. Rome says, you're sure they know all they have to do to avoid death is to step on the cross. Pliny says, of course, I tell them over and over, just step on the cross and drink a toast and you can live. That's it. It totally flummoxed him. And of course, in the end, the Christians won."

"I have a feeling there's something to be learned from that," Fred said.

Adrian patted him on the shoulder, smiling the knowing smile that had shaped all other aspects of his face. "The classics, my boy. We are doomed to repeat them."

EIGHT.

THEY WERE ABOUT TO pass over the pontoon bridge into the chaos of the marketplace. Virginia was bracing herself for the onslaught of young men in black windbreakers and asymmetrical haircuts. The inevitable crush of thick covered women pushing toward piles of formless underwear. They were headed for the City's ancient heart, Fred convinced that in a few months it would become inaccessible, tourist-clogged with the coming warm weather.

"We'll walk to the Starch neighborhood then, when we don't have a choice." He was holding her hand. The Starch neighborhood was where the city's old money was. It had sidewalks, the only place near High Field that did.

In spite of himself, Fred had to admit that things at the apartment had declined. They saw the Greeks occasionally, in the early mornings or the middle of the night, but there was a tacit agreement that there be no talking. Everyone kept their eyes down, even the child. It was like the two worlds of their dailiness were superimposed over one another, unable to touch. But other aspects of life permeated that barrier. After the first few weeks, Virginia proclaimed she would not clean another grain of rice from the stovetop, so now they stuck in the nooks of the burners like grubs, glued down by grime.

The ring around the tub was charcoal, and they left it that way since neither of them took baths. When they showered, the drain would clog and spit up little dark, curly hairs that made Virginia jump. The child seemed ethereally quiet, but Fred swore some afternoons he could hear the woman's soft moans coming from Virginia's studio. Virginia said she didn't want to know.

When they had first arrived in the City, they intended to walk to a different neighborhood each Saturday. It was, as people said, a city of villages. A walk among the gutted, weed-sprouting churches of the Lighthouse district was a world away from an afternoon rounding the Fashion neighborhood's wide promontory with nothing but the glittering Marble Sea before you. These neighborhoods were on different continents, of different worlds. But the most ready contrast was between walking north to the Starch or south across the inlet to the ancient city.

The marketplace spilled like a bucket down the sloping hill. At the top, the rug and gold sellers lolled beneath the blue archways romanticised by the Orientalists. Below them, the City's new splendors were piled in concrete arcades: spangled wedding gowns, pre-ripped jeans, cardigans with high collars, variegated headscarves, a T-shirt that read "There's life and there's loving you." Twenty years before, the United Nation's geological survey warned that the City's population could not exceed seven million, twice what it was at the time of the survey, without catastrophic ecological consequences and earth-quake risk. Thanks to shirts like "There's life and there's loving you," the City was fourteen million and growing. At the inlet's edge, stalls of salt cheese and pepper paste butted against the piers where the famous fish sandwich sellers had long ago swapped in frozen fish from Iceland for the fruit of the oil-slicked Strait.

Fred and Virginia passed along their usual route, moving through the market's least popular streets: bead street, cleaning liquid street, all-wood kitchen supply street. They used to walk the street of wedding gowns, where the most piously dressed women would create human gridlock studying tube tops like butterflies under glass.

"They aren't leaving, are they?" Virginia said as they hooked the sharp turn onto the street of buttons, snaps, and eyes.

"We're not either."

"You never heard from Marvin?"

"When he said he would be unreachable for twenty-four months, he must have meant it. I stopped paying him."

"What?"

"I didn't pay him rent this month. I saved it, don't worry. I thought he'd miss it."

"That's not honest."

"Well, we're not getting what we signed on for. Besides, if the Greek guy really does own the place, what if he asks us for back rent or something?" Fred studied the boards in each shop window, buttons in descending order of size, fasteners hanging limply.

"What about getting rid of them, with the cops?"

"Ata said it's tough. The cops are a non-starter, and we can't seem to figure out when they go out. A lawyer might work. But you know, what's gross for us is gross for them too. Eventually they might not think it's worth it, living this way."

"But they're not leaving."

Once up the hill, the market gave way to a kind of silence. The rabbit warren opened up to spaces of imperial grandeur, the seat of power of three empires, for eight thousand years. Only Damascus had been peopled longer. They'd only ever dared venture here when cool breezes crossed the spaces much of the world thought were full of camels and palm trees. In the summer, thousands of the benighted and fanny-packed would disembark their cruise liners and fill the squares. Looming above it all was the Holy Wisdom, the world's biggest building, tombs aside, for a millennium. It was a bad millennium for most people, but through it all the thing hulked like the engorged womb of the Earth.

Across from it was the first imperial mosque to be built with taxes, as opposed to pillage. It was controversial too for having a blasphemous number of minarets. The sultan had asked for gold minarets, and the architect, to save tax money perhaps, "heard" six minarets. In Turkish the two sounded similar, gold and six. The trouble was, the only mosque permitted six minarets was the one built around the Kaaba, in Mecca. The sultan added a seventh minaret to the Sacred Mosque, problem solved. Tourists called it the Blue Mosque, but every great Islamic city had one of those. It was built atop the colonnades of the Byzantine Grand Palace, sunk into the silt and broken by tree roots. Somewhere down there was the amethyst birthing room, where the empire's royal children were born into the purple—now probably home or tomb to the vagrants said to live in the tunnels and cisterns of the ancient City.

Fred and Virginia had a bench they preferred. It sat at the tip of what was the ancient horse track and gave a decent view of the grey sky between the two landmarks. They watched as sparrows got caught between the dull warmer air of the Marble Sea and the gusts from the north. Flocks would rip, contort, and crease up like someone fiddling with a piece of paper.

"Do you think about what's next for us?" Virginia asked as she watched the flocks disperse.

"The idea."

"Can you remind me?"

"We make enough money here to let us go after the things we really want."

"Right." Virginia didn't make eye contact. "Is that why you're saving the rent?"

"I'm not going to pretend to love what I do. You're not either, I know. So why not put away all we can?"

"What were we planning before we decided to come here?"

"Just to get jobs in New York, something like that. I mean, it wasn't that long ago." Fred's mother was an amateur astrologer, full of unbidden advice. She had, over lunch, opined that the couple might live abroad before settling down. That they ended up, six months later, taking these positions in the City was a coincidence. An email from April. But it could come off as Fred bowing to either his mother or his horoscope.

"Sometimes I can hardly remember before." Virginia didn't sound at all like Scarlett O'Hara. "But I can imagine our house. If it is in California, it will have an orange tree. If it is somewhere else, it will smell like wood smoke in the winter."

"We've got a couple fun things coming up." Fred broke the silence

They'd rounded the back of the Six Minaret Mosque and were strolling past shuttered hostels and laundromats. They'd walk down to the Sand Gate, cross the Coast Road, and walk back along the edge of the Marble Sea.

"Dinner with Eddie, and that gypsy fundraiser," he continued.

Virginia was mulling things over. When they finally caught the whips of salt air, she spoke.

"I need you to do something."

"Anything, babe."

"I need you to promise you are not letting this thing with the apartment go on just because it is saving money. Or providing material. Or any other secret reason."

She was giving him the look. At least that's how he thought of it. He remembered it from the first time he turned up shit-faced at her apartment. He'd been out in Providence with some of the artist-musicians on the make he'd shared a loft with and really let the drinks get on top of him. The look wasn't one of anger, or disappointment, or disdain, or pity. It was disenchantment. The unvarnished look of a painter examining a subject and seeing just what is there.

"It's saving us time," he blurted. "If we live for free, we can leave with our down payment in two years instead of three."

"Years we still have to live with ghosts. Ghosts who leave their laundry in the machine and their garbage in front of our door. I haven't picked up a brush in the past weeks, and I haven't seen you working on your script."

"I've just been pinched for time."

"Pinched for time trying to find ways to be out of the house? It doesn't add up."

The wake of a rusty tanker lapped up on the breakwater. The tanker itself had long enjoyed being free of the Strait and was gliding toward the grey horizon.

"Fred, I know you're trying to do what's right for us, but I need you to make sure you've done everything you can to get our apartment back. April said Ata would be happy to take you wherever so you can tell someone there are people living in our apartment who don't belong there. I know it doesn't mean anything will happen immediately, or ever, even, but I want to be on the right side of this. And if I have to live away from home, on the other side of the world from home, I need a place I can be myself, and be with you."

They came to the mouth of the Strait. At their feet, beneath the water, was the greatest shipwreck graveyard in the world. Since the peoples of the first alphabet, sailors had drowned in the ripping currents within sight of the City they hoped they could despoil, or save, or merely touch foot to.

From here they could see the financial district spring out of the distant hills like a cave quartz. The taut bow of the transcontinental suspension bridge arched to the hills on the other side. They could see the old train station across the strait, which daily dispatched passengers east to the holiest sites of all religions. Ferryboats, seagulls trailing them, puttered between the shores.

"I know I'm going to miss it, when the time comes to leave," Virginia said.

NINE.

FRED KNEW HE'D FOUND the right garage when he heard "Every Rose Has Its Thorn," the extended cut, blasting. Ata had taken him over once before, on a scooter. Fred figured himself for having a good sense of direction. But when he entered the campus of the Auto-Palace from the metro, he panicked. Stacks of garages were set into the hillside like an Anasazi site, full of mechanics ministering to the city's terrible drivers and delivery boys ministering to the mechanics with meatball sandwiches and beers. No one he looked at looked at him like he belonged there.

Ata's motorcycle gang might have ranked among the world's most adorable. The young bearded and bandanaed members would take their freshly tuned bikes out and return to declare his work "orgasmic." They kept the beer fridge full. They also kept the garage warm. Ata had rigged an old oil heater to burn their used motor oil.

The garage's bay was ajar, so Fred just walked in. A couple of the young guys were gathered around a massive bike, taller than most cars, with a profusion of pipe flowing from its sides. One of them, a doe-eyed junior rider, recognized Fred and went off to fetch Ata. Another turned to say something to him.

"Excuse me?"

"I said, you've got to have a dick like a jackhammer if you want to ride this bitch. Soviet, all mechanical."

"Wow," Fred said. He knew better than to make some stab about performance or durability. He'd be out of his depth in a minute.

Ata clapped him on the shoulder and with his free hand offered an uncapped beer. "What do you think of my new baby?" he asked.

"Big."

"Yeah, all mechanical. No fucking computer to go wrong. You can put anything in the tank. Whale oil if you like. Anything short of firewood, though you have to imagine the Russians tried that too. I got one with a sidecar, for when I have children with April, isn't it."

"You guys are having kids?"

"Of course. Isn't that why we are together?"

What could Fred say? Sometimes, in the moment, Virginia said things like *put your babies in me*, but they always used protection, so it was just a manner of speaking. Other times they'd joke about raising a baby in the Cage of their apartment. It was all in an abstract future, one that didn't include living with Greeks.

"Cheers to that," was all Fred ended up saying.

"You want to take something out for a ride? I'm sure the boys can lend you a bike. You can go through the woods as far as the European Lighthouse and be back before dark for the grill." Ata was known for the grill, serving up piles of smoky meatballs and chicken wings from negligible contributions. It was something he lived for.

"No," Fred said, "a lot less fun. I was wondering if you could come with me to the Housing Directorate. April said you'd be okay with it."

"Hmm. They are still in your apartment. I can send some of the boys down with you. We can just take them out, you know. Throw their asses in the street, isn't it?"

"But what if it really is their apartment? I wouldn't want you to do something that would get you, or us, in trouble. And you know, really, it isn't as bad as it sounds, there's plenty of space."

"So if you don't notice them, why do anything. Nothing happens at the Housing Directorate, certainly nothing for free."

Fred was aware that bureaucratic procedures could cost hundreds in small fees. It was the lifeblood of the City. "Virginia wants me to take care of this thing."

"Then it must be done."

They took Ata's old bike. He'd built it by hand, piece by piece in the bad old days, even welding a cavalry saber to the bitch seat, forming a kind of backrest/warning to tailgaters. Fred found the perfect arc of the saber against his back chilling, so he gripped Ata's riding jacket in real bitch style. The engine could have hauled an eighteen-wheeler, but it topped out at a hundred kilometers an hour. All noise and torque.

"I should lend it to you," Ata said when they arrived at the Directorate building. "It's slow, but it's loud. No one fucks with you. Maybe because of the sword."

When they entered the Housing Directorate, they were greeted with abandoned lobby: bits of plywood in one corner with sawdust, an unplugged water cooler, you'd think a plague had struck. Ata paid it no mind, walking right over to the only elevator in the bank without a sign taped across its doors. "Everything happens upstairs," he said.

Upstairs was all body odor and cigarette smoke. It was filled with a steady murmur punctuated by the smack of stamp blocks. There were cracked plastic chairs in loose rows. A few dejected people sat studying the linoleum floor.

"Just wait here," Ata said. "I'll figure out who we need to see."

Fred sat next to a man in a brown suit, who bobbed a little as he worked his way through his worry beads. To look busy, Fred pulled out all the documentation he'd brought along. It amounted to the lease, some emails, and some instructions Marvin had left concerning his whereabouts. He didn't have a copy of the Ottoman deed, so if the occupiers wanted it considered, they'd have to bring it down themselves.

Without much ceremony, two uniformed men grasped an old man who had been sitting at one of the kiosks, and, taking him by the armpits, removed him as he whimpered. Fred became aware of a kind of brown quality to the air. A kind of taupe hanging there. A desperate yawn opened up in him, like his body knew there was only so much air to be had.

"Tea or coffee?"

The woman said it in perfect English. She had full cheeks and soft eyes despite being drawn and broken by age.

"I'm okay," Fred said, a little desperate for Ata to return. The body odor coming off the man in the brown suit was coming into focus, and now this woman had him boxed in. There were plenty of other seats.

After a few minutes of looking him over, the woman said, "I'll get you a coffee, Americans like coffee."

"No, really, I'm okay. My friend will be back in a minute." But the woman was already up, headed with surprising agility toward a little galley in the corner of the waiting area. Fred popped up to try and track down Ata, but one look at the fractured hallways lined with offices and kiosks numbered out of order had him back in the waiting room. He switched seats, sat in the back like a bad student.

The woman returned with his coffee. It was the boiled tar in a blue and white porcelain thimble he'd become accustomed to. He took the saucer it sat upon from the lady. "What do I owe you?"

"It is just hospitality."

"Well, thank you then." Fred put it on the seat next to him. The woman remained standing beside him.

"I'm just going to let it cool."

"No problem." She didn't even lean against the wall, just stood with her back slightly hunched. He tried reading the few documents he had, the jocular emails from Marvin. He could feel her look.

"Are you sure I can't give you something for this?" Fred said.

"No," the woman replied. "It is simply our desire that you enjoy yourself."

Ata was nowhere to be seen. Fred was reading Marvin's message: I know this city will speak to you two. Don't forget to tell Mustafa the fishmonger that Marvin said he should sell you the god's-truth sea bass, not the farmed stuff. *Fine*, Fred thought to himself. *Fine*. He took the little cup and drained the strong syrup until the grounds hit his teeth. He gave the cup to the lady, who scurried back to her galley. He figured their little interaction was complete, but just as quickly she was standing back beside him.

"Where'd you learn English?"

"It was required for the job."

"You're kidding."

"There used to be very high standards." She sighed. "See, look at this."

It was a brochure, timeworn. The faded image showed three figures holding hands crossing the inlet bridge, behind them the gray profile of the New Mosque. On the left, a stylish Turkish man in a light jacket. In the center, a Turkish woman in a black dress and orange scarf with a Mary Tyler Moore vibe. And looking like the hat she's about to toss in the air, James Baldwin. If Fred hadn't been able to recognize him from his undergraduate years, the caption below would have given it away. "Istanbul is a place where I can find out again where I am, and to find out what I must do"—Jimmy Baldwin, the famous black American novelist, and his friend the great Turkish actor Engin Cezzar.

The brochure was titled "Istanbul for the Black American Traveler." It began by describing Baldwin's flight from racism, first American and then French. The Turks understand, the French were racist towards them too. If this weren't reason enough to cancel that trip to Paris, those curious about Islam, members of the Nation or no, could get a taste for it in the religion's fourth-most holy site. But what really caught Fred's attention was the brochure's final missive.

"The dream told Mehmet, you must conquer this city, or it will conquer you. This is commonly known. But who conquers this city? The strong have tried, twentyfold times. They only succeeded twice. Even the companions of the prophet died outside its walls. Here it is the slaves who conquer. The black eunuchs, the Viking guards, the kidnapped boys of the New Troop, the kidnapped girls of the harem. Even the Christians and the Turks began as slaves. So we welcome you!"

The old woman smiled. "I really wish we were as welcoming now as we were back then. Sure there was less money, and more gangsters, but I miss the sweet sadness of the old City." Her hands passed lightly over Fred's, retrieving the brochure. She had the long tapered fingers of a young musician. Once she started back toward her galley, a long shudder passed through him.

Ata arrived after a minute. "I'm not sure we can do anything without the original deed, but if you want, we can both go to the clerk and you can try and explain what's going on better," he said.

"Is it true slaves are the only ones who can make it in this city?" Fred asked distractedly.

"Maybe." Ata was philosophical. "Just look where you are."

Fred watched the woman tend the galley, checking the strength of the tea in the top kettle. He certainly didn't feel like trying to explain his home situation to a series of clerks, even through what he imagined would be Ata's vivid translations.

Fred had done something like this before. After a month living in the City, it was clear he and Virginia were ill prepared. The few palm trees that seemed to feature in all the trademark postcards of the City thrived in spite of the cold rains that set in with fall's arrival. Along with the Mexican hot sauce and packed brown sugar that could not be had for any money in the megacity, Virginia's mother had sent her the winter coat from her Chicago days in their first care package. Unfortunately, Virginia's mother had a Midwestern honest streak and put the coat's full value, new, on the customs declaration. When the package failed to reach their High Field apartment, Fred got on the phone with the postal authorities. The first few phone calls ended with what Fred would later learn to be diatribes against the ignorance of foreigners. After weeks of being on the other side of these, he picked up the few words they all had in common. Finally he got a reply in halting English. The box was being held at the Cannonball Gate postal depot pending payment of customs duty.

The afternoon they made it out to the Cannonball Gate was typical late fall: getting out of the tram, the cloth of their umbrellas was flayed from the frames. They stood for a moment before the vast walls that had been grotesquely restored to look as they had a millennium and a half ago. The descendants of the conquerors had filled the holes their cannons made and now flew their own flags from the battlements: red, for the West, and the moon as seen by the Lion Warrior, reflected in the blood of those he'd defeated. Instead of holding back besieging hordes, the walls loomed above public fitness equipment painted in primary colors.

The depot was set behind a little muddy parking lot, not far from the highway or the famous gypsy neighborhood of the Water Tower. Walking in, they were greeted by a modest line in front of a kiosk marked 1. When they were finally standing in front of the jaundiced clerk, he took Fred's reference number and entered it on a keyboard like someone picking lice from a child's head. He printed out a slip on an old dot-matrix machine, tearing the perforations with agonizing delicacy. Then he said a word, presumably a number. Fred just assumed it was two. But at the kiosk marked 2, the clerk looked at the slip as if he had never seen the like. After turning it back to front and examining it under a light, he called over to the clerk in kiosk 8, across the hallway. The clerk at 8 recognized the slip and even spoke English. He told the couple they either had to go to room 10 or room 30, where the package would be.

They came upon room 30 first. All the while Fred was thanking the Father of Turks, who switched the country from Arabic script to Latin script by fiat. He also gave the City its name: Istanbul. It was through a law of postal reform. Istanbul, slang for "to the city," officially replaced the kaleidoscope of what the place meant to the world. The post office would no longer deliver letters to Stambol, or Constantinople, or Al-Asitana, or Kostandina, or Bâb-i-Âlî, or Takht-e Rum. Nevertheless, to this day you could catch a plane from Moscow to Tsargrad and end up in the City. The Father of Turks changed the name to take away the city's history. And his successors did their best to get rid of any people who might remind them of that past: the Greeks who had founded it, the Armenians who'd built it, and the Jews who tied it to the rest of the world.

Three men were at a card table, smoking and eating sunflower seeds. They'd been at it a while; the floor was scattered with husks and butts. Fred presented the slip to one, who eyed it with mild disgust. He handed it to another, probably the youngest, who rose and shuffled into a caged-off area full of parcels. He came back with one—the one, as Virginia's sigh confirmed. Another of the men cleared the table with a few hand sweeps. Then he pulled out a knife. The package was placed before him. Instead of cutting the tape, he went after the box with a butcher's precision. He even cut off the customs declaration, which he handed to the only man yet to move. That man examined the declaration as the knife man took items out of the box and handed them to the youngest man. First were a pile of circulars from Virginia's Illinois hometown, full of stories of restaurateurs and their recipes of the month or motions passed by the city council or record livestock auctions. These attracted no interest. Then came the socks: Virginia's mother bought holiday-themed socks for the two of them, and in this package were the socks for Christmas, Easter, and St. Patrick's Day. The men were slightly confused; perhaps they couldn't figure out the corresponding items on the declaration. Or they wondered why anyone would import socks into a City where they were incredibly, almost preternaturally, common. Then came the food items. Then the raincoat. They looked it over a few times, maybe to make sure it wasn't undervalued.

The knife man put everything back as the seated man filled out a form, occasionally punching numbers into a large-format calculator. The standing man used cable ties to close up the box, except for the hole where the customs declaration once was.

"You take this to seven," the seated man said, giving the receipt to Fred. Virginia got the box.

"Is this what I pay?"

"You take this to seven."

"Okay, thank you."

"You take this to seven." It was, apparently, the only thing he knew how to say in English.

At kiosk 7, the clerk asked for the equivalent of $200. Fred was speechless.

"What if I just leave it with you?" he asked.

The clerk looked blank. Virginia was going to kick Fred in the shins. It was her stuff, after all, from her mother. She would have happily handed over two hundred bucks to feel closer to home.

"Fine, do you take a credit card?" Fred asked, producing an example. The clerk shook his head.

"Fuck." Fred turned to Virginia. "I need to go to an ATM, I don't carry that much around."

Once he returned, mildly soaked, many of the kiosks were shuttered. Virginia was still there, arm over her package defensively as the clerk leered at her. She quietly thanked god at Fred's return. He handed the money to the clerk, who counted it and put it in a drawer.

"Receipt?" Fred asked. "Receipt, receipt?"

But the clerk just turned his attention elsewhere. Fred guessed the money was going home with him that night. That was how things got done in the City, a lesson he couldn't help but take to heart.

———

"Okay," Fred said to Ata, "is there anything we can leave with, you know, just so I can tell Virginia we did something."

Ata was pensive for a moment. "I'll write up your complaint. We can get it stamped and filed. Nothing will happen, and it will cost you fifty for the stamp."

"Great. I'll tell you all the details."

"But you know nothing will happen."

"That's okay. Just please don't tell Virginia that."

TEN.

"HAVE YOU EVER HAD this stuff? It's hooch from the Caucasus."

Eddie poured the straw-colored liquor from a plastic Coke bottle. He had pulled it from the back of the vast liquor cabinet, the work of a half lifetime of duty-free. Fred kept glancing over at it hungrily as Eddie was salting the lamb stew. Fred would pick out a bottle from behind the glass, Laphroaig, say, and guess its price at the nearest hypermarket—$200 at least. But Eddie was more interested in things without price, like this white brandy distilled in the land of the Golden Fleece. It drank like Brut aftershave.

Eddie lived in an Ottoman wood house in the neighborhood of Little Raven. The neighborhood's name could also be translated "Barred Window of a Prison Door," but few people thought of it that way. Mainly thanks to Eddie's work. He was a contractor specializing in connecting traditional craftspeople with moneyed foreign property buyers. While the locals still flocked to stacked villas in gated suburbs, Italians and Gulf Arabs were snatching up the grand, tired wooden mansions of the empire's "little lords." Eddie's army of stooped masters and their skinny apprentices from the east sanded, patched, and spit-shined until grandeur was restored. Then Eddie would dip into the vast stockpile of push-button light switches and brass faucets he bought up upon first arriving, the ones stripped from "abandoned" downtown apartments like Fred and Virginia's. He sold these to the new owners at "vintage prices." While most expatriates cycled through the City as journalists or teachers or election observers, Eddie's business was the City. He was an expat's expat—a fixture.

Little Raven was in Asia, a short walk up from the ferry port of the Golden Town. Golden Town because it was where Alcibiades, pederast and Socratic disciple, set up the first tollbooth on the Strait. Golden also for being the town where the Christian emperor defeated his last pagan co-ruler and gave his name to the City. Looking back from the ferry, through the formations of seagulls, Fred silently watched the City: the hulking mass of Holy Wisdom set between hillocks, behind it the sparse forest of minarets. No matter how many times he saw it, with the sun extinguishing itself in the Marble Sea, it still awed him. From within, the City was a catastrophe of little streets, stacked too densely to hold the various desires of those who lived within them. But from the water, it was itself, the sum total of power, wealth, history, and death. So Fred thought, turning to watch Virginia tossing bits of cheap bread to the trailing gulls. With each toss, her ass would flex a little in her jeans. Fred had to lighten up.

Eddie plated the Lady's Command—lamb stew on a bed of eggplant puree—and they walked the short distance to his dining-room table. He explained that the dish had been presented to Lady Wortley Montagu, the great Orientalist. After eating it, she asked for the recipe. And though she was told the only text the sultan's chef followed was the Koran, the dish was subsequently named after her. Fred had heard the story, but in his version it was named after the Empress of France. Eddie was probably right; he'd written a book on the local cuisine. He also had an old-school hip-hop radio show

("Nothing From After I Left the States") syndicated on a few local stations. Rumor was he was writing a book of linked short stories based on the goodbye parties he'd attended. If the rumor was true, it would already be a long book with no end in sight.

"You two are some of the luckiest newcomers I've known," he said, raising a glass of wine. It was, he explained, communion wine. It was made by obscure Christians in the east who still aged it in clay amphorae. Made using techniques from the time of Homer. It tasted like dirt. Good dirt.

Fred and Virginia must have looked a little taken aback, because Eddie felt the need to clarify his toast. "I mean your place. Marvin had me under contract to do a turn-around on it. If we'd gone ahead and finished, he probably could have asked any price to rent it. As it is, you're getting it for a steal."

Fred nearly spit his Lady's Command in a laugh. He didn't look over, but he knew what Virginia had in mind. They had talked about bringing the subject up with Eddie, and now it seemed they'd have their chance.

"What, did I say something wrong? It's not like Marvin's going to kick you out. He might not even go through with the renovations, with this new assignment and all."

The food was good, the way the local food could be. Rich, salty, but ultimately simple, like something from the Midwest, substituting eggplant for potatoes. It didn't look like much either. Having tasted it before at the Castle's faculty welcome dinner, Virginia termed it "barf atop vomit." Fred ate so he could keep drinking. Virginia artfully rearranged her food until, turning to Fred, she said, "Are you going to say something or shall I?"

Mouth full, Fred nodded.

"Eddie," she continued, "there are other people living in Marvin's apartment."

"You moved out?"

Fred shook his head.

"No," Virginia continued. "Other people just showed up. They moved in when we were out to dinner and they are not going away. Sometimes I go to the bathroom and I know what they had for lunch."

"Previous owners?" Eddie swigged his wine knowingly. "That happens. Not much you can do. Most of them are just peasants who don't have a deed. They'll 'sell' the place, then show up again when the money runs out, claiming squatter's rights. Problem is, foreigners aren't supposed to be buying in High Field. Or in the Water Tower. Or here, for that matter. The property is undervalued, but none of the generals or ministers have put together enough capital, political or otherwise, to buy up the place wholesale. At least High Field. Water Tower is looking to be a different story. Anyway, you're just renting. I'll find you another place and Marvin can sort it out. It won't be as nice, or as cheap, but what are you going to do?"

Fred poured himself another glass. Maybe the white brandy was kicking in, because he didn't much care if Eddie could solve their problem. It was seeming less and less like a problem and more just a part of what it was to live in the City. A challenge, an experience. He gazed off at a trio of photographs: a crowd of fully covered women against a cloudless sky, a half-finished carpet still on the loom, a fat, turbaned man with a jeweled sword.

"You like that one?" Eddie was looking at him. "That's the Emir of Bukhara."

Fred was actually looking at the difference in the wall shade. A large rectangular frame had occupied that space before. Virginia was waiting for him to pick up the conversation.

"Well," Fred said, "it's not the previous owners. It's this guy and his wife and kid, and they claim to be the original owners."

"The original owners?"

"They're Greek, or something." Virginia filled her own glass, since that was the direction the night was going.

"That's different," Eddie said, leaning in on his elbow. "I got this place from its original owners, if I get what you mean by original. I mean, original could go back millennia here. Mine were Levantine Italians. Family went back to one of the big Genoese trading houses, from before the conquest, before the Turks. They were shipping silks to the Medici princes. Pretty unbelievable."

"Wow," was all Fred could say. He was still glancing at the faintly lighter wall space near the Emir of Bukhara, and occasionally at the Emir, who looked like a sweaty and unpleasant fat child, hardly able to move with his weight, yet hardly able to keep still out of spite.

"Yeah, the Levantines, the Greeks, the Jews, the Armenians. The so-called 'classical minorities,' whom the generals finally succeeded in driving out of here. Replaced them with eastern minorities: the Kurds, the Laz, the Circassians. Thought they'd like them better, but they've turned out to be more trouble than the old ones. But these two Italians stuck around until the bitter end. It was their home, I guess."

"Why did all the classical minorities go?" Virginia had her legs up on the chair, cat-like. She was going to bring this back around even if it meant slogging through the past. With Fred, she was used to it.

"The short answer is the pogroms. I mean, that was thirty years after the generals founded the Republic. The generals always saw the

minorities as both a fifth column and a cash cow. With the Armenians, sad to say, both things were probably true. The Turks marched
out to the Caucasus border, declared them traitors, and shipped them out
into the Syrian desert. And that was all done in the east, where no
one was looking. Probably since they got away with it with the Armenians, they went ahead with the Jews and the Greeks. I mean, the
Greeks had actually invaded before the foundation of the Republic,
so I guess they fall in that fifth column category too. The place was
a mess before the Father of Turks. Britain, Italy, Greece, Armenia—
they were all after a piece. This was after the Great War. Before the
War, everyone minded their own business from here to Baghdad.
The point is, most all the classical minorities in this city left after the
riots in 1955.

"When I was looking over the house to buy it, there were these
huge crates in the attic. I asked the couple what was in them because they looked a little termite-ridden. You know, those little
cones of wood granules. Termites are a disaster for a house like this,
I'm sure you can understand. They talked among themselves a little,
then the wife finally said, 'That box belongs to the Tavitians, that
box belongs to the Nestors, and that one the Goldbergs. Tavitans
ran the sweet shop, Nestors was the butcher, and Goldbergs worked
in the bank branch in Gold Town.' I said, okay, I'd be happy to get
them sent to these people. That's how you have to do business in
a country like this. A little of the personal touch. But the wife got
this melancholy look, one she must have done a lot since it fit her
face very naturally. We don't know where they are, she said. They
left all these things with us after the riots, and they never came
back. It was like that. And at the same time the City was growing,
the generals were trying to build an economy on cheap textiles, re-

cruiting out-of-work farmers from the east to work the mills. Same as generals all over the world, really. And they weren't as bad as the Nazis or the Soviets, in terms of scale. To make it easier for the easterners, the generals created squatters-rights laws so loose your overnight guest could put in a fair claim to a use-based ownership of your flat. Soon enough, you had places like High Field full of people selling off the plumbing from a banker's apartment because they'd never used running water before. This in a place with a long history of despoiling and being despoiled."

"The Byzantines sold the lead roof off the grand palace to pay the Genoese!" Fred chimed in. There was something almost comforting in rehashing history's disasters, as if it made you safe from them. Sort of the converse of "Those who cannot remember the past are doomed to repeat it."

"So when you bought this place from the Italians, they must have given you a deed or something like that?" Virginia wasn't going to let the conversation spiral back through the centuries just when it had nearly come round to contemporaneity.

"Yeah, actually. It's such a wild document, written in Ottoman. No one can read it today; the Father of Turks changed the alphabet with the founding of the Republic. I had to basically take their word that it said what they said it said. I framed it, it's in the hallway by the bathroom."

Virginia didn't quite leap out of her chair, but she was over by the bathroom before Fred really noticed.

"The people," Fred started explaining, "when they arrived in our place, Marvin's place, were waving around this illegible document claiming it's the deed to the apartment."

"Fuck," Virginia said.

"I guess we have something of a match." Eddie was almost smug, pouring out the rest of the bottle into three glasses. Fred could see this was going to make a good episode in his book of goodbyes.

"What do you think we should do?"

Eddie shifted in his seat. Virginia slunk back to the table like someone who just ended a bad job interview. Fred looked at the artful way the roof had been vaulted, the almost lace-like filigree decorating the ribs.

"The thing is, and I hate to say it, but I don't think their deed, even if it's real, will matter much. I don't think my deed really protects my right to this house. If I did, it would be in the bank. My friend, Sheik al Monsour, who bought up the rest of the block for me to restore, he protects me. But it would be a joke for me to try and defend my ownership of this house with that document. For one, there are maybe ten scholars in the city who can still read Ottoman. Under the generals, this place was in such a hurry to forget its past that it actually succeeded. For two, I can't imagine the general's government would welcome Greek property claims, however legitimate. They already gave that land away for political gain, and now that it might be worth something, they are working to get it back for themselves. Nowhere in that equation is anything about restoring stripped property rights to minorities they thought they dealt with fifty years ago. They have their hands full with the minorities they thought they liked. No one here is going to risk setting a precedent. And no one is watching from outside—this isn't like Nazi gold. Even in Greece, no one is demanding remuneration. Maybe because they kicked out their Turks. So I don't see these people walking in one day and telling you they sorted out their ownership. On the other hand, you're not supposed to be there either."

Fred felt oddly free. It was like they were totally unattached, like back when he was living rent free in that loft in Providence. They could stay as long as they liked or walk away tomorrow. The Greeks couldn't eject them, Marvin probably couldn't eject them or the Greeks. They were all squatters now.

"Do you have any more wine, Eddie?" Virginia asked.

Eddie hadn't always been a property restorer. At first, he only passed through the City traveling to points further east. He was working around the solitary inland sea, the Sea of Islands or the Sea of Thickets. The sea which, to irrigate cotton for the Communist bloc, had been dried nearly to a poison sludge. He was teaching people there what it meant to be a nation, and what it meant to be rich off petrochemicals after the fall of the Soviet Union. He made it sound like a hopeless, if humorous, job. His first assignment was in a place that claimed to be the Turks' homeland: the paradise of apples and tulips, a kind of static Eden from which flowed the nomads who would one day conquer the City. The first volume of the president-for-life's spiritual guide for the nation had just been released, and it was impossible to get a cab because all the drivers had to pass a written exam on the book's principles before being issued new licenses.

"Supposedly I was there to hold seminars on natural gas workers' rights, to protect them from exploitation by the West. But instead I was taking testimony from my pupils on the various injustices meted out against them by the Ministry of Fairness. I had six Russian engineers tell me they were removed from their jobs after being forced to train local ethnic replacements. When they asked why, the Ministry of Fairness said it was reparations for the Battle of the Blue Hill. None of the engineers had ever heard of the Battle of the Blue Hill.

Turns out it happened in 1880, when the Russians invaded, though it's hard to 'invade' a nomadic people, right? Anyway, it was my first brush with this kind of long memory. As Americans, we don't have it. I know there are some Southerners who natter on about 'the War of Northern Aggression,' 'the South will rise again,' etcetera, but this whole part of the world, east of Italy, went through something like the Civil War every twenty years. And no one forgets."

What had started as a lilting sway on Virginia's part developed into a full narcoleptic teeter.

"You guys can stay here," Eddie said. "There's a guest room made up. You'll probably have to wait two hours for a ferry right now anyway."

"It's not that I don't like your stories, Eddie. Really. It's just with all these things, I haven't been sleeping so well," Victoria said, snapping out of it.

"Let's get you set up. I might come back down and have a whiskey to settle all this wine in my stomach. Care to join me, Fred?"

"Absolutely."

They sat on a sofa below the photo of the Emir of Bukhara. Eddie poured them two fingers each of White Label. Perhaps because it was closer to the front of the bar than the Laphroaig, perhaps because they'd already dulled their palates with wine. Fred was not complaining.

"How's life in the City treating you?" Eddie asked.

"The bread is salty and the stairs are steep," Fred replied through his glass.

"*Purgatorio*, eh. Well, it could be worse. At least you feel like the steps are going up."

"You don't?" There was something in Eddie's tone.

"It's not that exactly, but if you are here long enough, things will go one of two ways."

"You'll conquer the City, or the City will conquer you?"

Eddie smiled. "I should tell you that some people find you obnoxious. In the community, you know. They like Virginia for all the obvious physical reasons, and she's genuine. You come off as smug, a know-it-all. You think you're quick, but really you're just fast."

Emptying his drink, Fred tried to short circuit the connection between his tongue and his ego. If Eddie refilled him, he'd know it wasn't personal, just what he deserved. He hadn't made it almost thirty years in this world unaware of how he could come off.

Eddie poured them both back up to the tumbler's edge. It was one of those duty-free bottles with the tiny ball-bearing regulator, so this took a minute. When he finished, he said, "Do you know who the Turks are?"

"Well, according to the generals, they are everyone who is born in this country, whether they like it or not. Kurds included. Others would say they are the descendants of Central Asian nomads, sons of the wolf, from the valley of the apple and the tulip. Still others see them as the slaves of the Arabs, who, like the Mamluks, turned out to be stronger and smarter than their masters."

"See, that's all wrong." Eddie took a formidable tug on his drink. "When I visited the ancestral homeland of the Turks, I found out there are no Turks. Sure there are a handful, probably, who somewhere in the world could trace their blood back to the little tribe of the apple and the tulip. But really there were never more than a few hundred. Nomadic populations don't grow large. You don't have a farm, you don't have a farmhouse, you don't have six kids. It's just that simple. The Turks are people who decided to become Turks.

That's the beauty of it. People who saw the freedom of becoming something else, becoming a word with nothing really behind it but the breeze of the steppes and the feeling of the horse. It was shaking off Zoroaster, Christ, the plow, the wife. Being a Turk meant eating the cattle you hadn't husbanded, literally. Turning Turk is turning pirate. To be a corsair, that was literally to 'turn Turk.' It's taking only what you can carry, but really taking it."

"I guess it's worked out for you." Fred figured this was a sales pitch.

"I'd say. Better than trying to save distant peoples through education."

Fred let the ice hit his teeth. He thought about Ata and his motorcycle gang. In a city with all the molasses traffic of the Third World, they moved as freely as water through the Strait. In the shadow of oil sheiks' high-rises, they grilled meatballs and downed aniseed liquor. While the City weighed on April, Ata moved through it like tall grass.

"There's just one thing, and then I'm going to pass out," Fred said.

"Wait, don't you want to know what I'm getting at? It has to do with the people living in your house." Eddie was clearly just winding up.

"No, I'm there. I got it. I see it just fine. But I have to ask you, what was up on the wall there, where the Emir of Bukhara is, before?"

Eddie let a little spit out of the edge of his mouth. By accident, certainly. "My wife hung a kilim there."

"Where's your wife?"

"She ran off with the fish guy."

Fred closed his eyes. He knew the idea was somewhere back there, the one that set all the City's impossible alleys to a grid. The conquering idea. But all he could say was, "I guess she turned Turk too."

ELEVEN.

No one can truly hate teaching. Hating teaching is like hating the growth of plants. But it is easy to hate the job of the teacher, easy to hate all those parts that happen outside the classroom.

It was the mid-semester meeting and the blackness of Fred's hangover was still with him, though the rest of it had passed. He'd arrived early so he could sit as far from Dean Rose-Eyes as possible. Fred had slipped up where it came to the dean. On a faculty satisfaction survey at the end of the fall semester, Fred had suggested a wine co-op as a way to raise the standard of living. It was a joke, though Fred and Virginia had been desperate to find affordable wine made from grapes with recognizable names and low headache potential. The dean had pulled Fred's response out at the last meeting to show how foreign faculty weren't working to integrate themselves within the university. Foreign faculty were always demanding more money, larger housing supplements, schedules which allowed them less time on campus and longer vacations. Turkish academics came to campus five days a week and worked through the summer. They aspired to live in the Castle housing, not in the dingy downtown neighborhoods of High Field, Friday Gully, Hunchback, and Tavern. Because this was their career and their country, and they had nowhere else to go. The dean simply wished his foreign colleagues could respect that. After that, Virginia tried not to sit with Fred.

Not long before Fred and Virginia joined the department, the foreign writing teachers only had to meet with the dean once a year. Things were good back then. The money, good to be sure, was better. It went farther in a poorer city. Teachers were given free rein. Fred and Virginia had heard all about it from Paula, who'd spent twenty years teaching in their department. They'd met her at a Christmas party. She was stirring her glass of wine with something that looked like a pen. When Virginia asked what she was doing, she answered, "Energy." She went on to explain the properties of the energy stick, by way of how good things once had been at the Castle. She was moving on. What she did not tell them was that she had been recently fired for teaching her students "emotional freedom techniques" instead of essay writing. Along with Paula, they fired another instructor who taught the concept of "process" by having the students make her cocktails. She would host meetings at her on-campus housing after 8 p.m. where she'd ask the boys to kiss her "just once." Things like this came to light in a series of articles in the conservative newspaper favored by the ministers. Fred and Virginia, with their reputable American masters' degrees, were hired to counter the tarnish these accusations put on a Castle education, but now they had to suffer for the sins of the past. It seemed like they were doing a lot of that these days.

Kiki, the department coordinator, asked for reports from various committee heads, hijacking their accounts to note her own contributions to discipline, evaluation, and curriculum development. She knew how to garb her own derivative thinking in the ideas of others, just as she knew to reapply her lipstick during the meeting break. She would go far.

The meeting got a bit more interesting in the second half. The dean wanted to discuss a serious issue. It had come to his attention that a new paper-writing service had been advertising itself specifically to students at this university. It guaranteed that these custom-written papers would be successful and avoid detection. How could it guarantee this? Because the papers would be written by a former staff member of the writing department. Did anyone have any idea who might be behind this?

Some of the older staff members who had survived the firings squirmed in their seats. "It must be Paula," Kiki said with the tone of someone who might say "in the conservatory with the candlestick" next.

"What makes you so sure." Charlie, the old Irish teacher who had somehow dodged the ax, now emerged as from under a rock.

"She's living down on the coast, supposedly selling her pottery. But you all have seen her pottery, right? I mean, no one is going to buy that. I have one of her espresso cups—thing doesn't even hold a shot of espresso. She's gotta be the one cashing in."

"Cashing in?" Charlie might have been trying too hard to sound skeptical.

"Whoever is running this so-called service is charging $400 a paper, and it seems like they are getting plenty of business." Dean Rose-Eyes added.

Fred's jaw was going all tight. How many hours of extra work, unpaid, was he going to have to put in, and just to follow up on a stupid kid like Oguzhan? Meanwhile, Paula or whoever was sitting by the beach probably sucking down some vitality-enhancing fruit beverage.

"Fred," Kiki said, "I want you to chair a committee on this. Anyone who thinks they have a Paula paper, give it to Fred. Fred, I want you to go through the papers and look for signs they were written by the same person—similar diction, sentence length. You can report to me."

The dean's smirk, which always seemed plastered across his face, now settled on Fred like a bad moon.

Fred wasn't going to give them the satisfaction of objecting. He almost teared up at the thought of the piles of essays, stacked high as the walls that once defended the City. This time it was Virginia who was shaking her head. Coming back from Eddie's, she'd wondered, through the hammering in her brain, whether this was all worth it.

With the matter settled, the dean released them, though not quickly enough for Fred and Virginia to catch the last university bus down the mountain. As they began the hike up the long driveway, Virginia suggested they sleep in their offices. "I don't see why we'd go nearly two hours just to shack up at our house. I mean, the place is like a hostel now. There's more privacy here."

Turning back to object, Fred beheld the whole Castle dark against the reflecting sea. There was no menace in it, maybe because it had already done its worst. And there was Virginia, in one of those neck-to-toe work dresses, her hair up in a bun. She was like a soldier in full camouflage, braced against her pack of gym clothes and un-marked essays. Maybe they had been peaceless too long.

They couldn't get back to their offices fast enough. Moving through the windowless hallways, giddy, they tried not to trip any of the automatic lights. Fred cleared his desk the way he'd seen Richard Gere clear his at the outset of many a doomed affair. The stapler hit the ground and exploded with a twang. Virginia tasted of weak tea. She was up on the desk. His hands ran the dress up her thighs, stopping at her underwear. She was working on his belt. Moving the crotch of her panties to the side with one hand, he opened her up with the other. He wanted to tear his way in, to put all the shit from inside him into her, like she were some nuclear waste disposal site deep in the desert.

"Take it off me," she said.

"No, I can't wait."

"Take it off me."

"No, just let me in."

"I have to wear it tomorrow."

Fred pretended not to hear. The dress came off over her head. For a minute, he took her in, almost quizzically.

"Yes," she said, "this is me."

Hard as he fucked her, he couldn't void himself. So instead when he came, he took her in: the lavender oil smell of her untied hair, the film of loneliness that rubbed off her skin like a wax.

TWELVE.

As FRED EXPECTED, THE Greek emerged from Virginia's old studio and made his way to the fridge. Fred had been sitting in the dark kitchen the past few hours. Partly because he couldn't sleep. He couldn't sleep partly because he was thinking about sitting up in the dark kitchen waiting for the Greek to emerge. This was how he was going to play his hand. He had to put things back to how they were. Or, if he couldn't, he had to know tonight.

The Greek stood in front of the open fridge for a minute. Fred had almost forgotten the man's physical form, he'd been so long a phantom. But there he was: a bit thickset, a bit balding, goatee frayed around those girlish lips. Nothing of legend. Fred noted that he seemed careful to only examine his section of the fridge, insofar as any of it was his. Fred had made a point of moving his own beer to the front of his and Virginia's section. Bait. But the Greek settled on a plastic container full of rice and cabbage. He closed the door quietly and turned, which was Fred's cue.

"They're going to kick you out again."

"Who?" the Greek said. His mouth was full, and nothing fell out. Not Fred's desired effect.

"The Turks, of course. The police."

"They never kicked me out," he answered simply.

"Well, have you ever been in a Turkish prison?"

The Greek eyed Fred for a minute. He was wearing a terrycloth bathrobe, and even though it was dark and he was soft-eyed, his air was of utter confidence.

"You realize you just quoted *Airplane*" he said and took another bite of cabbage.

Fred snorted the beer he had been swigging. It went all over the apartment's hundred-year-old floorboards, mostly right through the gaps and down into the dusty secrets below. The Greek chuckled, softly to keep those sleeping asleep.

"Okay." Fred laughed in spite of the beer stinging the inside of his nose. "But really, this isn't working for us."

"Isn't working for you? How do you think it is for us? Only emerging when you are at work or after dark. I hope you appreciate it's like being a vampire. Except vampires don't have to pee. We are working pretty hard to make this as easy as possible on you."

Fred felt a little like he was a teenager again. Having stood firm, he was left not with righteous anger but guilt.

"But what should we do about it? I mean, I tried getting you all kicked out. And clearly you haven't gotten any traction with your deed." Fred let that last bit linger, but the Greek didn't contradict him. Instead, he opened the fridge and removed an orange soda.

"I guess the thing is," Fred continued, "we're at an impasse. But Virginia and I have jobs here, decent jobs. We wouldn't even be here but for the jobs. I mean, we like it here, but we were never planning on dying here. We could work something out, I mean just until you get yourself sorted or we leave. We were paying Marvin a thousand dollars a month. We could, I guess, give you guys that money. That would set you up pretty nicely out in the suburbs. And when we're done you can have the whole place to yourselves." Virginia would be proud of him. He was being practical.

"Can't do it," the Greek said. "Our claim is based on residence. We leave, we've got nothing. And really, I can't emphasize this enough, we have done everything we can to make this a comfortable situation for you."

"Except leave."

"We can't. I just explained."

"Look," Fred said, "we're only going to be here another two years, three years tops. That's what we promised each other when we left. We're doing it for the money, see. Money and adventure. Then we're going back."

"What are you going to do when you get back?" The Greek took one of the stools at the kitchen table, the orange soda and cabbage set in front of him.

"Write for TV. Virginia's going to paint."

"Did you write for TV before?"

"I'm working on a treatment. It's a comedy show about expatriates. You know, their funny missteps with the local culture. I sort of see it like Seinfeld."

"Seinfeld is really funny. Do you think you're that funny?"

"It's not about being funny, it's about identifying a funny situation. I can do that."

"Have you written about this situation yet?"

"I have, a little."

"Well, when you get back you'll be surprised how little people in America care about what goes on in the rest of the world. I mean, my old man would talk to anybody who'd listen for hours about this

City. It was an obsession for him. If you opened him up, his blood vessels would look like a map of these avenues and backstreets. But most people he knew would rather talk about last night's Dodger game."

"You all moved from LA?"

There was some stirring from one of the bedrooms. The Greek seemed on edge, maybe because he expected to hear his kid. Fred kept forgetting about the child, that the three of them fit where Virginia had stored an easel, a stool, and a stack of notebooks.

"Things must have been really bad for you all to have moved here."

"Were they really bad for you?" the Greek asked.

"No, I told you. We moved for money and adventure. We couldn't get either back home. Neither of us comes from money. It was the recession. No jobs."

"Well, we moved because we owned an apartment here, a pretty spacious one too." He whispered this, as if on kid alert. "You know, if you want to continue this conversation, we should go to the laundry porch. Otherwise you should go back to bed. I've got to do some cooking."

The laundry porch was a narrow outdoor space shared by the apartments. Its entrance was off the stairwell. Fred always had a mind to put a chair out there, but it was impossible to sit without someone's bed sheets threatening to blow over your head. Also the view was of the blind wall of the building opposite. The two men managed to perch with some comfort on the clothes-folding table, Fred with his beer, the Greek with his orange soda.

"So you must have had a job back in California?" Fred asked

"You're from the East Coast, aren't you? East Coasters always start with the job. If you ever move to California, just know people will find it annoying."

"But you came here to do something for money. Or are you living off inheritance?"

"No, my father didn't leave me anything. He was a union pipefitter. Not saying it's a bad job, but it wasn't more than enough. No, he left me a life insurance policy, the deed to this place, and a decent head for schemes."

"Schematics?"

"No, schemes. The get-rich-quick kind."

"Doesn't seem like it worked out for him."

Fred thought the Greek might get up and pace. Or just leave. He was actually enjoying the conversation. The Greek had a kind of easy toughness Fred wished came more naturally to himself.

"Actually, you're a lot like my dad. You're working a wage job figuring you're gaming the system. In two, three years you figure you'll have a hundred grand that'll buy you into that house. Then you'll really start your life. When I was flipping houses in LA, I was clearing twenty-five grand a house with three crews at two months a flip. Do you know how much that is?"

"No."

"It's nine hundred grand a year, a good year, and I was pocketing a half million."

"But then the market crashed."

A breeze came off the alleyway, ghosting the sheets.

"The market crashed over there. But just like movie runs, what closed over in the States is just opening here."

Fred got it. Usually that felt good. The Greek continued.

"I was sitting in my offices in the Valley. Northridge, you know it? I'd just gotten off the phone with the twentieth mortgage guy to run dry. This was last fall, you know, when the other shoe dropped. My father had given me the deed, and I had it framed above my desk, a kind of conversation piece. That's when it hit me. I got on the Internet, started looking at building prices here, started making discreet inquiries to Turkish banks. Turns out they have a lot of money to loan. And I know among my father's friends and their kids, all the Greeks with diners, all the Armenians with collision shops, there have got to be hundreds of these deeds in Southern California alone. They belong to families driven out of this neighborhood, out of Friday Gully and Hunchback. I could get them for garage-sale prices or less. Most people in LA have no time for history."

"But you had to see if it'd work first."

"If it does, it'll be the biggest real estate coup since Manhattan was bought for beads."

The Greek finished up his orange soda. Moonlight was slitting through the gap between the buildings, and there was the sound of alley cats pre-fucking in the distance.

"If you were clearing a half million a year, why do your wife and kid live vampire lives in a single room?"

"It's all tied up in foreclosures now. The music stopped and I didn't have a chair. We left with the shirts on our backs."

"But you'd start all over?"

"I went abroad to find my fortune. Isn't that what you were saying? Anyway, now you know what's up. You should go to bed."

Virginia was snoring faintly. Fred curled up next to her, aware of his beer breath on her neck. The room felt tight, whereas before their modest dreams were snug within it.

THIRTEEN.

THE RUMOR WAS THE government wouldn't allow dancing bears in the housing projects, so the gypsies were forced to take them behind the ancient city walls and shoot them. This is how it all got started. The gypsies had been there for a thousand years, at a small crossroads near the City's Second-Most Important Gate. For a thousand years, they ran a few dozen fun houses with their dancing bears and dancing daughters. The walls had formed the edge of the City from 300 AD to the 1960s, so no one much cared what happened there. After all, within the walls were Abraham's pot, Joseph's turban, Moses's staff, David's sword, scrolls belonging to John, and the Prophet's footprint. So if there were a few gypsy "houses of love" within the walls as well, so be it. That was before they built a highway just outside the walls—Paris was their model. The gypsies' little crossroads now was "twenty minutes from anywhere." And so the gypsies had to go, to a housing project in the distant and appropriately named Rocky district. Their houses would be demolished to make way for a development of Ottoman-style luxury villas: washer-dryer, fitness room, twenty-four-hour concierge.

The protests to stop the eviction of the gypsies were scheduled for Hidirellez, the holiday welcoming spring. This was both a brilliant and flawed plan, since it ensured that a big crowd would show up, and ensured that the crowd would be drunk. The cartoonist was getting a head start, sucking on a beer as the taxi took them up the inlet, past the patriarch of all Christendom, toward the burial place of the Prophet's standard-bearer.

"If you tie your wish to the Hidirellez tree, it will come true," the cartoonist was telling Fred and Virginia. "You should wish for a child."

"Shouldn't we wish for the gypsies not to be evicted?" Fred asked.

"I know I'm going to wish for some people to be evicted," Virginia countered. The cartoonist looked at them, but the last thing they wanted to do was explain.

The cab could only get as far as the Church of Saint Mary of the Mongols, which some called the bloody church, before hitting the crowds of red-sashed protesters. The red was that of the wedding sheet, signifying the end of virgin winter, the start of spring's new life. Paying, Fred, Virginia, and the cartoonist hopped out to join them. The cartoonist's long-suffering wife had decided to stay home. "They are gypsies," she had said. "They get kicked out of everywhere else without a fuss."

They followed the stream of red-sashed protesters up the hill through the doglegged streets. The cartoonist had his red sash too. It seemed everyone in the City had one lying around the house. Fred and Virginia were without, of course. The wooden bow-houses loomed over them like a canopy, letting in just a sliver of grey sky. Some were scorched by fires that might have happened a hundred years ago. Behind drawn curtains, hooded women were either praying for the immoral pleasure houses to be bulldozed or praying that their neighborhood would not be bulldozed next for development.

The three of them passed a sad little mosque, a hooded raven perched squarely on the tin-capped minaret.

"If the cops break it up, don't come back through here," the cartoonist said. He had perpetually tired eyes.

"Why not?"

"The cops just come after you with gas and sticks. The men here, if they think you're trying to help the gypsies, they'll come at you with a knife or worse. It happened like that in the eighties all the time. The cops would drive the students right into a conservative neighborhood, and the men there would trap them in an alley or tea house, knock their teeth out." The cartoonist took a tug on his beer to punctuate this point.

They reached the Second-Most Important Gate in the city walls. It too had recently been restored, against the wishes of archeologists. The government wanted to show how massive the walls had been at this point, how thick and tall, because they associated themselves with the horse warriors who penetrated them here a half millennia ago. In redoing them, they overdid them; it was the historical equivalent of buying your wife a facelift and silicon boobs. Already this restored section was lined with protesters, many shaking banners from marginal left-wing parties or giant teddy bears. The cartoonist tossed his beer bottle down an alleyway and pulled out an already dated digital camera. "This will be the first cell for this week's installment of The Wolfman."

The cartoonist was there on research. His readership was either at the protest or eager to hear about it. Fred and Virginia were there out of vague liberal sensibilities. They shared a sad mental image of crimson-vested, MC Hammer pants–wearing gypsies being bused out to remote housing projects. They'd heard the stories about the bears; maybe it was only the one bear. Even if it were only one bear, it was one irreplaceable glimmer of the mythic City that was going to be concreted over. One more thing turned ordinary.

The mass of the crowd was on the wall's windward side, occupying a thin strip of parkland between the wall and the highway. Once the three of them managed to pass through the City's Second-Most Important Gate, they could appreciate the vastness of the protest. The crowd was thick as the audience of a stadium show, facing the restored section of the wall as if to ask, when will Roger Waters take the stage? Along the fringes, at a completely unthreatening distance, were busloads of riot cops, smoking and lolling on the grass. "The cops love protests," the cartoonist said. "At worst they make weekend pay, at best they get to crack some heads."

They began to wade into the crowd, the cartoonist clearly looking for Nil of the deep cleavage and "huge huge fundraiser party." The communists had set up a little booth from which they distributed leaflets touching on a variety of somewhat related grievances. Beside them, some kids were trying to take pictures of themselves with a cellphone, struggling to all fit in the frame with the wall for background. Girls who would never be mistaken for gypsies wore handkerchiefs in their hair and earrings in only one ear. Off in the distance there was desultory drumming.

The fundraiser had staked out a knoll closer to the highway. Orange construction-area fencing was meant to keep the beer and bathrooms for paying supporters, but it was pretty clear from its low sag that pretenses of exclusivity had been dropped. Along with the cartoonist, Fred and Virginia presented their tickets. The cartoonist inquired about Nil and was pointed back toward a tent. Fred was going to follow, but Virginia held him back. "I don't want to see anything," she said. "If his wife asks, I don't want to have to lie."

Instead they headed for what they imagined were the refreshments, where the crowd was thickest. Working their way through sweat-slicked backs, they came upon the vast troughs that once held beer and ice. A few empties bobbed. All around them boys and girls half their age were flirting or thumbing away at their phones. It could have been any afternoon outside the back-alley beer joints off Independence Avenue. At least it didn't smell. Fred didn't want to feel old, but all the same he couldn't forget he could be getting his grading done instead. At the minimum, they could have hung the laundry in the machine before rushing out. The cartoonist had made it sound like they needed to get to the protest before all the gypsies were rounded up and put on freight cars to the suburbs. But instead the suburbs had shown up, and there were no gypsies in sight.

"Hey." Someone was vying for Fred's attention. "You want a beer?"

The perfectly pronounced English should have thrown him more, but when it is your own language you are not used to hearing, you accept it readily. It was hard to locate the voice because it belonged to a scrunched-faced man a head shorter than the milling teenagers. "Come on, I have a beer for you."

Reaching through the crowd, Fred grabbed Virginia's hand and pulled her along in pursuit of the man and his promised beer. Only once they were well clear of the kids and headed for an obscure nook over the fundraiser's plastic fence did Fred reconsider the wisdom of following the guy. It was probably too late, but at least Fred had a little reach and a little weight on the shorter man. The man probably had a knife. Who wouldn't have a knife in this City? Fred took mental account of his wallet's contents: the few banknotes, the transit card, the Band-Aids for Virginia's inevitable blisters. It wouldn't be the end of the world to hand them over. But how the hell would he replace his driver's license?

They reached a waste disposal area with a couple of dumpsters hidden behind a wooden blind. The man indicated they should take a seat among some rundown lawn chairs set out just in front of the blind. He reemerged from the dumpster area with three cold beers.

"I should charge you for these, but I don't want to give you the wrong impression about us."

"Us?" Fred was worrying the bottle cap with a house key. The man popped one off with his teeth, what teeth he had, handing it to Virginia. She did a good job hiding how she felt about putting her mouth where his had been.

"Gypsies, of course." He took Fred's beer and toothed it open as well. He was wearing khaki pants and a checked shirt, both probably in need of a wash. "You're journalists?"

"Teachers," Virginia said. The man was clearly disappointed.

"We know some journalists," Fred added.

"Are they here?"

Fred shook his head. Out among the protesters, a beach ball had begun to bounce lazily above the crowd.

Pausing, the man said, "Do you know how I know English?"

"You sound like you've been to America," Virginia hazarded.

"America has been to me. My father ran the funhouse where *James Bond* was filmed? You know him? Bond, James Bond. We staged a girl-fight for him, right on the other side of the wall. If you were journalists, I could really tell you some stories."

Fred felt a little bad about the beer in his hands, but really for all he knew it was taken from the fundraiser in the first place.

"If you tell us one," Virginia said, "I'll write it up and give it to one of our journalist friends."

"Why aren't they here?"

"I guess there are other things happening."

"There are always other things happening. How does it go: While someone else is eating or opening a window or just walking dully along? That's when you are getting screwed. That's what my sisters always told me."

It seemed to be a joke or some kind of quotation, but neither Fred nor Virginia could summon a laugh.

"Well, fine," he said. "I'll tell you about my father's funhouse. Maybe you can learn something about this place before it's finished. The old saying about Turks is, and I'll translate, 'Everything is fine except for words—you can fuck them in the ass and they will thank you, but if you call them gay you're dead.' This was how we operated for a thousand years. This City is full of whores, all kinds of whores. But our whores had a tradition, our whores could make you feel, through the aniseed liquor and firelight, that wagon wheels were turning beneath you. That you were moving. That you were free. It was our gift to this City and all its sedentary nomads. Our particular poetry. But it all had to happen without words. When they started saying we ran brothels, that we were squatters, that we were gypsies, that was the end for us. And the end for us is the beginning of the end for the whole place. That's what the Byzantines said. We are like the rooks of the Tower of London, if you know about them."

"I thought that was the dogs? Isn't it the end of the dogs, the end of the place?" Fred wasn't quite sure if that just applied to the Turks, or everyone in the City.

Ignoring him, the gypsy said, "Let me take you to the Hidirellez tree. The best one is right in the crossroads of our neighborhood."

Virginia agreed before Fred could say something about finding the cartoonist. *Great*, he thought to himself, *now the knife will come out*.

The cops hardly noticed them as they passed. The sun was lower in the sky now, and most of them were using their flak jackets as pillows for an afternoon nap. A few of the younger, perhaps less jaded ones milled about with fingers on the safeties of their tear gas launchers. That there were over two hundred riot cops gathered for this event was no surprise; animal rights demonstrations of fifty people on Independence Avenue were overseen by at least a busload of cops, shields at the ready.

They passed back across the wall, scrambling over an unrestored section. Working their way through the ratty garden plots of the shanties abutting the toppled stones, Fred was struck with the sensation of passing through ruins rising from ruins. He could almost understand the developers at that point, their desire to free the earth from all this history. To wipe from the land all the traces of the saints, the companions of the Prophet, the knights and nomads who died trying to get on one side of the wall or the other, the spring where the Virgin Mary appeared that now fed the cabbages of the gypsies, the dust that rises from the ground like corpses on judgment day, the leering faces from the funhouse windows and all the guilty secrets behind them. All these things that had meant something to people through time were not merely interesting but sad or even dangerous. It was easy to be in over your head. Who wouldn't prefer a blank slate.

They reached the crossroads through the small alleys between weatherworn wooden tenements. Passing so close, they caught snatches of wild laughter and clarinet. The occasional clear note of a finger cymbal.

"The tree is there. They say it sprung from a seed planted in the skull of a Sufi."

It was a warped thing, its leaves replaced with tied lengths of what looked to be ribbon, but on closer examination turned out to be plastic water bottle labels bleached by the sun. Fred was hesitant to touch it, like it were someone else's grandmother. But Virginia approached it tenderly.

"So many wishes," she said.

"I mean, the tree looks dead, probably from all that plastic," Fred blurted.

"You should tie something to it, so you'll have a child. Plastic is good, makes the wish last longer and it's harder for someone else to take off," the gypsy added helpfully.

"Can you wish for something other than children?" Virginia asked.

"You can wish for whatever you want, but children are the only safe wish."

"Children aren't safe. Plenty of kids are disappointments," Fred muttered. He was picturing the house he and Virginia would buy. The little house where they would have time to do what they wanted. With the orange tree. He added a child to the picture and both time and space collapsed.

"Only someone who has never had one could say—" Fred couldn't make out the rest of what the gypsy said as his words were swallowed by a swell of noise that spilled over from the other side of the wall. It was like those first few moments of a live recording that amplify the collective chatter of the audience. But instead of the music coming on overtop, the sound of commotion only grew louder and more imminent. Fred walked up from the crossroads to get a sense of what was happening. He had gotten about twenty meters when the first red-sashed protester barreled past him. There was a faint unnatural smell, just a waft carried on the backs of people hurrying past. He thought to run too, but the action was clearly on the other side of the wall. So he stood for a while off to the side as a thin stream of people fled through the military gate, like an invasion in reverse. In the next day's newspaper, there would be no pictures of teens pasted against the wall by police water cannon. The incident would only be mentioned in a few editorials about the danger of consuming alcohol at public events. The cartoonist would tell it like it was, but it wouldn't surprise any of The Wolfman's readership. The images of crispy chicks partying with dancing bears in one frame, getting whacked by riot cops in the next.

The mass of protesters driven through the wall's Second-Most Important Gate had nearly made it to where Fred was standing before he could get his legs to start forward. Then he was running with the rest, down through the crossroads, where he grabbed Virginia's arm and continued running down toward the inlet.

Reaching the water's edge, they finally felt safe. There were other protesters trying to wash the gas out of their eyes using the tops of plastic water bottles. There was a four-lane road between them and the cops, them and the conservative neighborhoods. They began their long walk home, not saying much. As they passed the Iron Church of the Bulgars, Fred noticed a tear at the hem of Virginia's dress.

"Are you okay?" he asked.

"Huh?"

"Did you catch yourself on something while we were running? There were all sorts of old wood and nails. You might need a tetanus shot."

"Oh, that. No. I didn't have anything else to tie to the tree."

Fred couldn't help himself. "Did you wish for a kid?"

She looked through him. "If I tell you, it won't come true."

FOURTEEN.

VIRGINIA SUGGESTED SHE AND April try something different this time. She'd take the bus up to Therapy and they could walk down the Strait. She'd do this on the condition that they put certain restrictions on their conversation, namely that they not discuss Ata or Fred. "Do you think they spend their time talking about us?" she asked on the phone.

April had to agree. She'd have tea and cheese-stuffed breakfast pastry waiting on the deck. Ata would be at the garage.

"You owe me a glass of wine where we decide to end our walk," Virginia said.

"Excuse me?"

"There is a penalty, for breaking my rule."

"Is this just a ploy to get us drunk?" April asked.

"If it turns out that way, fine."

Therapy had one of the nicer bays on the European side of the Strait. It was almost entirely reserved for yacht mooring, and many famous fish restaurants lined the pier to serve that particular class of traveler. Setting off along the water, Virginia noticed a boat, the *Anna Maria*, of Newport, Rhode Island. She'd been there. Her parents had come out to Providence for a visit. It wasn't something they did regularly, traveling. She didn't think either of them had a passport. They'd come after things with Fred seemed serious. Not serious like he proposed, but they'd been together for a year and things seemed to be moving in a direction. Virginia took them down to Newport to see the mansions of the Gilded Age that lined the waterfront. It was supposed to provide a nice contrast to Providence, that hollowed-out industrial city. She and Fred were living in a subdivided Victorian in need of a new coat of paint. The first night at dinner, Fred had waxed poetic about how he'd spent six months living rent-free in an abandoned factory by the highly flammable Woonasquatucket River. It was an "artists collective," though mostly the residents just got high and thrashed two-note chords on electric guitars for hours. The courtyard was full of stripped cars abandoned there by two-bit mobsters. They did throw great parties. Virginia had been to one where they turned three floors of lofts into a booze-soaked maze. Rumor was that the daughter of some Boston developer had also attended these parties, gone home and told Daddy about all the cool kids living there. The place had been bought up, along with nine adjacent mills, to be transformed into condos, offices, and a supermarket. Fred and the rest of the "artists" were evicted. The developer's daughter became known as "Typhoid Mary."

Virginia's parents listened politely, but the romance of living with just cold water and extension cords didn't capture their imagination. Her dad sold insurance and her mom taught first grade. They were from farmers. They still knew people who lived without utilities, none of them by choice.

In Newport, she took them on the cliff walk, a strange echo of what she was doing with April, though much shorter and more picturesque. As they walked between the great houses and the crashing waves, Virginia had figured her parents would want to talk about

Fred, maybe raise concerns: he had served himself a lot of wine. Or voice approval: he had been smart, or at least charming, with them. He expressed genuine interest in their lives, which were provincial if well read. But they didn't talk about him at all. Instead they marveled at the houses, their sweep and grandeur, the meticulous elements of their façades and the care taken with the grounds. They wondered, what had changed such that the people who built these monuments to luxury no longer lived here? Virginia confessed to having no idea. Well, if there was nothing to learn, why drag them out there? It wasn't the first time they'd expressed some nagging doubt about her ability to understand why things happened in the world. Her disconnection from money and the things people did for it.

I just thought you'd like to see something beautiful, she'd said. Someday the waves will erode the cliffs and all this will fall into the sea. So think of them like giant stone magnolias teetering on the branch. Their season is almost over.

To her surprise, her parents nodded. They were good parents like that occasionally, though mostly a pain in the ass.

"I'm thinking of asking the Castle for some new furniture," April said cautiously. She was like a chess player trying to think several moves ahead.

"Really? Is it any better than the stuff we have? I'd love to have a couch that didn't look like it was lifted from a dentist's office."

"No, the new stuff is institutional too. It's just that after four years, my stuff is beginning to look ratty. They have these new leather-backed dining room chairs. They look like they're out of *Beetlejuice*, but still they beat the orange upholstery on the ones I have now."

"Will they replace stuff just any time, or does it have to be a special occasion?"

"We're coming up on contract renewal period. You know that, right? I figured it's a small request compared to signing away the next two years of my life." April laughed weakly.

"You know, I bet you could get a job back in the States at this point, as an instructor." Virginia said. "You've got a lot of experience and you've sold some work. You ever think about trying?"

"Putting aside factors that cannot be mentioned in this conversation," April smiled, "I just don't know if I can deal with the money thing. I strung together jobs for a while in Chicago after you left. I'm too old now to watch my checking account scrape bottom waiting for my bosses at the ESL program to give me another class. Even if I could get a full-time gig now, it's not going to pay anywhere close to the Castle. And even if it did, the cash doesn't go as far in America. Maybe it's a golden handcuff, but they're good at making things like that here. Implements of bondage. I feel like I saw one in the Cannonball Palace harem exhibit."

"You did not." Virginia chuckled a little.

They had walked to New Town, a pretty enclave where the shore was lined with the ornate wooden waterside mansions built by the Ottoman little lords. They walked along an inland road lined with linden trees. Cats scurried among the abandoned grandeur.

"There seem to be a lot of these old mansions in this part of town," Virginia hazarded.

"It's because the shore is south-facing. They used to line pretty much the whole Strait, but the ones facing north had a nasty habit of catching stray oil tankers coming down from the Caucasus. Wood house, full tanker, you put it together. People used to go up into the hills to watch them burn."

"And where did you pick up this little authoritative tidbit?" Virginia giggled. She could almost taste that second glass of wine.

"Actually, it was in Mr. Cotton's memoir of the City. I'm surprised you haven't read it; everyone who comes here picks it up."

"I leave those kinds of things to Fred."

She bit her tongue.

"Got you. Got you fair and square." April cocked her elbows back in victory.

"Well, we are only at one-one. I didn't want to drink alone anyway."

"Yeah, right." April continued with a little spring in her step. She was always one for competition; it was her reputation back in art school. They hadn't been friends back then, only known one another through that strange coincidence that they'd both dated the same guy. They were not unique in having dated him. He was older, tall and sort of a saint of the scene in Chicago. It was an art school rite of passage to get involved with him. He was a fixture at the dive bar frequented by the prog rockers and performance artists churned out every year with their BFAs. Virginia had dated him later, and for longer, a fact which might have been a bone of contention except that they'd both dumped him. April, apparently, in a public flameout lovingly recalled by his friends at the bar. The split with Virginia was quieter, almost informal. She didn't even know she'd moved on until she told him not to come visit her in Providence, where she was moving for graduate school.

It was a strange bond to share, the feeling that they'd both woken up in that same apartment with the stacked books, that certain quality of grey Chicago light demurely entering through the greasy window. The brackish taste of him alongside the flavor of stale cigarettes. It was a particular place in time and space. Everybody, especially him, suffused with ridiculous hopes and expectations that the outside world couldn't touch. In many ways, it was the polar opposite of being here: no one working, everyone broke, cold, totally free of the past. But in many ways it was the same. Here they were still the special ones, the different ones, the people who weren't of the place but used it to feel alienated or superior even if they weren't in full control of those feelings.

Lost in thought, she almost crashed into a group of locals. They were "Strait-staring" at the head of Safe Sheep Bay. There was something people found mesmerizing about the Strait. They'd stand in each other's arms, looking out intently like they were waiting for a Molly Ringwald film to be screened on the water's surface. Maybe it was the currents, the strange conflicts caused by varying depths, temperatures, and eddies. The activity fit somewhere into reading tea leaves, coffee grounds, hands, cards, and so forth. All extremely popular, especially with young women. In seeing a particular current, you could understand the course of your future. Fred would be prone to explaining it as a throwback to those happy ages which saw the starry sky as the map of all possible paths.

Virginia mentally pinched herself. The Strait was sort of like a river but sadder. It was not a thing itself, just a conduit. It had no source or mouth, it made no particular journey. If it were in a new part of the world, it would just be another heavily trafficked waterway. No one romanticized the Straits of Mackinac. Not even Gordon Lightfoot.

"I hate to ask," April said, "but have you resolved your housing situation yet? It's just that I know someone who is moving and she's leaving behind a pretty nice apartment. It's not downtown, and it's probably not as big, but it has a patio. Up around here the air is better, you know. And it's less of a commute to work. You'll last longer."

"You don't think we're going to last?"

Virginia caught herself. The doubt that inflected the words had come from her, not April, who looked like she'd touched a hot pan and spilled the cookies out onto the kitchen linoleum.

Verbally stooping, April said, "I mean, people get burnt out. Or maybe the better analogy is fed up. Or hungover. That's maybe the best. You develop this perpetually thin skin. All it takes is some tourist standing on the edge of the inlet asking, 'Is that Asia over there,' when clearly it is the Black Town and Asia is the distant brown smudge to their right, and you just snap. Because who the hell could be so ignorant. I've seen it happen. Or you go back to America and people ask if you have to wear a veil, or if there is alcohol, or Sharia law, or camels. And they've never heard of the Byzantine Empire, or the Ottoman Empire, they think the country is named after the bird. After that, you either cut ties completely with your home country or you come back wondering if the whole thing is a sham. It's just not good for your sense of perspective. You move out of the center, you realize that while this is the City, it is also just another city. There's a great grocery store here. It's not Whole Foods, but you can get approximations of Mexican beans and Thai curry, put things together like you were back home. Makes it easier to go back and forth."

"You were back last summer?"

"Yeah, I sold a piece to a museum in El Paso. It was a crafts museum, but still. They paid for me to take it to them, there was a reception. It was nice, though I got really tired of talking about the tradition of Ottoman miniatures. Went to New Mexico, where my parents settled in a golf and pool development. I ate my fill of Mexican food and I think I came back just before I overdid it."

"Overdid what? America?"

"Mexican. I love it, but enchilada sauce goes right to my thighs. Are you going back this summer?"

"I don't know, I guess we've been distracted."

"Does that count?"

They'd reached a particularly desolate stretch of the walk, where the coast was too steep for anything but the roadway. Cars careened along this stretch at Formula One speeds. Virginia flinched every time one passed like it would be the one to jump the curb and take itself and them to a watery grave. It would probably be one of their students. He'd be racing along in his Audi, dreaming of taking over their father's business, while another student gave him head, dreaming of a huge family in her suburban villa. Or taking over his father's business, if that were the case. She didn't want to assume. There'd be a massive funeral, clothing rent at the thought of all that potential squandered. And probably open wonderment at what those silly American women were doing walking on that desolate stretch. If they wanted exercise, they could use the equipment the ministers had installed in parks. Or the wonderful school gymnasium where the students changed into their imported yoga clothes to smoke cigarettes out front.

What would Fred do? Probably go on a bender with Ata. They'd resolve to ride the Silk Road, something that would begin as a flight from loss but turn into a journey of self-discovery in ancient lands. They'd be in Bukhara or something when they'd realize that so much of human existence since the dawn of time has been premised on accident, happy or otherwise. It would be the basis for a memoir of tragedy and redemption. He'd sell the film rights, become a millionaire, meet someone much younger with fake lashes and an Art History degree from a women's college. She'd find his stories charming and would put him to bed after a few drinks. He'd probably even have an orange tree, though that was Virginia's idea first. She privately promised herself she would not die in the City, not with people using her studio to struggle with their history. Fred could, if he wanted to.

"Well, you should get your ticket soon. Summer is just around the corner and the prices go way up."

FIFTEEN.

FRED TOLD VIRGINIA THAT he was going to stay up grading. They'd had a little tiff about the summer. He'd been formulating another road trip, just the two of them. Drive south around the Marble Sea to the ruins of Troy, that first great literary city. Then farther south to the once-glorious coastal cities that had been silted in by the Meander River. Places where Anthony and Cleopatra had dined, thinking themselves on the edge of inheriting the empire. The trip would end at the White Sea resort of Eyebrow: a beautiful little turquoise bay with pebble beaches, and just across the water an island still belonging to Greece. An island that specialized in selling tax-free booze to vacationers. They hadn't discussed it, he was waiting for the right moment, but then she said they ought to buy their plane tickets back to the States. He started by suggesting that they might not go back this summer, since they had basically just moved. He ended saying she could go if she wanted to. When he told her about Eyebrow, all she said was, "Isn't that where that lunatic Paula is holed up, making our life hell?" Then she said she was going to bed. Not "going to sleep on it," but "going to bed." He'd apologize in the morning. He always did.

He had a big stack of papers on abortion rights, most of which were too depressing to evaluate. ("The woman who opens her legs

once for a man must open them again for her child. It is only fair.")
They were bad but not the worst. The opinions were disgusting, but
not as blatantly contradictory as the essays about the just use of violence. He also had a big stack of suspected Paula papers that he was
supposed to read over for common vocabulary and constructions. He
was staying up because of these. Not to read them though. Virginia
had given him an idea.

The Greek showed up about when Fred expected, 11:30. He
went straight for the fridge and pulled out an orange soda.

"Why orange soda?" Fred announced himself.

"I used to drink. Not AA level, but more than my wife liked," the
Greek said. "Orange soda is the only thing no one mixes with booze,
so it doesn't make me nostalgic."

Fred nodded. The Greek began pulling things out of the fridge,
lengths of carrot, leeks. A bag of dry lentils.

"No luck with the deed yet?"

"You'd be the first to know." The Greek dug around for the stock-
pot.

Fred couldn't quite figure out how to broach the subject, so he
went back to the essay in front of him: Abortion should be legal because it is legal in modern countries, and we are a modern country
thanks to the generals. But no one should be allowed to have abortions
because the generals say the country needs a new strong youth. The
religious men and the ministers say abortion is against God, which
means it should be legal because we are a secular state and so should
do the opposite of what the religious men say. But still no one should
be allowed to have abortions because God is on the side of our country and we need to keep him happy. Women have rights in our country
thanks to the generals. We were the first country to let women vote. So

women should have the right to an abortion. But they still shouldn't be allowed to have an abortion without asking their husband or father first, because their husband or father is paying for them and so they should listen. So, in conclusion, abortion should be legal, but women shouldn't be allowed to have one.

That was the whole essay. Fred wrote some marginal notes: needs paragraphs; some contradictions; what are your sources? He gave it a D. It at least addressed the assignment. The Greek was chopping away, his water already set to boil.

"So, um, do you need money?" Fred asked.

"You can't pay us to leave. I thought I'd explained that already."

"No, I mean, I have an idea about how you can make some money."

The Greek stopped chopping. "Don't get me wrong, but I don't think you could afford me. Plus, you all are saving for your down payment, remember?"

"Money from an outside source. Decent money too. The work isn't hard, you can do it all from home. Something to tide you over while you work out the big real estate caper."

"What's in it for you?"

"A couple things, and a cut, of course."

The Greek looked at him with some disbelief. It was true, Fred was winging this. His body felt too big to be the source of something sly.

"So long as your hand is in the pot, I'm interested. Never trust someone without skin in the game." The Greek was playing along. Perhaps just for entertainment.

Fred laid it out for the Greek. They were going into the paper-writing business. The Greek would write the papers working off models Fred supplied him with. Describing it, it seemed incredibly simple and powerful. It was a kind of slave revolt on his part, taking command of the contradictions of his situation instead of being ruled by them. The more he talked about it, the more real it became to him. The more it seemed not only possible, but perhaps the only way to take hold of the future for himself and Virginia. His mouth was full of adrenaline.

"How am I going to make them different enough?"

He couldn't tell if the Greek was stringing him along. "I don't know, use a thesaurus. I'll give you one. Most essays are basically the same, that's how we know we've taught them right. No one is looking for elegant variation."

The general course of action would be: the Greek would send a cold solicitation to some of Fred's students, the ones he already knew were cheating. If they bought the Greek's papers, they'd get through. If they didn't, he'd come down on them hard.

The Greek sat. Was it beginning to sound more realistic? "That's only your students, your cheating students. How many is that? And how many papers? Sounds like a lot of work not moving a lot of units."

"It's probably twenty-five students in four classes, three papers each. At up to $400 a pop, that's not a bad start. And when the good students see that they could get away with buying their papers, that number will grow. These kids are paying to have BMWs shipped over; they'd happily pay to have more time to drive them. It's just human nature."

"Still," the Greek said, pulling his chair closer, "there's an upper limit. The business can't grow beyond your classes. Plus, if word gets out that these papers only fool you, then it's not going to take Sherlock Holmes to connect you to the source. The whole thing could be over before it started, which for me, you know, I don't really care. But you are putting it all on the table. If you are going to scheme for real, you've got to draw things out more."

"But that's the thing. We are going to expand across the college. See, I'm supposed to root out this woman who began an essays-for-hire business after she was fired. So everyone who thinks they have a fishy paper is just dumping it on me, expecting me to tell them which are homemade and which are store-bought. I'll serve up hers and let yours slide. When the students figure out her shit is rotten and yours is good, they'll switch over. That's got to be a market of at least three hundred students at three essays a semester. I'd value it at $540,000 a year if the papers average three hundred a pop. You could grease some palms down at the General Directorate of Foundations with that."

"How much is some?"

"I'd want forty percent."

"Seems little, since the risk is all yours."

"You'll have to do the writing. It'll probably take some practice at first. Besides, knowing who's cheating and who's not is worth something to me. You don't know what it's like, trying to teach ten kids and police fifteen. Especially when you don't know exactly which fifteen to police and which ten to teach. This simplifies my job. The extra money is icing on the cake."

"Someone at your school is going to figure it out eventually. Some student will talk. These sorts of things never last, I'm telling you from experience."

"Remember, we only want to stay here two years. Except this way we could buy the house outright instead of putting in a down payment."

The Greek's water had been boiling for a while now, coating the darkened windows with mist. The City was out there, and across the centuries countless other kitchen tables were hosting schemes, greater or lesser. The Monophysites, the black eunuchs, the Sultanate of Women, the Janissaries, the Committee of Union and Progress, the drug lords among the Grey Wolves—every marginal person talking themselves into making a play for the whole pie—all of them had sat as Fred and the Greek did.

"What about your wife?" the Greek asked.

"We're not married," Fred corrected, and then added, "She won't have to know. I mean, she wouldn't like it. But she wants this situation with you guys resolved and I'm just doing my part to resolve it. If she finds out, that's what I'll tell her."

"If that's what you'll tell her, she better not find out."

"Right, but like I said, she won't have to know. If this thing takes off, who knows, we might find the money to move somewhere else in the neighborhood. Somewhere fully restored. That'd make everyone happy."

"The only thing is, I'm not much of a writer," the Greek said.

"Don't worry." Fred handed him the paper he'd been marking. "The bar is low."

The Greek read and chuckled. He put out his hand. Fred took it, silently. With this concluded, the Greek returned to his soup pot.

Fred let his mind wander. How would he tell Virginia about the extra money? She knew there were no rich relatives. He didn't gamble, except now. Class-action lawsuit? He'd think of something, or just confess to the whole thing once it was done. He was doing this for them. With the house out of the way, there'd be nothing for them to do except write and paint, eat and drink, have each other. Peering through the hole in each zero he had written when calculating the cheating ring's worth, he had seen them planting an orange tree or fucking in the kitchen. Their kitchen, where no one would make soup, not them, not anyone else.

SIXTEEN.

THE DAY CAME WHEN all the tables outside the back-alley beer joints and fish houses were confiscated. The tourist police came through with dump trucks and tossed them all in. If the bar had built a little platform to level out the sloping roadway, make a little space for the crispy chicks and their secular dudes to blow some suds without slipping down the hillside, the police attacked it with childlike viciousness. Within the day, the two biggest nightlife areas, Vine Clad Mosque Street and Modern Music Street, were cleared of any "patio seating." Teahouses were left unmolested.

As with most unpublicized crackdowns, Fred and Virginia didn't find out about it until they tried going out to a restaurant they liked on Vine Clad Mosque Street. He'd asked her out, to her surprise. The Greek had sold the first papers. They were belabored efforts about the death penalty. But the Paypal payments to CapturetheCastleEssays were banked. They were in business. Fred now had the chance to celebrate and seem spontaneous at the same time. Virginia'd even dug out a backless blouse she hadn't felt like wearing since they'd returned from Bulgaria.

The City was convulsing its way through spring. Each day would be a little hotter than the last until a storm would come through and lower the temperature again. Eventually, they were told, the storms would cease, and nothing would stop the heat from creeping into permanence. Then summer would come with its unbroken blue haze of sky.

They'd noticed something was off when they turned onto the normally impassible street. Before, the fish houses there had set up long tables on either side of the road, leaving space for only two abreast to pass. At peak hours, you had to travel single file, the tips of your fingers prone to dip into some diner's eggplant puree. But this evening the street was desolate, like Clint Eastwood was about to have a shootout.

"Probably just one of those religious holidays," Fred said. Even he didn't know them all. But when they got to their restaurant, which specialized in the spice-laden flavors of the country's southeast, they knew something was up. The restaurant had claimed a whole elbow of an alleyway. The interior could only hold three tables. And those were packed close to the built-in charcoal grill, comfortable only in deepest winter.

On any given night, the tables were packed, particularly with expats. The food from the southeast was closer to what most Americans knew as Middle Eastern food. It was a welcome reprieve from the cheese pastries and yogurt-soaked dumplings that were the city's Eastern European staples. The restaurant also brought in cheap wine made in Syria. It was surprisingly good, but sometimes you got a bottle that had been cut by the smugglers. Those reminded Virginia of grape Dimetapp. Still, a cold carafe alongside a plate of rosemary salad and spicy shaved kebab took you a thousand miles away from a day of jockeying for space in the dusty City.

But first you had to deal with the saddest waiter in the world. His sadness seemed to sprout from having his restaurant filled with foreigners. Foreigners, to his mind, never ordered enough food. Fred and Virginia originally tried to cheer him up, ordering far more than they intended to eat. But even then he was disappointed they passed on dessert. So they went back to ordering average quantities, which was even sadder since it was backsliding.

They were just preparing themselves to face the waiter's disappointment when they saw him sitting on a lonely stool in the alleyway. There was no one, and nothing, else.

"Greetings," Fred said in his bad Turkish. "Open?"

The waiter gave Fred a disgusted look. In English, he said, "Where have you been, the Himalayas?"

It had been a little while since they'd been out. Work was getting the better of them again, even though after the fall semester they promised each other it wouldn't. Virginia especially was finding her days consumed. She'd had a student confess to cheating, and then when the student faced the disciplinary council she claimed Virginia had forced her to sign a confession. So Virginia had to go back through all the student's work and build a case. She sat up in bed with a highlighter, identifying sentences with divergent constructions. The kind of work Fred was supposed to be doing for his Paula committee. She occasionally muttered things like *No orange tree is worth this.*

The waiter went on. "That son of a bitch prime minister had all our tables taken away."

"How can he do that?"

"He just did it, and the police came and took them away."

"But you own them."

"They said the tables were in the public street. The prime minister was trying to get through here with his motorcade, they say, coming from the restored tomb of the minor seer. He was blocked, or at least thought he was. But you know he's always hated it up here. He grew up down the hill, on the wrong side. Down on the little port on the inlet where the barges dropped the meat for the restaurants and hotels. They say the prime minister's father was a butcher, too poor to buy meat for his own family. They say the prime minister worked in a basement stuffing mussels with rice until his hands bled into the stuffing. He still has scars from the shelling knife. And each night he'd watch the little truck full of meat and mussels putter up the steep slope to the Taverns neighborhood. He knew his work, his blood, was going to be eaten by drunken infidels and, worse, lapsed believers. He swore revenge, and now he is taking it. The generals may be bad, but God save us from the pious ministers."

"Jesus," Fred said. He'd always thought something was off about those stuffed mussels.

"Some are saying he will calm down and in a few weeks we can put the tables out again. But I think he has been waiting his whole life for this. Until we can put our tables back, we are closed."

"I'm sorry," Virginia said. She almost added that she wished she'd ordered more while she had the chance, but it might have come off as cruel.

After an unsatisfying plate of rice, chickpeas, and chicken, Fred suggested they salvage the night with a visit to the expat cocktail bar. The place was the brainchild of a glad-handing American whose Turkish wife footed the bill for this quixotic hobby. His vision was a real cocktail bar: him, tied and vested, shaking up a round of sidecars. He sold the drinks at cost, so they were merely expensive rather than exorbitant. The true price was having to make small talk with him as he labored over his creations. Fred and Virginia usually preferred the cheap anonymity of the London Orient Express Hotel. But it had been so long since they'd been out. There was more appeal being in a place where you might run into a friend instead of a Russian hooker.

The bar was illegally situated in a building of law offices and shipping concerns. You had to buzz the intercom three times and give the password (rosebud) to get in. It was all a little much. Alex the bartender was giving a large nickel shaker a vigorous go with both hands when they walked in.

"You are just in time. You have to tell me what you think of this," he said.

Fred bridled against being told what he was to drink. No booze on the rocks here, just "mixology." Alex poured the shaker out into a row of cocktail glasses, most of which were for a group of blond hippies who were probably German and probably taught preschool art at the German school. They thanked Alex with blown kisses and retreated with their drinks to one of the card tables next to the blacked-out window.

"So, how good is that?" he asked as Fred and Virginia hazarded a sip. It tasted like lemon tea, under-steeped. "Earl Grey Martini," he added. "This sort of thing is hot right now in the East Village."

"It's nice," Virginia said. "I think my grandmother would like it."

"An instant classic." Alex put his thumbs in the watch pockets of his vest.

But for the German girls and one dark, well-groomed man conspicuously reading Proust, the bar was empty. Most people would drink at home to save money, then come out at the last minute for one drink on the town. So it seemed they were destined to be stuck with Alex for another two hours.

"What's going on with the tables?" Fred broke the silence.

"Yeah, how 'bout that," Alex said.

"We heard it was the prime minister's revenge," Virginia chimed in. "The man hates foreigners, drinkers, meat, and stuffed mussels."

"I'm with him on those stuffed mussels," Alex replied. "They are a public health menace. But I don't think it's a personal thing."

"What do you think it is?" Fred kept the conversation going so he wouldn't drink too quickly.

"It's just how it is here. You have a good idea, then someone copies it. I mean there used to be no tables outside in Vine Clad Mosque. It was where the drug lords took their mistresses, the ones they didn't like. Then "fish house one" puts a few tables out one summer. It seems more people go to fish house one so they can sit outside, watch the people pass, whatever. So then fish house two puts out a bunch of tables too. If it worked for fish house one to have four tables, then fish house two will put out eight. And so on until you get the situation we used to have, where every inch of the alleyway that can fit a table has one. Then you get the government involved, because there's money in it. Word has it they are going to make the owners rent the spaces in the alley for their tables. Rent the tables too, like the government runs some kind of beach cabana. That's why I have to keep this place quiet. Bunch of people start copying me, who knows what's going to happen."

"I don't think you have to worry about it," Fred said, searching his palate for some evidence that his expensive drink contained alcohol.

"I figure two years tops," Alex said, "then you'll find a bar like this hidden in every office building. Except the guys running them won't know an Old Fashioned from a whiskey sour."

Virginia was staring off into a corner.

"What are you thinking about?" Fred asked.

"Two years," Virginia said. "It's a long time."

"Not long enough," Alex said, but she wasn't listening to him.

After something Alex called a Bronx, which tasted like orange juice, Fred and Virginia were ready to go. Other expats had trickled in: young English teachers in cargo shorts, troll-like wire journalists, even a group of wives who were known as the expat harem and did things like this together to remind each other of the outside world they had once called home. As Fred settled the bill, Virginia looked around. "God, don't let me die here," she said to herself. Someone who didn't know her might think she was just being snide.

Eddie rosebudded his way into the bar just as they were leaving.

"Come on," he said, "I'll buy you one. Alex actually takes requests from me."

They sat at a card table. Eddie returned with three ample Old Fashioneds.

"You are a prince among men," Fred said as he clinked his glass with Eddie's.

This was one drink too many for Virginia; she'd feel it tomorrow morning. But any escape from the anxiety of prosecuting the recanting cheater was welcome. Deep down she knew the dean would have to let the cheat go free, evidence or no. The Castle was selling its students an education, and it wanted satisfied customers. She also knew that if the cheat went free, any other confessions she got would be thrown out as entrapment for consistency's sake. She understood why Fred liked whiskey. It tasted like forgetting.

"So," Fred said, "do you know about this thing with the tables?"

"Know the thing…" Eddie took a sip for emphasis. "I know the guy."

"The prime minister?"

"No, that's just a cover story. The guy's name is Furkan Soz. He's a developer backing General Yazgan. Those two were trying to make a play for the Water Tower development project. But this other guy, Demir or something, got the money in first, paid the right people and the cops. So the cops cleared the place out for him under guise of controlling a riot, and the bulldozers rolled in."

"Wait," Virginia said. "They've already bulldozed it? I hadn't heard."

"Only took an afternoon. Before you know it, there are going to be nice clean Ottoman-style townhouses by the wall. I hear they are building a strip mall next to the Second-Most Important Gate. Just another neighborhood now."

"But what does that have to do with the tables?"

"Yazgan and Soz were stuck with all the ready cash they were going to spend on Water Tower, but there wasn't the same kind of opportunity just lying about. It took five years to turn the public against the gypsies. So they came up with the tables idea. Property values in Vine Clad Mosque and Modern Music are low, but rents have gone high off all the al fresco dining. If you take away the tables, the fish houses won't make rent. Some of them do eighty percent of their business outdoors. They'll fail, leaving the building owners without rents. That's when Yazgan and Soz swoop in and buy the property. If they catch any static, they can count on the prime minister to rail about districts reserved for the debauchery of foreigners and apostates."

"Then what?" Virginia asked.

"Once they've bought up all they can, the tables will return. Like they were never gone. Except now the rents will go into the pockets of Yazgan and Soz. Simple, right?"

"Won't people see right through that?" Virginia said.

"There are enough other rumors. Yazgan and Soz did well by the prime minister, and it doesn't hurt that this lets him stoke anti-foreigner feelings in this district. No one likes the idea of foreigners having a good time at their expense."

A sugary sickness was settling into Virginia's stomach. Eddie sounded so safe in his feeling that things were like this, that this was the way things worked. Fred too seemed surprisingly comfortable with this cynicism about how things happened in the City. She almost thought he was nodding in appreciation of the developer's cleverness. But what about the saddest waiter in the world? Even if he knew what was happening, what good would it do him? His job might come back with the tables, it might not. In the meantime, what would he tell his wife? Maybe these were pitiful thoughts, but she was feeling more in common with the saddest waiter in the world than the buyers and sellers of buildings.

SEVENTEEN.

[OPENING ON "THE APARTMENT WITH GREEKS," except set up in the same way as Nick Adams' apartment in previous episodes, with a teal couch being the central focus and a much nicer kitchenette with two stools. There is a lot of unstained wood and exposed brick, we are kind of going for the aesthetic values of a Chelsea loft, which should contrast with the more humble furniture from earlier episodes. There should also be some kind of sign of Greeks: a blue and white flag, a hexagonal bottle of Ouzo standing out on the bar, a large framed portrait of Lord Byron in his Greek War of Independence gear. We open on Jake Barnes at the bar, poring over the bottles. Nick Adams sits on the couch in his classic pose, resting the ankle of his right foot on his left knee, his elbows up and his hands cradling the back of his neck. The audience understands that he is "on the couch" while on the couch]

Jake: Do you think the Greeks would miss a little of the Ouzo?

Nick: No, but what's the point. There's plenty of aniseed liquor. It's the same thing, just made by Turks.

Jake: Turkish-made booze gives worse hangovers. I secretly think they want to feel God's disapproval the next morning. Or at least feel like they got their money's worth. But even if they are basically the same, don't you ever just crave some variety?

Nick: You're just saying that because you dumped Merve. And what'd you dump her for?

Jake: She kept insisting we play backgammon, and she kept winning. And you know, that would put her in the mood.

Nick: Terrible.

Jake: I'll say. She'd be running her fingers through my hair and I'd be replaying her moves in my head.

Nick: I can't imagine either of those activities really took any time at all.

Jake: Finally I just said, you're cheating, and walked out.

Nick: Good for you.

Jake: Didn't you break up with Catherine Barkley because she couldn't handle the Greek thing?

Nick: Yeah. She said she didn't know how I could do it, living with the Greeks. Really pissed me off, like I don't know how to bathe or something. Finally I just told her she was a racist and walked out.

Jake: Greeks aren't a race.

[Nick is distracted. Jake, sensing the lapse in attention, pours himself a double Ouzo, Nick a single.]

Nick: What are we doing?

Jake: [Opens the freezer, removes ice cubes, plops them in the drinks, and walks to the couch] We're doing drinks.

Nick: No, I mean with our lives. Here we are in this place, with these drinks and these women. We're just children. We're running around this place from rooftop bar to dark alley like kids around playground equipment. And all around us people are actually living life, going to offices, taking their kids to school. Are we going to die here? If we did, do you think the City would care?

Jake: [Actually caught up in this] You're right. You know, years have passed. I've watched my Turkish ex-girlfriends get married, move into condos and have kids. I've sat on the other end of Skype talking to the people I used to know who'd become lawyers or moved to the country, listening to them talk about how their kid has trouble with Spanish or how they'd really like to come visit but things are just so busy with work and the dog. Am I never going to have that?

Nick: I'm living in an apartment with Greeks. What am I, in a fraternity? I just want to be normal.

Jake: Yeah, normal.

Nick: I mean it, starting today I'm going to take active steps. First thing, I'm going to call up Catherine Barkley and talk to her about moving back to the States.

Jake: I'm going to call up Merve, tell her that I really do want to have dinner with her parents on the Asian side.

Nick: I'm not kidding.

Jake: I'm not, too.

[Jake downs his drink, salutes Nick, and marches out of the apartment. Nick gets his cellphone off the tea table and dials. As he has his conversation, Reyhann enters quietly and cruises over to the fridge for a beer. Nick doesn't hear him.]

Nick: Hi, is this Catherine? Yes this is Nick… Funny you should ask, I was actually thinking about moving… No, moving back to the States… Yeah, I was thinking of settling. It's not the kind of thing you can do here…That's right, there are no Whole Foods… It is really hard to get kale chips, I mean you'd practically have to make them yourself. Well, I'd love to talk more about it…over dinner, of course.

Let's say eight, at the Photographer's Cafe…Great, bye. [He hangs up].

Reyhann: [Surprised] You're moving back to the States?

Nick: [Surprised] When'd you come in?

Reyhann: I have to help another foreigner. If you want to marry a Turkish woman, you have to write her a poem. A classic poem, like they wrote in Persia. But it must also be original, or she will think you don't mean it. It is very difficult. I said I would translate the poem if he wrote it, but it has been three hours now and he hasn't been able to do it. So I needed a beer to help him think, isn't it?

Nick: Why don't you just write it for him?

Reyhann: The woman wants English. She wants a foreigner. I just make a translation so she knows he's saying true things.

Nick: And all foreigners who want to marry Turkish need one of these poems?

Reyhann: The Directorate of Marriages requires it. For foreigners only. Turks are born with poetry in their souls. Is that why you are going back to United States, no poetry in your soul?

Nick: No. I'm getting older and I just think that it's time I took some steps to settle down. I mean, as it is, it would take me years to get to a place back home where I could afford to have a dog, let alone a kid. If I don't start now, it'll never happen.

Reyhann: What do you want a dog for? Here there are many dogs, the dogs that live in the City. In the City, everyone has a dog and no one has a dog. This is the better way. What do you get when you own the dog? You don't get to pet it more, you can pet the dogs of the City as much as you like. You can walk with them as much as you like. If you like, you can have one come up to your apartment and lay on the floor. The only thing you get for owning the dog is the right to pick up its shit. Same with kid, isn't it?

Nick: I'm glad we had this talk.

Reyhann: I go back to see if the man is done with his poem.

[Reyhann exits. Nick picks up the phone again, looks at it, then puts it back on the tea table. He does this a few times. Then he finally picks it up and dials. As he waits through the rings, the Greek comes in and heads for the fridge, where he pulls out a half-eaten gyro. He is reciting poetry to himself quietly so as not to disturb Nick. Maybe a snippet of Byron's "The Isles of Greece."]

Nick: Hi, yes, is this Catherine? Hi, yes, this is Nick again. I'm sorry, I think I need to cancel our dinner...Yeah, it is unfortunate... No I'm not sure when we can reschedule... Why? I need to see a man about a dog... Yes, I know what that sounds like... Well, at least I'm not a racist.

[Nick pulls the phone away from his ear. The audience can hear the dial tone. The Greek continues his recitation.]

Nick: [To the Greek] Excuse me, is that poetry?

Greek: [Between bites] Why yes. I love poetry. Reciting it, writing it. I find it elevating. Have you been eating my tzatziki?

Nick: [Ignoring him] Do you like classical Persian poetry? Do you think you could write some?

Greek: Sure, though I don't know why I would.

Nick: What if I said there was money in it?

[CUT TO Jake Barnes sitting at a family dinner with Merve. Merve is an attractive Turkish woman in the "Green Pine" style. This means a sort of seventies look, bouffant hair and liquid eyeliner. The scene is shot from the perspective of Merve's parents. The decor is Turkish nouveau riche: crimson with gold accents on the furniture. There may be a portrait of the Father of Turks in a tuxedo.]

Merve: They say they are so pleased by your proposal. To be honest, when I told them that I was seeing a foreigner, they thought I was just rebelling. But I told them how you told me you wanted to settle down immediately and start a family, and that you wouldn't mind moving over here to the Asian side so we can be closer to them. They were impressed. They said they'll be happy to say yes after they read your poem.

Jake: My poem?

Merve: You must write me a poem. To prove your love. Don't worry, it can be in English. After all the nice things you said to me, it should be easy.

Jake: Yes, well, I'm not much of a poet.

Merve: Just say all those things you said to me earlier, just as a Ghazal.

Jake: A Ghazal?

Merve: It is the only form the Directorate of Marriages accepts.

Jake: Can I have another drink?

Merve: Of course, my beloved. But keep your head: we will all play backgammon once dinner is over. I'm sure you will win this time. Even if you lose, you win, isn't it?

[CUT BACK to Nick Adams' apartment. Nick is on the couch with John, another foreigner. They are drinking beers. Up at the breakfast counter, the Greek is scribbling away.]

Greek: Eye color?

John: Green

[The Greek scribbles some more.]

Greek: Hair color?

John: Dark, brown I guess.

[The Greek scribbles.]

Nick: So what made you want to settle down?

John: You know, I spent a long time being bothered by the patriarchal culture here. All the macho shit, keep the women at home, you know. But when you are on the other side of that, you start to really see the advantages. I never worry what's for dinner or who's going to make it. If I have to work late, no problem. If I go out with the guys, no problem. She doesn't fetch slippers, but I'm sure if I made a point of it, she would. And you know what's great, even with all that I'm still treating her with ten times the respect she'd get from a Turkish guy. It's a win-win.

Greek: Cup size?

John: They're a handful, if you know what I mean.

[The Greek pauses, then goes back to scribbling. Jake busts in]

Jake: You'll never believe it. If I want to marry Merve, I have to write her a goddamned poem. A Ghazal!

Greek: The going rate is two hundred a stanza.

Jake: Excuse me?

Nick: It's a little business venture.

Greek: A Ghazal is five stanzas.

John: It's entirely worth it. What's a thousand bits against a lifetime of happiness?

Jake: What does Catherine Barkley think of this little racket?

Nick: [Ignoring him] You know, with all the money this scheme stands to make, we can have Scotch anytime we want. Come by tonight, we'll tie one on.

Jake: Sounds great, but Merve has us slated to watch *From Russia with Love.*

John: Don't humor her, they can smell weakness.

[CUT TO later, a group of expatriate men drinking in the apartment as the Greek scribbles away.]

EIGHTEEN.

THE SEMESTER WAS FINALLY coming to an end. They were up at the Castle giving a final round of MICs. It was getting warm enough for the scrub pines to weep resin. It was one of Virginia's new favorite smells, but it was lost to her once within the perpetually fluorescent hallways. Things with the cheating student had gone worse than she'd expected. The dean had been convinced, and passed her case up the ladder. But looking over her evidence, the vice president for student affairs lectured her about holding vendettas against students. "You have to stop using grades and allegations to punish students you don't like. You are here to give these students an education in a language you were born speaking and they weren't. If you can't do that without judging them, I think you should work elsewhere." She'd almost cried. Fred had always said Virginia was the better teacher because her heart was in it. She always thought he was the better teacher because of his relative indifference.

After her meeting, she peeked in Fred's office. He was in the midst of a MIC, but he seemed relaxed. Usually he'd have a pen clamped in his mouth as the student asked him questions about the marginal notes. But today he looked like he could almost put his feet up on the desk. Good for him. Whenever he was stressed out, she could feel it. It was like getting into bed with a tight rubber band, or a fault line.

Looking at her list of MICs gave her that same feeling. If the VP was going to let the cheats claim she had a vendetta against them, what was the point? Usually she looked forward to talking with the good students one on one. Giving them a boost of confidence. But today she didn't know where she'd find the energy. It reminded her of the story Fred told about the conquest of the City, how the Turks had imagined it was all they needed to complete their empire. They had everything east to the Atlas, everything west to the White City on the Danube. They just needed the center, whose conquest was prophesied in the Koran and would begin the end times. But the City they conquered was a ruin. The throne of Solomon had been broken centuries earlier when a fat usurper sat in it. The Grand Palace was a roofless prison. The icons had been blinded, then stripped of their gold leaf. The Venetians had carried off the bronze horses of the chariot track and the jewels of the treasury. The Genoese had taken the rest, and they claimed to be the City's allies. There were only five thousand men to guard the City at the time of the conquest. It was, as someone said, nothing more than a shadow in a vineyard. Once the Turks had it, they had to pour all they had into it. They had to pay people to live in it; they had to bring in slaves. They had to let the sons of their enemies reproduce such that two hundred years after the conquest the Greeks were again the City's most powerful denizens. Their Janissaries, kidnapped Christian boys, turned into fat tradesmen. The Sultans' mothers and viziers ruled while the Sultans scoured the palace for the horsetails they lost among the harem girls. They had exhausted themselves fighting for an idea. When the idea was revealed to be false, they lost all they had trying to make it true.

That was her takeaway. Fred seemed to think it meant something else.

Kiki knocked on her door. She was, as usual, overdressed with a string of pearls over a black blouse. "Sorry, Virginia. I was on my way to the rector's office. They are putting together the next set of contracts. I'm just checking, but you and Fred said you would renew for two more years? There'll be a chance for you to look at the details over the summer, but they say everything is about the same. Have you guys made travel plans, or are you interested in teaching summer school? It's five weeks, eight hour days, but the money is great."

"Actually," Virginia said, "I don't think Fred and I are renewing our contracts."

"What? But I thought—I mean, do you have another job or something?"

"No."

"But you aren't renewing your contract here?"

"No, we're not."

"Okay, well Jesus, you guys could have told me earlier. When did you decide?"

"Just now."

"Just now?"

Virginia felt light as a feather. She felt like she could throw a bridle on Kiki and ride her west past the last shanty on the City's edge. As close to home as she could get—she'd hitch the rest of the way.

"Wait until April hears this."

Virginia locked her office door behind her before the first student arrived. Fred was still in the midst of an MIC, so she went to see Adrian. Her fingers were tingling.

"Do you think I could have one of your cigarettes in your office?" she asked.

"Certainly, but I assure you the experience is more pleasant outside. And the students smoke finer cigarettes."

"I think I just quit my job."

"Well then, come in, come in. This calls for a celebration. I'm certain I still have a few fingers of Haig and Haig somewhere around here. I did my best to forget where I put it, since it's for victories, not to treat depression."

"The cigarette is just fine."

"Well then, truly spoken. Forgive me if I can't help but imagine it will feel post-coital."

"Actually, I'm a bit worried. I haven't told Fred."

"Fred will be happy, though it might take him a while to realize it." Adrian lit the two cigarettes on his lips and cranked open the window. "When the Greeks were first settling the Strait, they built their first town on the Asian side, where today's Town of the Judge is. It's farther south, so they came on it first. They didn't bother to look at this side, where the inlet formed a great natural harbor. So when the City was founded, the Greeks here began to call the first town the 'land of the blind.' The name stuck, because it was true."

"Are you saying that Fred is going to see there is a better place to leave for?"

"I don't know. One hopes. Just because the place is the land of the blind doesn't mean people didn't keep living there. The fashion district is quite nice."

Virginia sucked hard on her cigarette. It had been five years since she quit smoking, but it could have been yesterday. Outside, the students struck her as perfect strangers. The outcome of their lives, the comforts they enjoyed, and the challenges they undertook or avoided were as foreign to her as their mother language. She had been in another country the whole time. It would still be there, though she would no longer go to it.

She flicked the butt out Adrian's window. She hoped it would hit a student.

"Hey," he stammered, but with a smile. "Not everyone here is quitting."

"Thanks for everything, Adrian."

She wasn't exactly sure how to start with Fred, so she just sat in the chair across from him and twirled her hair tight. His office was stark, some postcards on the wall, a bookcase largely empty but for a few reference volumes. He had a stack of about ten papers in front of him and he was lazily writing marginal notes on another one.

"How are MICs going, babe?" she finally asked.

"Fine," he said, looking up. "Same as always."

"Cheats?"

"Yup, but thankfully I don't have to meet any today."

He looked at her, but not really. He was closed up on his work like a boa constrictor, crushing it to death at his own pace. She considered not telling him. He wasn't in the right mind frame. He was finding the work boring but tolerable. But there was a good chance Kiki would stop by. Kiki would love to see the two of them out of sync. It would be like finding out they only did it missionary.

"I've told Kiki we're not renewing." Her voice didn't waver.

"What?"

"I told her we weren't going to be coming back next fall."

"Why'd you do that?"

"She came around to ask, I thought about it, and I just went with my heart."

"I'm sorry," he said. "I'm right in the middle of this stuff right now. I know it sucks, but it's going to be over in a week tops. We have the summer then. We'll head back home. Really, I'm sorry I suggested otherwise. We'll head back home to the States, you'll see it's still all there in one piece. We'll eat sushi, watch some independent films, come back refreshed and ready to go. And we'll know the ropes this time. The next two years will fly by."

If he was going to present his case, then she'd present hers.

"Fred, listen. We can live out on the farm with my folks. They wouldn't mind. There's space. Chicago is only an hour and a half away. We could do the things we talked about. You could sit down and write your treatments, teach a class at the local college if you feel like you have to. But why not do it now? Who knows what we'll become in two more years—whether we could ever get back to who we are now, or who we were before we first came."

He pressed the tips of his fingers together. She felt exposed, like she'd asked him to marry her and he was weighing the pros and cons. She remembered him as they'd first met: in a class together, and through some icebreaker it came out that they both loved *The Mutiny on the Bounty*. But later they couldn't agree on which film version of Fletcher Christian was better. She liked Brando, he liked Gable. In the Brando version, after the mutineers land on Pitcairn Island, Christian wants to sail back for England to seek justice against the evil Captain Bligh. His followers burn the *Bounty*, and Brando dies trying to save his only way off the island. In the Gable version, Gable burns the ship himself, happy to live out his days on the uncharted island paradise. She could never have guessed this would be the difference between them.

"We can talk about this some more," he said finally. "I just don't think we can walk away from two good jobs."

"Not one of the things you said just now is true."

There was a student at the door, a bleach job with a Michael Kors bag pretending to demure but listening intently.

"Come in," Fred said. "Ms. Hammond was just leaving."

This, at least, was true.

NINETEEN.

THE APARTMENT SEEMED HUGE again, like it did when they'd first moved in. It wasn't that Virginia had so much stuff. She hadn't even taken most of it with her: the work dresses, the black pumps. She left the carefully selected tchotchkes she'd assembled with an art school eye. She didn't even take her half of the money, though Fred swore he'd keep it for her.

Time was what made the place big again. Fred sat in the living room with a book and a beer as the Greek and his family ate dinner in the kitchen at a normal time. They'd even made him a plate, though he felt strange sitting with the ever-silent wife and child. The bedroom doors stayed open during the day and an early summer breeze played in the hallway. The Greek had set up a desk in the Cage that Fred was planning to use to revise his spec scripts until summer session began, when the Greek would be using it to write papers full time again. The bed too struck Fred as being huge, but he was trying not to think too hard about it.

He met Eddie for a drink in the lobby bar of the London Orient Express. Trunks with colorful travel labels were stacked throughout the lobby. A plaster statue of Athena anchored the wide and worn wooden banister. The concierge in his cap and suspenders seemed to

be less a person and more an exhibit. Most Turks avoided the hotel—
a reminder of the bad old fez and smoking jacket days. Unless they
were there to solicit.

The hotel had two bars, the lobby bar and the party bar. The
party bar, with its tiki torches and decorative BMW motorcycle, had
been closed for many years. Some said after an incident. The lobby
bar was a series of grand salons whose sagging couches had their trim
freshly painted gold. There were parakeets, a cockatoo, and, inevitably, a blond woman sitting in the farthest salon intently reading an
in-flight magazine upside down. When they used to come together,
Virginia would flip the magazine over for the woman, as a kind of
favor. Then they'd laugh about it all the way home.

Eddie was at the bar drinking a tall, milky glass of aniseed liquor.
Fred had called him after Virginia left, but now he was feeling reluc-
tant to talk. He indicated to the bartender that he'd have the same.

"I drink it with soda water," Eddie said. "Most places won't let
you. It's not traditional. But here you can do whatever you want."

The bartender poured the drink strong. He was an old man, and
the veins in his hand showed as he tipped the liquor over the ice.
Then he poured in the tiny medicine bottle of soda. That was how
mineral water was sold in the City, as a cure. The most famous brand
was bottled at "the true Mount Olympus," the only mountain in the
ancient world too tall to climb.

"Where's Virginia tonight?" Eddie asked.

Fred took a moment to imagine the hotel at its peak. A night here
marked the beginning of a journey to Cairo or Tehran or Bombay.
To the sweltering riches of the Orient or the stark desert salvation of
Jerusalem or Mecca. You came here with the mists of the Balkans in
your clothes. You came here, but you were going somewhere else.

"Virginia is back in the States."

"Oh. Is everything all right? No one died, right?"

Fred shook his head. He tried to imagine the salons full, but he could only fill them with caricatures: the pith-helmeted imperialist, the Brylcreem spy, the fez, the pilgrim, the long lady in the long dress with the long cigarette holder. It was probably never like that, and if it was it must have been truly boring. A book he and everyone else had read before.

"So when are you going back to join her?" Eddie was playing dumb. Fred deserved it. Virginia was always picking up his conversational slack. She hated doing it. But it had meant Fred could skip conversations he didn't want to have, like this one.

"I don't know," he said. "I'm going to teach summer school."

"Sounds terrible. Virginia opted out?"

"Of the whole thing."

"As in she left?"

"A week ago. She's with her parents." Fred had already finished his drink.

"And you just let her go?"

"I didn't think she was serious. I mean, I guess I still don't." But he did. She'd left his spec scripts open on his computer before she left. He doubted they made any sense to her, but he recognized they signified a rift. Maybe she'd been looking for evidence of an affair, something to explain why he was so determined to stay. He probably would have done the same. He felt a little superior that he hadn't been cheating.

"Why didn't you go with her? At least figure out what's going on."

"I've got this money thing going on here, I didn't tell her about it. But I don't want to leave it either."

"Money thing?"

"Nothing illegal, just something extra on the side. It's kind of a once-in-a-lifetime opportunity. It's the kind of thing where I could walk away in a year or two and not have to think about money for a long time."

The bartender put a bowl of bar nuts in front of them. He was listening, not that Fred cared. Fred was going to go for a handful when he caught himself. There were whole pistachios in the mix, a great way to crack a tooth. Virginia had joked they were there to punish the drunks in a country of tea drinkers. He picked one out and forced its halves open.

"You and Allen Iverson. You hear he's coming to shoot hoops for the Cradle Stone professional team? Some people are saying Kobe Bryant will come if the NBA players go on strike. Seems everyone is coming to make their fortune here. You wouldn't have guessed it five years ago." Eddie finished his drink. "I'm guessing you'll have another."

Fred nodded. "She wanted us to go live with her parents, on their farm in Illinois. I didn't think she was serious. I mean, after a few weeks I feel like we can talk about her coming back for the fall."

"I'm guessing you're telling me this because you want to know what happened with my wife," Eddie said.

It had crossed Fred's mind.

"My wife was the quiet one. She was Australian and came here to teach nursery school. She had the big eyes of a forest animal. We were both living over here; I was just getting started in contracting. Sort of a winning situation. The money, compared with what I was used to. We met at one of those going-away parties with all the expats. The cherries had just come into the markets and I was joking with the host, who was moving to New York, that he'd never be able to afford so many cherries again in his life. You forget just how expensive they are in the States. Then she, my wife-to-be, said, 'With all the money he'll save on wine, he'll be able to have cherries.'

"I don't think I'd even noticed she was there. She was like that, my wife, one of those people who took things in. I think I made her happy. We sort of fell into our own world here—I'd tell her the histories of the places we'd visit and she'd make up stories about the people who lived there. And so maybe I got to thinking I was all she needed. When we had the chance to move into that house in Little Raven, I figured it would be perfect. All our friends were here on the European side of the Strait, sure, but we were going to set ourselves up in a swank little house. And for a while things seemed just as they had been. I remember sitting on the shore with her, drinking pomegranate juice and telling her the story of the Red Tower. That's the strange little fort that's built out into the Strait. It kind of looks like a lighthouse. Now they've built a lux restaurant in there and everyone calls it by its Greek name, the Maiden's Tower. The story was that a fortuneteller told the emperor his daughter would die by a snakebite. So to save her, he built her that tower in the Strait. Surrounded on all sides by water. Totally snake-free. The thing was, the emperor didn't know the daughter had a secret lover in the court. His name, of course, translated to something like snake. Viper maybe, a sort of ancient River Phoenix. Anyway, there are lots of ways the story can go from there, but if I tell you the princess dies, you get the point."

"The guy bit her to death? Sounds kinky," Fred joked. The bartender perked up. But since nothing followed, he went over to feed the parakeets. They were starting to whistle and curse in French.

"Anyway, we used to go to this fish guy. I don't know if I'd call him a handsome guy. He'd got impacted teeth on one side. But he was wire strong with soft eyes like you might see on a sailor. I could tell my wife was attracted to him. He'd teach her little phrases in Turkish when she'd go and get the bream for dinner. You know, those everyday things expats love because they translate so weirdly: health to your hands, I'm unarmed, hope for better weather, your smile is like a boiled sheep's head. That sort of thing. So one day I asked her if she was attracted to him, to the fish man. She said yes. Thinking about it now, I don't know if she said yes with any conviction. Just as a matter of fact. But it ate away at me. I didn't feel like I could tell her not to go buy fish from him. He has the best fish in the neighborhood, to this day. But each time she'd come home and share the little phrase he taught her, it'd be like he had his hand in her pants. Finally one bad night I told her that if she wanted to, she could get with the fish guy. I think she was surprised. I wanted her to say that she'd never want to do that. That the idea disgusted her. But instead she said, okay. Not with any passion, in retrospect. And then, for all I know she did get with him. I couldn't ask. And she didn't say. Finally I just changed the locks. I mean, I couldn't even look at her."

"And so she's with the fish guy now?"

"I don't know. I don't buy fish from him anymore."

All the ice had melted in Eddie's glass. The sun had been down now for two hours. But the concrete on the land and the water in the air kept the early summer heat. Perhaps it was to recreate this sensation in the winter that the Turks built their steam baths. It didn't seem like anyone else was going to come in, so the bartender was leaning in close to see if their conversation was headed toward another drink. He was looking to cut his losses. Fred didn't know what to say, so he laid cash down for the drinks.

"You want to take a walk?" he said. "Maybe hit one more place before the last ferry?"

They walked down the old street of bars, beneath the Art Deco streetlamps and the framed photos of the Father of Turks. The hawkers called out drink specials, the only thing that distinguished the otherwise identical bars. They stopped in one and had a shot of hazelnut liquor, but decided not to stay. The place was full of cardboard nostalgia, like an Irish pub in an airport. Working their way through the back streets, they didn't say much. And whether by accident or on purpose, they ended up on Little Feasts Street.

The hookers on Little Feasts Street were by law not supposed to solicit. Everyone knew they were there, waiting behind the doors of unmarked buildings. But since it was a hot night, their barred windows were open, and they leaned out silently to watch the street below. Fred looked up at them and waved. They waved back. Then Eddie was there, up the few front steps, knocking at the door of one of the buildings. Number 23.

"What are you doing?" Fred hissed.

"I've never done this before," Eddie said, "but I don't see why I shouldn't."

"Well, I'm just going to head home."

"Because you're still with Virginia?"

Fred didn't respond, but he didn't keep walking either.

The door opened, revealing the madam, a hard-faced, piously kerchiefed woman in her forties. She took a quick look at Eddie, and at Fred, and said, "These are Turk girls, for Turks only. By law. You can go have a Russian girl in a hotel."

There were two things about the City that never changed, whoever conquered it. One was bread, the other was whores. Citizens were entitled to bread; under the empire, it was free. Today a loaf with a golden crust and a dense white crumb could be had for ten cents at any one of the public bakeries run by the government. The government also ran whores, whether they were temple brides or bath attendants. The generals had set up a system whereby rural girls could serve a turn, send money back to their families, and be returned in a marriageable state. How they managed the last part was anyone's guess, but keeping the clientele to citizens—pious, respectable men with wives, neighborhoods, and mosques to get back to—kept the whole system quiet.

She was about to close the door when Eddie said, in English, "We will be Turks."

The madam shook her head.

"Look," he said in his best Turkish, "you will make us Turks. Because we are going to sleep with these girls. And if only citizens can sleep with these girls, that makes us citizens. Would you do the honor of making us Turks?"

The madam gave a stern look, but in a way Eddie knew he had her. He was asking to turn Turk. And though there were no longer Western misfits lining up at the borders of the Ottoman Empire to step on a cross and join the corsairs, the sentiment must have rung true for the madam—a pride for what had once been the most desirable thing in the world. She would do them this honor.

The madam stepped aside, leaving the entryway open to the streetlight. Eddie looked down at Fred.

"C'mon," he said. "We're all Turks now."

AUTUMN

ONE.

FRED HAD JUST GOTTEN used to the idea of having the whole row to himself when the woman excused herself. She was in the window seat next to him. She crawled over, a mess of bags and boobs.

"I almost missed the flight," she said, straightening her blouse. She didn't strike Fred as the kind of woman who'd get left behind. He went back to his book, some new account of what "really happened" on the HMS *Bounty*, and settled into the heavy scent of her lotion.

"I'll have the salmon," Fred told the stewardess, "and another gin and tonic." He hadn't planned on going back to the States. Summer session had proved lucrative for him and the Greek. The shorter time frame put more pressure on even the good students to produce, and once they learned there was another way, they were all calling on the Greek's services. They wanted their summer back and were happy to pay. The Greek's summer was stressful, but Fred let him reuse the same papers across classes, which cut down on the work a little. It was dangerous; the chance of getting caught was a lot higher. But summer session had always been a kind of devil's bargain: everyone pretended they were doing a semester's work in five weeks, the instructors for vacation money, the students for higher grades. So a lot of the usual scrutiny was dropped. Still, they'd both resolved that if the scheme were to continue, they'd have to conceive of a more airtight way to handle demand.

When it was over, Fred figured on taking that trip to the south of the country. He could fly down and have a couple weeks watching Scandinavian blondes get sunburns ignoring their beer-drunk husbands. Maybe get out to some of the pirate coves, where people still dove for coins with Cleopatra's face on them. It wouldn't even put a dent in the down payment. He'd already surpassed the number he and Virginia were shooting for. In another two years, they wouldn't need a mortgage.

Virginia and he hadn't been talking, really. He'd send her occasional emails to see how she was and got brief, but not cruel, replies. She had set up a website to show the paintings she was doing on her parents' farm. They depicted broad open spaces, but across them were the shadows of tight alleyways and stovepipe minarets. He got in the habit of checking it at least once a day. Maybe there'd be some sign of him there.

Instead of the beach, he went back to the States. His grandmother was sick, and once the fall semester began, it would have been harder to make the trip. She was ninety-five and still living in the split-level house she'd bought with her husband outside Rye, New York. He'd passed a week with her and his mom, cooking, taking walks, and avoiding questions about Virginia. Even though his grandmother couldn't remember the day of the week or what pills she had or hadn't taken, she remembered Virginia. But she'd forget she'd asked where Virginia was, so Fred was forced to lie every few hours. "She's preparing for fall classes, Oma, she couldn't leave the City." "The city is only thirty minutes from here," she'd say. Then he would have to clarify, and she would say she couldn't understand why they had moved all that way away. When he said jobs, she'd pshaw. Though she was still too with it to say "money isn't everything." By the week's end, he was ready to return.

"You were right to choose the salmon. You just can't get decent salmon in the City," the woman in the seat next to him said. He turned in his seat to get a better look. She was put together, which made him suspicious. Her hair was perfectly bleached. It struck him as sort of beautiful in its unnaturality. She had a soft face and body, both of which were expensively presented. She wore gold bangles, but her fingers were bare.

"You live in the City?" Fred was noncommittal.

"I was born there," she said, and anticipating his next question, "I went to college in Coral Gables, Florida. Don't ask me where, because you haven't heard of it. It wasn't a good school, but that doesn't matter since, in the City, having gone to school in the States is enough. It doesn't matter that we'd wear our bikinis to class. It was that kind of place, but no one back home knows that."

She left Fred with that image, knowingly returning to picking at her salmon. Fred finished his drink.

Her name was Ayşe—the Turkish version of Jane, she'd said. Plain old Ayşe. She'd studied hospitality in Miami and had up until recently worked at the Four Seasons on the Strait. She'd lived in Little Raven but didn't know Eddie. She'd loved it there: the little cobblestone streets, the herbs she'd grow in her window planters. She loved the fish house on the water where all the old drug lords would go for Sunday lunch, their black American cars parked along the coastal road. They'd served the European market for a generation, growing modestly rich off the seventies heroin boom. There was a rogue's gallery of their mug shots proudly displayed in the restaurant's foyer. Her parents didn't think she was meeting the right people.

"I always figured I'd meet a young traveler, an heir who would pull his yacht right up to the hotel. And he'd take me away with him. But it was just years of fending off married men with expense accounts. I finally agreed to move back in with my parents," she said.

"Where are they?" The cabin lights had been dimmed, so they were alone among the rows of eye masks and blue-glowing individual movie screens. Their knees weren't quite touching.

"This is funny," she said. "They are in Little Raven." She let Fred puzzle at this, then laughed a bit at her own impossible riddle.

They lived in a development called Strait City, she explained. It was a prestigious gated community. It was built around a miniature version of the Strait, like a giant lap pool. Fred couldn't help but notice that she called the Strait by its Greek name, the "Ox-ford," instead of the Turkish, the "Throat." It was a sign of worldliness, no doubt. The miniature strait didn't have seas at either end, she explained. Instead, on either side and the back there were luxury high-rises that looked down on this stretch of water with its gentle willows and reproduction wooden boats. "Experience the Strait as it was a hundred years ago, no Ukrainian oil tankers, no Chinese container ships." She imitated the TV spot. But even more elite than these half-million-dollar condos with their pristine balconies were the Ottoman-style townhouses built on the manmade shores. Each of these was named after the neighborhood that corresponded with their relative location and had appropriate architectural accents.

"They built the Taverns house in the form of a tower, of course. And there's the Cannonball Palace with lots of small pavilions. Little

Raven is pretty ordinary. It's big and has some nice wood accents. Oh, and it came with a little wooden boat in a slip. But my family never uses it," Ayşe said. She added, "You should come see it, if you have time. The new Istanbul. It isn't far from the airport."

In the taxi, Fred didn't know what to do. He had helped the cabbie load her brushed aluminum luggage set into the trunk, fully expecting to say goodbye. But when the cabbie went for Fred's small suitcase, he let him take it, and he got in the car. Ayşe did not seem surprised.

It was the tail end of summer and a little film of sweat formed in her cleavage. Fred would glance at it, then look back out the cab's window at the endless factory outlet stores that lined the highway spur from the airport. She put on large Dior sunglasses and pulled a soft pack of Anadolus from her bag. Without asking the cabbie, she lit one with a high-pressure lighter, the kind ordinarily reserved for cigars. The blue flame sliced into the cigarette's tip. She rolled down her window.

"Do you smoke?"

Fred shook his head.

"You should. They say breathing the air in the City is like smoking a pack a day. You might as well get to feel something for it."

They were traveling a route Fred didn't know. He was used to following the Marble Sea, passing through the land walls at the Most Important Gate right at the Seven Towers Fortress. Then the cab would wrap around the back of Six Minaret Mosque and the Holy Wisdom, around the tip of the Palace Forest and across the inlet bridge. He knew there was a faster way to get to High Field, but this was the proper route to take. The way people had entered the city for nearly two thousand years. Now they were heading deeper and deeper into a landscape of warehouse stores and high-rises. Things he hadn't seen since driving to Bulgaria. The only familiar thing was the sun.

They passed the ride in silence. Though topics of conversation would rise from Fred's chest, his throat closed on them. By the time they arrived, Fred figured he'd say he had a meeting he'd forgotten about and just stay with the cab. Maybe he'd ask for her number. He hadn't done that in what seemed a lifetime. They pulled up to an anonymous gatehouse, the sort that might lead to a rail yard, and Ayşe told the cabbie the number code. Passing through, they emerged onto a large boulevard with heavily laden pomegranate bushes lining the median. At some distance down this drive, Fred could see the high-rises that formed the amphitheater for this new city. Ayşe was tersely guiding the cab through a series of roundabouts that tied together the spider web of roads. When they finally reached the banks of the miniature Strait, Fred was impressed. Mounds had been formed to mimic the City's rolling hills. Fred could make out among them familiar monuments, disproportionately reimagined as living spaces. There was even the covered bazaar, which seemed to be a kind of mall. People strolled along the shore with parasols. It was like they were enacting nineteenth-century prints Fred had seen of the City, except instead of sky on the horizon there was glass and steel.

The road left the "Strait" side and veered right, inland as it were. There were larger hillocks built to obscure the rolling shoreline from the rest of the compound's everyday life. On this side were the high-rises with their practicalities: entrances to parking structures, cafés, cab stands, signs for the fitness center. All they lacked in their imitation of the City's charmless sprawl were the massive garment factories and the poor rural migrants to work them.

It wasn't long before they veered left again. Toward the first bridge, Fred thought, right by Little Raven. He was getting pins and needles.

The Little Raven house was bigger than Fred had imagined. It was as if someone had taken one of the wooden mansions of the Ottoman little lords and filled it with helium until it was just off the ground. It wouldn't be a surprise if a red-fezed butler came out to meet them, closing the door behind him quickly to avoid letting any of the pomp out of the house. When the cab rounded the driveway and stopped before the double wooden doors, Fred did not immediately get out. Neither did Ayşe, leaving the cabbie to hop out and begin unloading. She went for her purse.

"I'll get this," Fred said uncertainly. She just continued into her bag, fishing about. Was he going to end up with her card, or just a banknote for her part of the trip? Finally she came up with her sunglasses case. The Diors came off, and Fred was back with the carefully kohled and shaded eyes he'd watched on the plane. Fred got out of the cab. He paid the cabbie, he even paid the arbitrary luggage fee, which was asked of everyone but which locals customarily ignored. Then he went to Ayşe's side and opened her door.

"I guess I should give you the tour," she said. They left her bags in the receiving room. The floor was dominated by a painstaking reproduction mosaic of Bacchus, complete with blank patches. It looked almost exactly like the one in the Rhode Island School of Design museum, ripped from the Villa Diana in Antioch sometime in the nineteenth century. The ceilings were surprisingly low, giving the otherwise large room the feel of a crypt. They proceeded directly toward the broad staircase, her heels clacking on the tile. But instead of mounting to the rest of the house, she suggested they check out the dock.

Fred followed Ayşe through a side door into a stretch of dark, carpeted hallway. As they went, Fred could hear the wash of the mock Strait against the side of the house. The Strait, the real one, had currents that ran strongest just below the water's surface. Not a summer's day went by without some poor kid being sucked under, getting carried the whole length and ending up blue and bloated, washed up on the shores of the Marble Sea. Fred was recalling the newspaper pictures as he bumped into Ayşe, who had stopped abruptly.

"Something wrong?" he asked, his hands on her black muslin dress just a bit longer than was necessary to steady himself. They rested there on her fleshy hips, just out of the light. She turned and Fred got his first taste of Anadolu cigarettes. The faint, dirty flavor faded quickly, or he forgot it as his hands migrated up to the hard breasts. What the hell, he thought. Then he realized they must be fake. It seemed completely appropriate, and his penis agreed. But she pulled away.

"My parents are home," she said. Her eyes were reading his. His pants belied his disposition. He probably should have been embarrassed, or maybe more assertive, but she was already walking away, opening a door to the exterior, their little moment of darkness washed out by the City's sun. He followed her out onto the dock, where a rowboat was moored. It struck him then how small the mock Strait really was, no more than the width of a backyard pool. It was similarly deep, with a cleverly rendered lining that gave the sloshy water more sense of movement. The "first bridge," a single-lane causeway with some suspension accents, was just to their right; the second, which carried traffic in the opposite direction, maybe a hundred yards beyond. Unlike the real transcontinental bridges, they were entirely free of traffic.

To the left, at the base of the Strait, were the three landmarks of the historic peninsula reimagined to house people instead of God, Allah and the Sublime Porte. The leftmost, the palace, made sense to Fred, though its "tower of justice" looked too small to room a person. The renditions of the Holy Wisdom and the Six Minaret Mosque, though massive, seemed uninhabitable. They came off as huge blocks capped by little domes that served as pincushions for the slim mock minarets.

"They get more light than you'd imagine," Ayşe said, following his puzzled gaze. "What do you think?"

"I think we should get back to the privacy of the hallway."

"No," she said, "what do you think about the Strait, the whole development."

"I don't know whether to laugh or cry," Fred said. He wasn't worried about coming off as charitable now.

"Well, don't tell my father that."

"He must like it. After all, he bought a place."

"He was the developer. The whole thing was his idea."

The rest of the tour passed quickly. Ayşe was more than capable of spending the afternoon telling Fred the pedigree of every carpet in every sitting room but opted not to. She also didn't take him to the family living quarters, saving him from having to meet her parents, and also, he suspected, not to further give him the wrong impression. She phoned him a cab as he milled, feigning interest in a set of framed miniatures.

"Do you have a card?" she asked.

He pulled out one of the high-gloss white on crimson ones the Castle had given him. They reminded him of Christmas, a strange feeling which he suppressed. Ayşe took the card and looked it over like she was studying one of the miniatures. The taxi announced its presence with two curt honks. Instead of retrieving a card of her own, she grabbed Fred's wrist, and overtop that vein that they say leads to the heart, she wrote her cellphone number in eyeliner.

"It's waterproof," she said, ushering him out the door without a kiss.

TWO.

FRED BROUGHT A KITCHEN stool into the Cage, the dark heart of CapturetheCastleEssays. The Greek was already there, composing the welcome back email that was going out to their customer list. It promised twenty-five percent off the first paper with proof of referral. It also outlined some changes in policy, which its founders were there to discuss.

The Greek was just back from a "roots" trip with his family and looked a little better for it. They'd flown to Athens, then island-hopped all the way back to Smyrna, now a pleasantly sophisticated Turkish metropolis happy to forget the Greek evacuation with its dead babies and mules drowned in shallow water.

"Some of those islands, man, it was like time stopped" was his takeaway.

The problem they faced was the volume of direct electronic communication between clients and the Greek. The cheats would email the Greek the assignment prompts, then email him six more times freaking out about whether he'd get the paper done on time. Over the summer, Fred had observed kids doing this in the Castle computer lab for anyone to see. He almost went over and smacked their stupid heads. Then they'd get the paper emailed to them and print it out without changing the parts in the heading that read "Your Name" and "Your Teacher's Name." And to top it off, some would pay with PayPal accounts linked to credit cards belonging to their parents, who'd dispute charges to CapturetheCastleEssays. Fred and the Greek had to let these go, since the arbitration processes meant revealing who they were and what they sold. Even putting all this aside, it would only take Dean Rose-Eyes asking the network administrators at the Castle to monitor IP traffic in order to track them to their doorstep.

"I think we need to take a more old-fashioned approach to this," Fred began. "Something a little more Ian Fleming."

"Who's that?"

"James Bond."

"Right. I love that guy. I loved reading spy novels at the beach. I used to do it all the time at the Malibu Lagoon. Between the sun and the sound of the water, you can just lose yourself in one of those. All those dark and sexy girls and their poisoned umbrellas."

"I was thinking more about how they communicate. Dead drops, never face to face."

Fred illustrated, crumpling up a sheet of scratch paper, and whistling "discreetly" while dropping it in one of the corners of the Cage.

"Okay." The Greek skeptically played this out. "So the cheats would drop the assignment and the cash. You'd pick it up, bring it here. I'd fill the order and you'd drop the essay off. Sounds good to me, no more whiny emails. But that's a lot of exposure for you. Let's say you have them drop things in some random locker, it's only a matter of time before someone notices. Or worse, you're there picking up when they drop off. Someone knowing you are running this operation blows the whole thing up. And then there's the matter of them picking up the cooked essays. If it's all in the same place, it's going to look like a Starbucks at the airport. Or the stupid Weeping Pillar in the Holy Wisdom. Maybe we should just switch email addresses every three months? I can work out of a coffee shop, if the IP thing is a problem. I'd rather, I think."

The Cage was tight and windowless, but they had outfitted it for the purpose. There were hanging files now with all the standard assignments given out by the writing faculty. Prompts and their variations, related readings and sample student essays Fred had nicked. Also legal pads where the Greek made "originality lists" of words and phrases he'd used more than three times writing any particular assignment. When he filled the page with fresh ones, he could use the old ones again, sort of a lexical hourglass. Even though the Greek was getting pretty good at this, trying to juggle all the variables in a coffee shop and not end up with identically written essays seemed unlikely.

"I'll think about it," Fred said. This meant extricating himself from the Cage and hitting the couch by way of the fridge. He looked at the bookshelf in disgust. He and Virginia had only brought twenty or so paperbacks from home, mostly for sentimental reasons. Things they wanted other people to see on their shelves, farewell gifts from parents, literature germane to their adventure abroad. Nothing that made particularly good light reading. Books, especially foreign language books, were highly taxed in the City. The rationale, Fred suspected, was the same as the booze taxes. The generals didn't like non-Turkish ideas, so they taxed foreign ideas. And untranslated books didn't go through the religious censors who prevented blasphemy from being printed in the country, so the ministers added another tax to keep the faithful well clear of unapproved texts.

He pulled out a short story collection, interconnected stories of expatriates in Morocco. He'd start to read a story, but as soon as it mentioned the souk or the casbah he'd skip to the next one. He'd burned through the book in fifteen minutes or so. At the back, there was a postcard jammed in the spine. Virginia must have been using it as a bookmark. It was from Rye Playland; he'd sent it to her when she was in Providence and he was down visiting his grandmother. All it said was, "We should do this sometime. Thinking of you. Love, Fred." He seized up a little. He could remember writing it: the want for Virginia there so they could ride the wooden coaster and he could win her the giant mint-colored teddy bear from the shooting gallery. The feeling that, without her, these same actions had no meaning. If he got on a plane tomorrow, she might have him back. "I was wrong, I have the down payment." But how much better would it be to apologize with the keys and the deed to the house with the orange tree? There's always less to be sorry for when you've won. He jammed the card back into the book's spine, which gave him the idea.

"We'll use the library," he told the Greek.

The Castle's library was a joke. It was a three-story building prominently situated on the central "quad," which was more of a giant tea garden patio packed with students smoking and taking their caffeine. The stacks on the upper floors were popular with students looking to nap among the sparse collection of Turkish reference volumes. Many of the shelves remained obscenely empty, like the university wanted to keep them cold and insecure. In the basement, there was a vast collection of bootlegged DVDs. Fred shouldn't have found any irony in this, but he did. The basement was also where the English-language books were shelved, off to one side. To say it was an eclectic collection was generous. It seemed more like the selection of books one might find at a beachside hotel: Danielle Steel, Atkins Diet, *How to Make Friends and Influence People*. Fred knew the collection well. He'd scoured it for decent reads more than once and come up short.

"The cheat will take an English book off the shelf and tuck in the assignment and cash. Then he, or she, will dump it in the book drop. The librarians will reshelve it, and I'll drop by and pick it off the shelf."

"I assume you realize, once they are reshelved, you won't be able to distinguish which ones contain the cheat's requests."

"The librarians don't know English. They just put the most recently returned books at the end of the shelves."

"What if the cheat's money falls out?"

"They'll tape it in."

The Greek raised an eyebrow. He had caterpillar thick eyebrows.

"It could happen, sure. But with no names, no instructions, the librarians will just pocket the cash. If they begin to intercept it, we'll have to change tactics. But I think you overestimate their curiosity, especially when it comes to books."

"Okay, so you'll be hauling twenty-five or more books out at a time. Nothing suspicious about that."

"Paperbacks. I'll just line the sack I use to haul student work home. Couldn't be more than fifteen extra pounds."

"And you'll haul them back too? You better put some of that money aside for chiropracty. Or bail."

"No." Fred had figured this aspect out too. Like a chess master, he had seen the full potential of his chosen move. Once the Greek had completed the plagiarized essay, he'd trot it down with the book to the photocopyists of Pirate's Boulevard. He'd ask them to include the essay as notes to the photocopies of the book, and they'd bind it in. The cheat would come to the photocopyists and say he or she was picking up the copy and the original. They'd pay the nominal fee and walk away with their essay and the book to return to the library, where it could undergo the same journey. There were so many ways this could go wrong, but Fred believed that an overwhelming lack of curiosity would keep the scheme safe, at least for its appointed run. And what indifference couldn't solve, he was sure mild corruption could.

"You're a writer, right?" the Greek finally asked after Fred laid the whole cycle out for him.

"For TV. Aspiring."

"And you don't feel bad using books to make a buck off the craven and insipid?"

"We'll be among the few to make any money off books whatsoever. Craven and insipid, eh? Looks like that thesaurus is coming in handy. But I don't think any Castle students would use either of those words, especially about themselves."

The Greek shrugged. When Fred had first conceived of this scheme, he thought of the Greek as a co-conspirator. But now Fred was wondering if the Greek had the stomach for it. Still, what was worse: helping kids buy a degree they were already paying for, or driving up home prices in Southern California? Fred could imagine the Greek rolling up to that little fixer-upper with the orange tree with a pile of cash. Bouncing Fred and Virginia's offer right out of contention, installing a Potemkin kitchen island. Where was the justice in that?

THREE.

IT TOOK FRED A few weeks to notice the tables were back. Whole alleyways that had been abandoned were packed again with patio furniture, filled to the gills with fish eaters and aniseed liquor drinkers. He should have noticed earlier. Truth was he'd been avoiding the places he used to go with Virginia. But he'd read there was a new hotel balcony bar open just over the old underground funicular. It was a fancy cocktail bar in the American style, with valet parking. Orient Express themed. Real American liquor. He figured this might be a venue acceptable to Ayşe. And he was prepared to pay, despite knowing full well the drinks would be stronger, the atmosphere more Orient Express at the Big London among the prostitutes.

His mind was on prices as he turned onto Vine Clad Mosque Street. He would go as high as twenty dollars a drink, depending on how crisp the view was of the historic peninsula and whether he could get a firm guarantee of a table with that view. There were plenty of rooftop places. Most averaged fifteen dollars a drink, though ones that had opened over ten years ago could only charge ten. Twenty dollars a drink was what they charged at the restaurant built into the Red Tower, the fairytale prison in the middle of the Strait. He and Virginia had joked about swimming to it. It was the only way they'd ever get a chance to try it, since its ten tables had been booked well into the next decade. They envisioned crawling up onto the tiny island and unzipping wetsuits to reveal eveningwear, and then ordering lemonade, since it would be all they could afford. He regretted that this never happened, even though it was impossible.

Though Vine Clad Mosque Street was again lined with diners, the atmosphere was different. Before, the tables' population split three ways: twenty-something art school graduates, sixty-something alcoholics, and expats of the ages in between. The three groups enjoyed reaching across to one another, clinking milky glasses to art and freedom and the worker's paradise before digging into ratty plates of grilled fish and mounds of dip the consistency of baby food. Now it was evening gowns and candelabras. There was no crush slowly passing between the lines of tables looking for an open one. This had become reservations territory. The food did look better—tamed and served on top of arugula or lentils. One could always have found those sorts of "international standards" in the posh Villages along the Strait. It was just as Eddie had predicted.

As if he'd spoken of the devil, there was Eddie in a nicely tailored blue suit, sitting with two older gentlemen, about to stick a toothy knife into a fatty lamb chop.

"You know, in Turkish they say, 'A good person shows up when you speak of them,'" Eddie said, standing and giving Fred the whole handshake and elbow grab.

"Were you talking about me?" Fred asked.

"Not exactly, but I was talking about some of the neighborhood's offerings for after dinner entertainment." He gave a rakish smile. They hadn't talked about that night on Little Feasts Street. And though Fred wasn't avoiding Eddie per se, he'd begged off seeing him again since before his trip to the US. Summer teaching, he'd said, was all-consuming.

The two men introduced themselves. Their generic but difficult to pronounce Turkish names passed between Fred's ears. "We're here celebrating," Eddie said. "Why don't you join us for a glass, unless you have somewhere else to be."

They were drinking Club brand aniseed liquor, the brand favored by the generals and industrialists. The label, unchanged since the glory days of single-party rule, portrayed two tuxedoed gentlemen, cigarette holders clenched in their teeth, poised over a drink-laden table with the hard bands of a Crayola sunset behind them. As much as things changed in the City, they stayed the same. Just as the label of the Club brand remained frozen in the violet hour.

Fred acquiesced. Luckily he'd worn a shirt and slacks for his Ayşe dry run.

"So what do you think of the new Vine Clad Mosque Street?" Eddie asked, pouring water into Fred's drink.

"It's like Baby or Dry Spring without the Strait views." Fred hadn't meant his comparison to the Villages to be favorable, but the two men nodded their approval.

"Just what I was going for," Eddie said, "but with a little more of an arty edge. The Villages create the illusion of openness, of being above the City and looking out. Of being somewhere else with a sanitized cosmopolitanism. Europe. This, this is in the City, in the press of its energies. With all its life piled right here on top of you. It's like you could turn a corner into an alley and find your lover, or your murderer. It's what people want now, the feel of real excitement, what the City is really like. What it's always been like."

The two men were eating this up in between bites of thick white fish fillet. Maybe it was the strength of the drink Eddie had poured him on an empty stomach, but Fred's gut was twisting. Around the corner had been the cartoonist's favorite spot, the one that always seemed to have some thin T-shirted girl puking her guts out as a friend held her hair back. Sometimes this happened in the bathroom, but mostly it was into a large planter set just beside the bar's countless rickety tables. Bade's Place was the name. The cartoonist said he liked it because every so often someone would get held up at knifepoint. This kept the yuppies and the business majors well clear. Fred and Virginia went there on the hottest nights of fall, when the lobby of the Big London smelled too much of rose musk and hooker snatch. They sat out with bottles of Bade's homemade wine, which Fred strongly suspected was white grape juice spiked with grain alcohol. It didn't matter after the second ice-filled glass. They staggered home and fucked sloppily in the kitchen, lying out on the tile after. It was the only cool surface in the whole apartment.

"How's that situation at your apartment going? I realize we haven't talked about it forever," Eddie said. The two men were palling around in Turkish.

"It's been resolved," Fred said.

"Really? You got them to move out?"

Fred shook his head. Funny, he hadn't even asked the Greek if he'd made any progress with the deed lately. Their time had been so consumed with running the essay operation, he doubted if either of them had given anything else much thought. The Greek hadn't even moved his things out of Virginia's studio. If Virginia came back tomorrow, she'd find the apartment as she'd left it. The chair they'd bought in the antiques market above the post office in the poor valley and carried a half-mile, right past the ten overpriced antique dealers leading to their block, was still in the corner. He'd have to do something about that chair, maybe sell it to the antique dealers. He'd make a profit and he'd be one step closer to ridding the place of its ghosts.

"So what's the deal? I mean, has it been a year of them living there yet?"

"Seven months."

"And nothing from Marvin?"

"I stopped trying to get hold of him. I also stopped paying rent."

"Are you going to pay if he gets back in touch?"

"I figured he and the Greek would sort it out. But he could be dead for all I know. He is in another country."

"Morbid." Eddie shook his head. "Thoughts of death can come up on you in this City. It's like Venice but bigger. Death is bigger here, more general, less personal, less romantic. Probably better. Did you get yourself a beaker of the warm south this summer? We've got the Black Sea up here, but it's only a short trip down to the White one."

"I didn't make it."

"Well, it's still nice through the fall. You can fly there in an hour. Fall's better—give you a chance to meet the people in this country who have nothing better to do than go to the beach."

"Can't I meet them here, on the new Vine Clad Mosque Street?" It was a bitter sentiment, its source the deep part of Fred that still saw wealth as the thief of authenticity. But it was one which rolled off Eddie's back. This wasn't Eddie's neighborhood anymore; he'd left its shabby bohemian streets a decade ago. And it wasn't Fred's anymore either, unless he was changing with it. Perhaps he was.

Eddie was saying something like, "In a month I'm sure, it takes time for word to reach…" when Fred cut him off.

"Do you know the owner of this place?"

Eddie pointed to one of the gentlemen, rousing him from his chatter.

"I'd like to make a reservation, two weeks from now, for Friday. For two. I'm sure you're already booked, but I want to have the full experience: braised artichoke heart, pounded octopus, god's-truth sea bass, and whatever else you think appropriate."

"End with the Palestinian cheesecake, she will like that," one said.

"Of course, for a friend of Eddie I will find you a table," the other, the owner, added.

"Don't count on any favors at the end of the night." Eddie smirked.

"I've got it covered," Fred said.

"I mean from the girl," Eddie jockeyed, once again all winks and nudges.

FOUR.

It was awkward for Fred, the first meeting of the fall semester with Dean Rose-Eyes. He'd asked to talk to Fred before the opening departmental meeting. Fred had to come up to his office, what turned out to be a sprawling compound on the top floor of the Humanities and Social Sciences building. Fred budgeted a half-hour to find it, the Castle sharing that distinctly Ottoman architectural tactic of reserving every window for private use. This meant one had to wander a warren of hallways with no sense of where one was in relation to the building itself. If the offices were numbered sequentially, this wouldn't matter, but Fred had learned from the post office not to expect this. He wandered the hallways slowly, thumbs in his belt loops. When he hit a dead end, he just bounced out of it like a marble in a maze. He knew this was a means of unsettling. The metaphor for power in the City had always been the door— who could open it, who it could be closed on. The Turks learned it from the Greek synod, the sultan becoming the "Sublime Porte." Last fall, he would have been panicked, like someone who'd taken a wrong turn from the tourist areas and entered the organic City. Now he had things in hand.

"You know, for us in this country, family comes first."

Fred nodded. The dean's office was beautiful, views on the Black Sea from three sides. The dean had his back to the windows, so Fred got to enjoy the afternoon sun playing the unbroken field of sky and water.

"And when a wife leaves her husband…"

"We never married."

"…and the husband lets her go, it raises questions about the husband. What kind of man is he? Is he in control? Or does he have other interests? Unhealthy interests?" Dean Rose-Eyes lisped this all out like a concerned parent with unhealthy interests of their own. Fred knew he was being insulted, but he kept his cool. Rose-Eyes was in charge, after all, no reason for him to believe otherwise.

"She didn't like it here," he said.

"Here the City or here the country or here the university?" the dean pressed.

"All three, I'd say."

"Why?"

"I'd ask her yourself. I like it here just fine. Is there a question about my performance?"

"No. Actually, you may not believe this, but I can understand having difficulty living here. It isn't widely known, but my family was of Jewish origin. From Salonica, once so thick with rabbinical schools people were convinced the next Messiah would be educated there. No more. The twentieth century was bad to it, like so many places. Anyway, we moved here and became Turks. Made it work. And so sometimes I'm saddened when someone feels like they can't live here. Then again, some people have more choices than others."

"Well." Fred felt a bit badly. He'd always figured the dean for a grown-up version of their students. Smug and silver spooned, happy to be teaching at the thirteenth-ranked university in the world among universities founded ten or fewer years ago. But Fred got things wrong. Things he thought he knew, that history had taught him, turned out false. Or worse, multiply true. No fixed story to learn and retell. "I like it here just fine. Is there some question about my performance?" he repeated.

After a minute of wondering if he'd revealed some sensitive aspect of his heritage to an unsympathetic listener, the dean said no. Fred had done well, was popular. "Except with the students you've exposed as cheats. But you must know by now, they've just been given warnings. In the end, they are good kids and it is our responsibility to give them an education. They are the future of the country."

Fred nodded, pushing a smile from his lips. The future of the country was learning that it was better to pay for something twice than do it once. It was a valuable lesson.

"But if you are going to stay here, you should keep an open mind. You know most foreigners who come here do so to find a partner."

Fred nodded.

Kiki was warming up the projector. She had kohled her eyes for this meeting.

"One of the secretaries showed me how to do it," she explained, a little too innocently.

"The secretary named Desire?" Fred half joked. There was a secretary whose name meant desire.

"I hope you don't intend to teach like that, Kiki," the little dean scoffed in his lispy fashion. "Your students are going to think you don't have a man in your life."

In the light of the projector, there was no hiding the blood rushing to her face. She was like a rosy sun rising over a white desert that read "Autumn Semester Policies and Goals." The dean sat, apparently oblivious that he'd cut Kiki off at the ankles. Fred made his way to the back of the room. He nodded as he went, as if to acknowledge the stares that followed him. There had been an assumption that Virginia had just taken the summer off. Fred neither confirmed nor denied. Her missing the semester's first meeting was news. Fred could feel a nebulous sense of contentment as this situation spread through his colleagues. The Beatles had broken up. Sonny and Cher split. Everyone was seemingly grateful. Fred was now just another lonely atom far from home. He felt dinner invitations coming on. No doubt at the cost of opening up about how things had gone spectacularly wrong and Virginia chickened out for America, with all its false promises and dead-end politics. Its recession-gutted economy and university adjuncts dying of the common cold. At first they'd dine on Schadenfreude, that expatriate delicacy, at his expense. But then he'd be allowed to dig in on the collective contempt for Virginia's decision. The prospect was amusing, but he'd have to pass.

The only person's eyes he met, accidently, were April's. Behind them was just a question mark. He couldn't imagine Virginia hadn't confided in her. They went back, Chicago back. But what Virginia'd said, how much or how little, Fred could only guess. When he and Virginia were new to the City, they'd crashed a freelance journalist's going-away party. Well into it, Fred asked the journalist, a guy about his age, what it was like to live in the City. "It's like Mario Brothers, the old one," the journalist had slurred. He'd obviously given this some thought and was happy to try it out on a fresh face. 'You're crashing along, grabbing what you can, taking it all in, land, sea, and air. It seems like a million discoveries are possible. But each time you think you've gotten somewhere, you're told, 'Our princess is in another castle.' Then comes the day you try and go back, try to retrace what you've done and get back to some point where you could have done differently. That's when you realize the game doesn't work that way, the screen only scrolls right, the past is an impermeable black wall." Fred had said something like, "Isn't life like that," thanked the guy for the party, and went to refill his cup with wine he already knew was bad, but wasn't sick of yet.

Fred was lost in thought when he realized he was being called upon. Kiki hadn't really recovered—the committees she'd wanted to form, the proposals she'd wanted to farm out, the draft grants she'd wanted volunteers to draft so she could take them to the faculty council all fell flat. Without the dean's underwriting, his smiling gaze, there wasn't much incentive for the department to take on extra work. Kiki looked hopelessly at the dean through her raccoon eyes, but he was busy with his smartphone. Just as distant as any of their students, making plans for when his real life could begin again. In what must have been a panic, she had called on Fred to report on the success of the Paula strike-force. Fred couldn't stifle a yawn.

"I think we've got the Paula situation under control. I've identified her tells, like in poker. The phrases and structures she depends on. I've been able to sift through the papers you all have given me, and with surprising accuracy I've identified those Paula wrote. I'm getting results with the disciplinary council, isn't that right, Dean?"

The dean nodded, not looking up from his phone.

"That's great, Fred," Kiki said, "but don't you feel like this is a lot of work? As the department chair, I'm only teaching one class. Maybe you could help me learn Paula's tells and I could take over the task of reviewing suspected plagiarism. You could have some more time with your students."

In this situation, someone might be worried. But Kiki didn't seem to be onto anything except that Fred had won his punishment. He'd beat the scaffolds like a game of hangman. If he'd figured a way to sift through Paula's handiwork, then why shouldn't Kiki take the task on and collect the gold stars for herself? And really, why shouldn't he let her?

"Okay," he said. "I'll come by your office with a couple of sample papers and show you how it works."

Kiki looked for the dean's approval, but there was nothing. The meeting was adjourned, to everyone's great relief. Fred was ready to make his escape, but Kiki and the dean converged awkwardly at the door like the pair of Cyanean rocks the ancient Greeks thought guarded the northern mouth of the Strait. You could almost see that mythic point from the Castle, the point where the rocks tried to close the Strait upon Jason and the Argonauts. After Jason penetrated them, they never closed again. Another one of those psychosexual Greek myths. Fred though he might be able to slip behind the dean and Kiki if he could shoot up the opposite side of the table. But there was April, standing in his way.

She was always more on the voluptuous side, with an hourglass figure that fluctuated between pizza and yoga. Not that he kept track, but Virginia had commented, mostly as an indictment of the thickening qualities of local food. But this time the change seemed more marked than the result of a few furtive pizza escapes.

"You're pregnant," Fred said a bit tenuously.

"Virginia didn't tell you?"

"We haven't been talking much lately." Fred resisted asking about Virginia. "Congratulations!"

"Thanks, I know you mean it." She had a bent sort of smile he couldn't place. Maybe she thought he was being insincere. "But you really should come over and see Ata, he's been asking about you."

Fred felt the embarrassment of a child being told to report his behavior to his father. Did Ata know about his failed relationship? Was that what it was, a failed relationship? If it was, the failure felt like his. "I've been out of town. I was planning on stopping in at the garage."

"You should come see us at home," April said. "Since we got pregnant, Ata's gone and got a job at the airport. He isn't spending much time at the garage these days. He's even talking about passing it off to one of the lieutenants."

"Huh. Well, I think I have some time this week before the semester really gets underway," Fred said noncommittally. He wondered what Ata thought of the phrase "We got pregnant."

"What are you doing tonight?"

"Laundry" was all he could think to say.

"You're already all the way up here, why not just come home with me? Ata's making dinner. There's always plenty of food."

April and Ata's apartment in Therapy was up in a gully, where the posh waterside restaurants and wooden Ottoman-era mansions gave way to modest, well-maintained apartment buildings housing the families of sailors and fishermen. Even though April and Ata were on the top floor, their rent was probably $500 and a three thousand feet short of a view of the sea. But they did have two terraces, one on either end of the living room. One was almost entirely filled with

April's vegetable vines, lured out of their pots and onto the tile by a web of string. The other was Ata's grilling porch, covered for all weather. The grill was built into the back wall like a fireplace raised to waist height. It was his stage, his blank canvas, his orchestra pit. Fred had watched him before, carefully building a jagged bed of hardwood charcoal, working beautiful curls of kindling among the coal. Then taking the top of a chopped onion and vigorously cleaning the ribs of the grill. Ata could put a fish fillet on that grate and peel it off in four minutes with perfect burn lines and no flaking. He could pull wads of ground meat from a giant ball and toss them haphazardly across the hot surface. In minutes, they were the juicy grilled meatballs beloved of all Turks when smothered in garlic yogurt. He had a similar aptitude with the giant improvised grill at the garage, but the intimacy of this hearth showcased his mastery best.

Between these two terraces, the apartment was the cozy meeting point of cultures, where pickled tomatoes from Ata's Bulgarian village lived beside bottles of Cholula and Liquid Smoke. Though they slept together in April's bedroom, Ata kept a bed in a spare room with tiger-striped silk sheets and a rack for his leather jackets of varying grade and thickness. April's aging cats moved freely among the university-provided furnishings and April's sculptures, tiny dioramas carved into the hearts of tree trunks. Ata showed his affection for the cats by slapping their asses hard and repeatedly, like he was beating a rug. As far as Fred could tell, the cats liked it.

He rode the minibus with April. Mercifully, she was offered a seat—her condition must have been obvious to the Turks, more obvious than to Fred. It was a public minibus with a route through several uniform apartment complexes that had sprung up amongst the hillside farms. When Fred first saw them, he thought they were housing projects, especially since herds of sheep and stray chickens passed between them. Rather, this was where those who cashed out of neighborhoods like High Field were moving. Here they had what seemed like fresh air and space, however stacked. The minibus quickly filled with cheaply but aspirationally appareled wives, some with children, some with shopping baskets, all headed for the blasted little Strait-side suburb of the Yellow Place.

The Yellow Place was the site of the last public stoning of a woman for adultery. Fred wondered if this fact ever occurred to these women who had packed themselves tightly around him. Over their cowled heads, he could peer out the left side of the bus as it crested the road. The glittering Strait seemed to loll through the hills, no grander than a river. Yet beneath it was the City's doom, the faults that spread like cracked glass from the continental meeting point.

Having worked its way through the market area of The Yellow Place, the minibus picked up speed on the coast road. Fred was jostled against the surrounding women. The bus careened around the eddy, passing an abandoned nightclub, an abandoned church, a plot where an Ottoman mansion had burned down and a swarthy crew of workers were pouring cement for what promised to be six stories of Strait views, private terraces, and walk-in closets. Rounding another promontory, they passed the rows and rows of fish restaurants Therapy was famous for. It was named Therapy by the Greeks, who believed that good air poured into its little gully from the forest above. The same forest which was slated to be clear cut to create a highway spur for a third transcontinental bridge over the Strait. It was estimated that twenty thousand trees would have to be removed for the bridge alone, leaving aside the inevitable development along the road. It was a grand forest, so vast the Magnificent Sultan dumped the surviving population of Belgrade there after he had razed that city. Environmentalists said the City's ecology wouldn't be able to withstand the loss of it. It was where the fresh water collected. But the ministers had the support of all those people who wanted to live in a part of the City never before lived in, of which there were many. Who wouldn't want to live somewhere safe, clean, and free of ghosts? Soon the breeze down the gully would bring the heat of concrete and the tar of petrol. It was just another change.

They got out at the ice cream shop where the mouth of the gully spilled into the small bay. Fred helped April down from the minibus. She seemed abstracted, like she had been lost in thought.

"How long do you think you'll live here?" she asked as they turned up her street.

"I don't know. A while longer. I mean, the money is good, there are still a lot of places I haven't been."

"Even without Virginia?"

"I don't know," Fred said again. He had already thought, in the two years remaining, that he'd travel to Egypt and Israel, the most ancient places. He'd add Italy to that list if it looked like Virginia would never forgive him. She'd always wanted to go to Italy. She'd even promised not to run off with a cute Italian guy. "I guess part of me is hoping she'll come back. I mean, she's with her parents now. I can't live like that, with them. Eating food out of their fridge. Sitting on their couch out in the middle of the plains. It's just not how I was raised."

"How were you raised?"

"To have a job."

"Having a job isn't like having a moral code. Going to work doesn't make you a better person. Ask Ata—he'll agree in a second."

"Living off the charity of your girlfriend's family doesn't make you a better person either."

She let some time and space pass. They had slowed with the grade, and the trees had shifted from the scrubby coastal variety to a grander prelude of the forest above.

"I don't think Ata would ever move to the United States," she said.

"Are you thinking of moving?"

"No. I mean, not immediately. Though I'd never imagined myself correcting the grammar of generation after generation of generals' kids into my dotage. Or until they toss me out like crazy Paula. I was getting some gallery shows before I moved here. Nothing much was selling, but I was getting some exposure. I moved here to add a little spice to my résumé. I thought I'd come back with a little forest of work, influenced by my exposure to Islamic miniatures. That's the sort of thing you need these days: an angle. And you can't just do it in Chicago studying a book of print reproductions—it has to be some part of your life experience or people just aren't interested."

Fred shrugged, but of course he had felt the same way about his screenplays. Firsthand experience was the coin of the realm. Otherwise you were just some kid with a master's degree and a library card. "And now that some people are interested, were you thinking of going back soon?"

"No. Same as you. Too many places left to visit on the back of Ata's bike. Whenever I think I'm done, he suggests we explore some corner, some valley where they still speak the dialect of Jesus. A place inevitably destined to be flooded by some grand new dam on the waters of the fertile crescent. Doomed like the world before Noah. How could you say no to that, even if it means another two semesters of grinding your teeth over the indignities of the job. But now there's this." She gestured to her stomach.

"You want to raise the kid in the States?"

"Is it wrong for me to say yes? Things are fine here now, but the guys who knocked Ata's teeth out are still around. They're among the generals now, making little nationalist wolf howls to each other in the halls of power. And if it isn't them running things, then it's the religious ministers—they'll take the wine glass right out of my mouth. God knows what that will mean for the kid. Everyone has money now, but that's bound to change. And when it does, there isn't going to be a lot of space for different sorts of people here. They had no problem getting rid of the minorities when things got tight before, setting up their own people in the houses they had just pogromed."

"You really thing that's going to happen to us?"

"Ata does. But he thinks we should go buy a gun, not move to America. All I know, this kid will have a set of loving grandparents in New Mexico and a chance to grow up in a country that learned to accept its minorities, not disappear them, as long a road as it was to get to that point."

They had nearly reached the apartment building, but April had slowed to a crawl. They stopped for a moment, both gazing up at the thin stream of smoke rising from Ata's grill.

"Will you talk to him about the States? I don't expect you to change his mind tonight, but try to pry him open. There's got to be a possible future where we go back, or there's no future for us at all."

They walked into the building's narrow marble foyer and mounted the age-slouched stairs. After two floors, April needed a breather. It was clearly a burden. Abortions were legal in the City, but not after the tenth week, and not without the man's consent. At least officially. Fred's impulse was to turn around right then, say he'd forgotten to turn the gas off on the stove, or had a long-standing dinner appointment with his shrink. Ata simply wouldn't understand. Why wouldn't his kid live his or her life in his country, among his people? The child was going to be heir to the great nomadic warriors, the only people in the world who could truly claim to carry on the glory of Rome. In America, people believed Turks spoke Arabic and rode camels.

Ata's hug in the doorway was no less warm than when Virginia had been on Fred's heels. Ata didn't act surprised. There was no twinge in his demeanor, none of the silent judgment Fred felt among others. It was a relief, and he gladly accepted the offer of cold plum brandy. April went to change out of her work clothes and put her feet up until the food was ready. Without Virginia, it was clear to Fred he was here to serve a purpose, a sort of tit for tat. It was April who'd gotten them over to the City, plucked them out of America's stumbling economy. Now she wanted Fred to open a way back for her.

Ata pulled a plastic soda bottle from the freezer, its label in Cyrillic. "My grandfather's recipe," he said. It was dirty and viscous. He served it without water or ice. Clinking glasses and meeting eyes, they both sipped. To Fred the taste was deeply sad. Not because it didn't taste good; it had a mellow fruit flavor beneath a touch of crisp anisette. But because it was something he would only have here and now. Something he'd never share with anyone back home.

"I have this very good Bulgarian pork to go with it. It has a nice smoke." Ata rummaged through the fridge, pulling out various bags of meat and then a half cabbage. "April will want a salad, though I know my baby will want meat."

Fred gathered up the meat, but Ata turned his attention to the cabbage first. It caught Fred a little off guard. He was ready to take his seat by Ata's hearth, shoot the shit about the garage and segue way into all the great motorcycle opportunities in the US. He wasn't sure which direction he was going to take it: that all the great 1% gangs had their origins in America, from the Hells Angels on down, or that even investment bankers were lining up for custom bikes. Instead, there was Ata, slicing up the cabbage. He looked wrung out. His eyes, those filial links to the great Khans, were puffy, and in the unforgiving kitchen light his face looked wan beneath his stubble. He was even showing a bit of a gut, the burden of an office job. He took a tablespoon of salt, spread it over the cabbage, and began working it with his hands. It struck Fred as a beautiful display of care. He didn't crush the cabbage or break its threads, but instead worked it so it released its water and became tender.

"How's the job?" Fred asked.

"It takes about an hour and a half to get out there, maybe two to get back."

"Do you ride?"

"I wish. Riding would be forty minutes tops. It's the traffic that is killing me. They've lent me a company car. I can eat my breakfast and listen to the radio, isn't it."

"You could leave suits in your office." Fred decided to jump to conclusions. "Then you could ride in and change before work."

"It's not that kind of office. They already look at me funny. I have this job only because one of my old club friends knows the airline's owner. They gave me a job that would bring in enough to pay for my baby. But that job has made me the boss of three people already. In Turkish, we say, 'There are many who throw stones at a red apple.' There are at least three with their stones at the ready."

"Well, it's not forever, right? I mean, you can use this to get a different job closer in. Or take some of the money and put it toward setting the garage up commercially. No reason you can't fix bikes for money."

"It's all right, you know. I'm going to be a father. With this job, I know I can be that. With the bikes and everything, maybe I couldn't be. To have another life is okay. My father left Bulgaria to keep me from becoming Stephan. Instead of denying me my connection to our glorious ancestors, he moved here with nothing. He still works in construction. Who am I to do less for my child than my father, isn't it?" He grated some carrots in with the cabbage and added a handful of olives. He then grabbed the bags of meat and the two of them headed out to his grill patio.

"Have you ever considered moving back to Bulgaria, if things get better?" This was Fred sticking his pinky toe in to test the waters. If Ata would consider moving back to his home country, maybe he'd consider moving to April's. "I mean," Fred continued, "it's your child's heritage."

Ata was flipping meatballs with one hand and taking a sip of his liquor with the other. This gave him some time to respond. "I'd like for him—it is a him—to know Bulgaria. But we are not from there, just as we are not from here. The only difference is that we once conquered there, and we still conquer here. And here is the greatest City ever built. The only one to be both east and west and rule three empires. Before meeting April, I thought to leave this City many times. I thought I might go to our ancestral homelands, you know. I hear it is like the Wild West, the Wild East rather. Vast space, chances for money in oil and gold. The lands where the apple and the tulip were born. I thought it would be good to get away from air that is being sucked into the mouths of millions, from soil that covers up millions more dead. But I would get out on that big bridge as the sun was rising and it would catch the waters of the Strait and the countless tips of the mosques, and I knew to leave here would be to leave the only place worth going. It is the world that comes to the City. That's why the Greeks gave it its name, isn't it?"

"Yeah, that's what they say," Fred said, a little distant. It had always bothered him that Istanbul translated to an action: "to the city." It was like the City was itself trying to reach itself, like the waves of its endless hilly suburbs were always inching toward the center. The center that was the watery void of the Strait. It was eternally moving toward its own end. It was in this way that the City could claim to be the most human city in the world.

Ata tossed the meatballs onto a plate and turned toward Fred. "Virginia is back home?" he asked.

Totally caught off guard, Fred almost launched into a lie about Virginia having some kind of stomach bug and being back in bed in High Field. But instead he just said, "Yeah."

"She didn't find the magic of the City." It wasn't a question.

"She didn't like the job." Fred was a little defensive.

"But you found the City's magic?"

"Something like that."

Ata nodded heavily, and it occurred to Fred that magic in this case might not translate as Disney magic or magic stain removal. One of those foresty gusts blew down the gully, bracingly "therapeutic" for early fall. Without any more talk, they headed in for dinner.

FIVE.

Ayşe lit her post-dinner cigarette. She held the lighter open perhaps longer than necessary, trying to get a better look at Fred. But the bright blue flame only darkened the alleyway more. They were splitting a whole bottle of Club brand, at her insistence, and the few she'd had already were taking hold.

It had been uncomfortable at first, for her. This was the neighborhood, in the films she watched growing up, where the assassins and heroin kingpins met in basement bars. Bars full of women with thin eyebrows and thick eyeliner, bouffant hair and boobs that would slip from their blouses when the men knocked them to the ground. Of course she'd been here before, cruised Independence Avenue in her younger days. Visited the record stores and sat on the famous benches in front of the French Culture Center. But girls raised as she was did not stray into the alleys at night. They could be mistaken for a prostitute or worse. So when Fred invited her to dinner on Vine Clad Mosque Street, she almost hung up the phone at the implication.

The meal had been nice. On the traditional side for her taste. But everything was perfectly presented, no bony fish that looked like a cat had already gotten to it tossed on a plate with some onions and arugula. The kind of thing the alley taverns had been known for—food for drunks, something so they could tell their wives they were at dinner. This was different. It was nostalgic for that idea, a place where the grown children of those drinkers could reenact the dark days when this was a poor City and their fathers drank and cursed the generals. But the chatter around her was all about the new design firm opening an office down the street or construction contracts flowing in for luxury condos in the Paper House district. The Paper House district, which when she was growing up had been synonymous with abandoned power stations and gypsy camps. Fred seemed totally oblivious to this, staring off at some dark corner of the alleyway. He was the only foreigner.

"Had you come here before?" she asked with her first post puff breath.

"I used to come to this neighborhood all the time. Before…" He trailed off.

"Before?"

"Before they took the tables away. I mean, they're back now, but there was a while when no one was allowed to have tables outside."

She helped herself to a disappointed puff. All night he'd dodged talking about his past. They'd talked about hers, she'd even told him half the funny stories she had collected working as a concierge. The half that didn't involve men propositioning her. He seemed to love the one about the imam who wore ladies' underwear. She'd walked in on him because he'd called earlier demanding fresh towels. Never demand fresh towels, not even at the Four Seasons. She'd let the imam stew, then having supposed he'd gone to dinner, she decided to go into his room and assess the towel situation. He was standing in the middle of the room in a black push-up bra and thong. She shut the door quickly, but he couldn't look her in the eye when he checked out the next morning.

She was happy to talk about the past, just as happy as he was to talk about the future. He was full of ideas for trips. Here they were, so close to Egypt, to India, to Italy. Had she ever been? Lots of things he wanted to do. Was he inviting her? She loved to travel, but he talked about it with a foreigner's ease. Did he know it could take months for her to get a European visa? Perhaps she should start proceedings in case. She asked him about his job; he dodged that one. She knew the university he taught at. It was for the generals' kids, the ones not smart enough to be schooled abroad. She'd had friends who went there, not close ones. She imagined it paid well, but really, was she going to be with an English teacher? Everyone knew they were rootless people. Worse than gypsies. At least gypsies traveled with their families.

"I remember reading about that," she said, lest they descend into another silence. "Wasn't it because one of the conservative ministers couldn't get his pious motorcade through here?"

"That was the official story."

"The official story? You have lived here for a while, haven't you?" People of the City loved a conspiracy. Often they loved them because they were true.

"The official story was that it was an affront to public piety. But what about public piety has changed in the last six months? I'll tell you what has changed: the owners of these restaurants. It was a shakedown."

"How do you know?"

"My friend was the contractor for the new owners."

Which went a long way to explain this new Vine Clad Mosque Street. It was the foreigners, after all, who had fallen in love with the dingy, uncouth center of the City. While her parents were constantly moving to newer, safer, cleaner constructions, the foreigners were setting up house alongside the transvestites and Kurds. They cleaned it up but kept the character, so now you could get a better cappuccino in some converted shoe factory than in the cafés on the Strait-side. It would take a foreigner to envision this, someone who could pick and choose history piecemeal rather than be forced to remember it all.

"Do you miss the way it was?" she ventured.

"I guess, but this is the way things go. In the end there are winners and losers, but the food gets better."

His nonchalance surprised her. He was a teacher, after all. She remembered her foreign teachers in prep school, mostly German girls. None of them spoke Turkish. They seemed constantly beleaguered, scrounging for a morsel of respect in their dun-colored smock dresses. They would arrive pretty and young with the light of travel in their eyes, but in a few years they'd be stooped and fat like those cowled mothers of five. She always thought it was because they cared too much, they came from a place where school was how you moved ahead. This man, with his stubble mustache and his arm hooked behind the back of his chair, looked more like one of those Green Pine film stars than a paper-grader. One of those actors who couldn't survive against Brad Pitt on looks alone but had attitude. Like the "Ugly King," posed with a pistol in his hand and a daisy in his teeth. There was something in her that could love an asshole. Maybe she was looking at this all the wrong way.

The waiter came by to freshen their drinks, filling their glasses a third of the way with clear liquor. Touching the glass's slick interior, little wisps of louche formed. It reminded her of cum. The clink of ice and pour of mineral water quickly turned the glass a uniform white, but she was already crossing her legs. Since moving into her father's development, she'd been celibate. She'd reclaimed herself for the marriage market. But here she was in a part of town no one she knew would ever consider visiting. Half of them would be afraid to catch a venereal disease. The other half probably ordered an airstrike on someone with relatives in the neighborhood. A sort of freedom washed over her. She looked around to check that she was truly alone with this foreign man. The faces surrounding her were fresh from college: no work, no reflective pancake covering their yet to emerge smoker's lines. Fred too was gazing out at the crowd.

"So, what do you think?" he said.

"I think we should get out of here," she replied.

Fred had told the Greek to clear out for the night, and mercifully when he was finally able to get the "do not duplicate" key to turn in the lock, the place was empty. The Cage and the Greek's family bedroom were closed up and dark. He helped Ayşe over the threshold and then fumbled for the switch to the small lamp that rested atop some bookshelves by the door. Virginia had outfitted the apartment with a comprehensive set of indirect lights, and though Fred had just used the overheads in the past months, he was grateful for another option now. Beside the lamp was the old rotary phone, that olive-green Bakelite monument to his one sincere attempt to evict the Greek.

"Oh, I love it," Ayşe said, touching the handset lightly. "We used to have the same one growing up. You could dial 203 to hear fairy tales told by that actress. She was so famous they named a tea glass after her. It had a bigger mouth, for her voice, and a rounder bottom too. There were like thirty stories to choose from. It must have been very expensive since I was forbidden to do it. But whenever my parents would put me to bed and go back to join their friends in the sitting room, I'd sneak into the kitchen where the phone was and dial up a story."

"Which was your favorite?" He'd braced himself against the now closed door. She was wearing that same lotion.

"The story of the girl in the Red Tower. I'd always think of her when we passed it on the ferry to Europe."

"The one with the snake?"

"No, the older Greek one. She lives in the tower and lights a candle so her lover can swim to her from the opposite shore. This works through the summer, but when the ill fall winds blow up the Strait, her candle is extinguished and her lover drowns. It was a very sexy story the way the actress told it. His name is something like a flower."

"Leander. He's gone; up bubbles all his amorous breath."

"What's that?"

"Keats. An English poet. Died of tuberculosis in Rome. Sad story, maybe even sadder than the snake one."

"We are a sad people, you must know that. Even the conqueror knew sadness when, after taking the City, he saw that its greatness had passed from it and that it would be his burden to carry on the weight of empire."

"His burden?"

"We say to have the sword of your desire is to have to carry it at your hip henceforth."

"Huh. Do you want another drink?" he said, shifting closer.

"No," she said, putting a hand to his rough cheek.

———

She was there when he awoke, her breasts like a pair of Eneolithic burial mounds under the sheet. It was the accordionist that must have woken him, winding his way through the back streets with his little daughter. Fred got up to toss the man a coin. He debated throwing away the condoms on the floor, but thought it would be better for everyone to know they had been safe. Pulling on jeans, he peeked out into the hallway. No sign of the Greek. Hopefully he'd taken his family back down to the islands. He wouldn't have to hurry her out, then. He put the kettle on and was about to open the kitchen window to make his contribution to the accordionist when he stopped. It was deja vu from the earliest days with Virginia—before work had begun, before the Greek, when they'd awake on a Sunday morning to the accordionist and sit with their French press, just being slow. Being in a new place, with all the possibility that implied. Making vague plans to visit this or that market or neighborhood but spending most of the day on the couch with a book or calling back home. He tried to imagine what it was like to be that person, devouring history books with Virginia's lean legs in his lap. He tried to recall the sense of obligation he cultivated for himself: he was going to make this adventure a success because he was going to learn what this place was all about. What bullshit. She was the one who put together this home, and he'd let it go without a fight.

He felt the tip of Ayşe's breasts on his back before her arms locked around his waist. He tensed, part surprise, part sucking in.

"That accordion is magical," she said to his shoulders.

"Yeah, he makes the rounds every Sunday."

"This is a really nice place, I mean I'd never guess walking through the neighborhood."

"I've been working on it," Fred lied. "Some of the rooms aren't done."

"A homemaker."

"A gentrifier. Lots of foreigners do it. And when I'm finished I can sell it to the next batch of foreigners."

"Is that your plan?" She let go. He turned. She had his robe on. With the added width of her bust, the cloth only came to mid-thigh.

"I just mean it's a good investment." The kettle started whistling. Fred dug the coffee from a drawer, popped the canister and spooned a bit into the French press before asking, "How strong do you take it?"

"Sometimes you just don't talk like an English teacher." She put her hands on her hips. "I like it strong, doesn't everyone?"

He scooped in a few more tablespoons, then poured the water over the coffee. She lit a cigarette and wandered through the kitchen–living room, admiring the flea market tchotchkes Virginia had picked out: framed photos of Green Pine cinema stars; coils and coils of prayer beads; a red crescent medicine cabinet that she'd filled with whirling dervish statues of various sizes and colors.

"You have quite the artist's touch," Ayşe mused.

Fred stirred the coffee. "I write screenplays."

"Hmm, shouldn't you be in Los Angeles?"

"I wanted to try something different." Fred poured two mugs of coffee. He wondered how he was coming off. How should he come off? He had this vision of the person he was trying to be: worldly, tough, with means. The kind of person who would look at a scheme to sell cooked essays as a business opportunity. The kind of person this woman, whose soft-focus beauty might have been created through a papier-mâché of banknotes, would want.

"So how'd you end up choosing the City?" she asked, flicking a dervish statue into a twirl.

"I think it chose me, you know. Once you find its magic, there is no other place in the world."

"Even though you can't get salmon."

"Even though you can't get scotch."

Walking over, she put her hands on what promised to become his love handles and on her toes went for a kiss. The taste of strong coffee and tar covered over the flavors of last night. She took his hand. "I want you to show me around the neighborhood when we finish." She started leading him into the hall.

"We can get coffee out," he said. "There's a good place. The Italians go there."

"After we finish." She led him back to the bedroom.

They sat in the new High Field coffee shop, their broad cappuccino cups drained, ringed with the evidence of foam, espresso dregs in the inaccessible recesses. Ayşe was safe behind her Diors, lighting her fifth Anadolu of the day. Fred was squinting a bit. The waitress had told him that the next time he wanted a table, he should call ahead and make a reservation. This was the coffee shop that, when it opened six months ago, had a "pay what you want" policy. Fred had always paid market rates. Maybe that was why the waitress with the asymmetrical haircut had taken pity on him. The people who were waiting for tables were young Turks in skinny Levi's. The place had a nice presentation: Viennese coffee served with water and a tiny cookie on a mock silver salver.

"You know, even a year ago these people wouldn't feel safe here." Ayşe said, gesturing to the clumps of youth. She pointed her cigarette at a waif clutching a large punk rock studded bag. "That's an Alexander McQueen. Probably costs more than a year lease on an apartment here."

"Not for long," Fred said wistfully.

"Are things heating up here? Real estate, I mean?"

Fred shook his head. "No, it's still just this side of dark and dingy. But it probably will soon. It's only a ten-minute walk from the metro."

"The metro." Ayşe half smiled. "You know they said it could never be finished. Whenever they would dig ten feet, they'd hit some stockpile of bronze armor or Greek pottery. Then hundreds of German archeologists would force the government to stop digging. It would take them ten months to clear out all the priceless stuff. That was back in the bad old days of student against fascist street wars and hyperinflation, back when everyone was feeling heavy with history. Now look at us: three full metro lines, a fourth being dug under the Strait. And for those who want to drive, a third bridge for their Audis."

"You almost sound nostalgic."

"Surely you know we are a nostalgic people. Some are nostalgic for the days of the closed economy, when anyone in a military uniform could get a free drink in a tavern. Others long for the empire that built domes and spires and brought the Prophet's footprint here from the holy cities. Still others I think wish we had never given up our horses and still sailed on seas of grass in the land of the apple tree. No one, except maybe those babies in their jeans over there, has any love for the present, let alone the future." She crushed her cigarette. "So, what should we do now?"

Fred wanted to suggest they go back to the apartment. He wanted to feel totally empty, like there was nothing left in him. But chances were the Greek was back. "Let me show you the rest of the neighborhood. There are some beautiful old buildings any nostalgist would enjoy."

Behind her glasses, she seemed disappointed. Fred kicked himself. But he nonchalantly laid down the nearly twenty dollars the place was charging for cappuccinos and went around to help Ayşe out of her seat. As she stood, he let a hand come to rest on her hip. She let it remain.

SIX.

[OPENING ON the now familiar Nick Adams' apartment. There are still the Greek accents but they are more backgrounded, like the bicycle hanging in Jerry Seinfeld's apartment that in defiance of Chekhov he never seems to ride. Jake Barnes is once again at the bar, lingering over his choices. Nick is on the sofa with Catherine Barkley, a slim brunette with large eyes and yellow leg warmers.]

Jake: So which rooftop bar do you want to hit tonight? Balcony is nicer, the view of the Holy Wisdom is pretty clean. But we can also go to Upper Tavern. They dust off some pretty good cheap white wine, made from the Sultan's grape.

Nick: You know what they call the Sultan's grape in America? Thompson seedless. But there are no rooftop bars in central Illinois, isn't that so Kit-Cat?

Catherine: So true, Tatie. That's why I decided to stay. I don't even notice the Greeks anymore. [There is some kissy-face between her and Nick]

Jake: Okay, pet names, Upper Tavern it is. It's near that new fish place that only serves the rich.

Nick: Is it possible, coming here for money and adventure, that we ended up rich? With our part of the Greek's poetry business?

Jake: Don't fool yourself, Nick. We'll only ever be foreign. But that might be enough to get us in the rich fish restaurant if we play our cards right.

Catherine: Tatie, remember we never wanted to be rich, just to have enough to do what we want. I've got Pilates now, so I'll see you boys at the bar [She leaves after some kissy-face.]

Jake: Great, glad that's over. Now let's call Brett and do this fish place.

Nick: I don't know. This fish place, it's got rules. It's for rich people, the generals' kids. They are sort of Nazis about it.

Jake: Are you saying you don't think we'll get away with it? Eating the rich fish.

Nick: No, we've gotten away with everything else. I don't see why this would be any different.

[Brett Ashley walks in, looking like Courtney Love if Courtney Love were fighting in the Spanish Civil War. She is also conspicuously wearing yellow leg warmers.]

Jake: Brett, you're coming with us to the rich fish restaurant.

Brett: Rich like covered in cream? Because I don't like it that way. That's how the fascists like it.

[NICK, JAKE, AND BRETT are in line for a table at the rich fish restaurant. There is a maitre d' at a small podium, which stands between them and the many outdoor tables of the rich fish restaurant. The maitre d' has a monocle, maybe epaulets. Needless to say, the audience should think: Nazi. Brett approaches.]

Brett: Phew, fancy place you got here. I am, uh, a British heiress, Lady Brett Ashley, and I, er, look forward to gracing your restaurant with my presence.

Maitre d': [In Turkish] I don't see your reservation.

Brett: [Trying to remember what Nick had coached her into saying] As a visitor to your country, I'd simply like to sample your culinary delights. I'll never fully apprehend the tortured history of iniquity that has some dining in luxury here while others live in shacks on distant hillsides. And perhaps it's my privilege not to care, not to judge, just to enjoy the experience of the exotic. [The maitre d' raises an eyebrow. Brett looks at Nick like, is this what you really believe?] Look here, my fine fellow or whatever, I've eaten fish up and down this stupid City. And I think I liked it better when this alley was full of communists and art students.

Maitre d': No fish for you.

Brett: [Turning to the two men] Well, I guess I torched that one. I can't pretend to care. Let's go to the Upper Tavern.

[The two men pretend not to know her. She storms off.]

Nick: [Says a few choice words in Turkish, then adds] And we would really like to sample your restaurant so we can tell our friends about it. As you know, foreigners fraternize with the country's elites.

Maitre d': [In Turkish] I don't see your reservation.

Nick: You know, as I know, this restaurant doesn't take reservations.

[The Nazi maitre d' invites them in.]

[LATER, AT THE UPPER TAVERN, Nick and Jake are regaling Brett and Catherine about the rich fish place. Upper Tavern is a dive bar crowded with students drinking beer on rough-hewn booths. The four occupy a coveted booth by a window. The lights of the City are visible through it, little pinholes of apartment windows whose combined light extinguishes the stars.]

Nick: And then they brought out this perfect walnut paste, with smoked peppers and pomegranate molasses. It was spicy, it was crunchy, it was sweet and sour.

Jake: I could have eaten the whole thing myself and had another. But then they brought out the eggplant. My god, you'd think it was cheesecake, smoky cheesecake.

Brett: Sounds vile, and yet I find myself salivating.

Nick: We'll just have to go back tomorrow so you can join us, isn't that right, Kit-Cat?

Catherine: Of course, Tatie, you know it for sure. But Tatie darling, you know I have work tomorrow. Won't you walk me home down Independence Avenue? Those young Turkish guys sure know how to let a girl know what they think of her.

Nick: I'm sure they think you're beautiful. You know I do.

Catherine: Oh Tatie, you're such a romantic. [They do some kissy-face in the booth.] See you two tomorrow for more rich fish. [They exit.]

Jake: I can't fucking stand the pet names. It's just disgusting.

Brett: You know what's disgusting? Pretending to be rich. There's nothing to being rich except having money.

Jake: You know Merve's pretty rich, one of those new rich Turks. It's actually kind of hot, her being rich. That and her fake boobs. Her family made a fortune flipping houses that once belonged to Greeks. You know the Greeks owned everything around here. My apartment, Nick's apartment, probably even the rich fish place. The one who owned Nick's apartment even came back. Can you imagine what it'd be like if the one who owned the rich fish place showed up? What a scene that would be.

[THE NEXT NIGHT, Nick, Jake, Catherine, and Merve at the rich fish maitre d' stand.]

Nick: Are you sure you don't want me to handle this, Kit-Cat?

Jake: Or better yet, Merve—she's actually rich, and Turkish.

Catherine: Oh Tatie, can't we just have a little fun with this? I know you secretly wish you were with a rich local girl, let me play one tonight. [She goes in for some kissy-face.]

Maitre d': Excuse me, but you should get a room. There are people here who are trying to eat a dignified fish dinner.

Catherine: Excuse you, I'll express my pure and beautiful American love wherever I choose in this morbid old City.

Maitre d': Not among my people. No fish for you.

Catherine: Oh, fuck this. Come on, Nick, let's go to the Upper Tavern.

Nick: I'm sorry, do I know you?

[Catherine, shocked, storms off.]

Jake: So you chose fish over a woman.

Nick: Rich fish. And I figure it'll be easier to patch things up between me and Catherine than with the Nazi over there.

Maitre d': What's that?

[Nick and Jake push Merve forward to get them into the restaurant.]

[CUT TO a scene of Brett talking to the Greek who lives in Nick's apartment. They are in the kitchen, sharing feta and clearly plotting.]

———

[CUT TO Nick Adam's apartment. Nick is on the couch. Jake is at the bar, pouring them drinks]

Nick: I just don't understand it.

Jake: Don't understand what? You said you didn't know her to get into a fish restaurant.

Nick: Rich fish! Rich fish!

Jake: Maybe it's a sign. I never knew what you saw in her.

Nick: She smelled of heather, and when we did it and my eyes were closed, the colors of the sun through my closed eyes were red and orange and gold. The earth moved.

Jake: Is that why you called her Kit-Cat?

Nick: We'd agreed, money and adventure. Enough to get us home after the recession with a down payment and stories to tell. I held up my part of the bargain, even if I had to play the asshole.

Jake: But you are an asshole.

Nick: I thought you were the asshole on the show. I'm the sympathetic, if exasperated, protagonist. I'm supposed to get away with things.

Jake: The show?

Brett: [Busting in] You'll never guess. I found the Greeks who really own the rich fish place. They're going to camp out until all the rich run away.

Nick: Ugh. That's never going to work.

Brett: What do you mean?

Nick: I mean, in real life, that's never going to work.

Brett: Why not?

Nick: Because no one who has money cares about the past. And if you don't have money, you don't care about the past either, unless there's something in it for you.

Brett: But what about the Greek in your apartment?

Nick: To be honest, I don't know what that's about anymore.

SEVEN.

"YOU WRITING?"

Fred was tempted to slap his laptop shut, like he'd been caught rifling his grandmother's purse. Instead he said, "You could call it that."

The Greek was undeterred. "How was your date?"

"I went to that new place on Vine Clad Mosque Street. It was crawling with young local money. And then we went for morning coffee, to that coffee place that all of two Italians ever patronized. At that place, they asked me if I had a reservation. For coffee."

"Is that your way of telling me you got laid? Because you could just say that. I've got a kid, so I'm familiar with the process."

"I'm just saying that the neighborhood is going to launch. If it turns out you own half of it, you won't be visiting the Greek islands, you'll have one to yourself."

"Well, funny you should bring that up," the Greek said, leaping on the opening he must have been hoping for. He left Fred in the living room, pinned to the couch by his laptop, then returned too quickly with an unmarked bottle of wine and two tumblers. He looked good, the Greek. Tan. Some of the doughy jowl that made his big eyes and full lips seem effete had cooked off too.

"I thought you didn't drink."

"This stuff is medicine. It's part of the island life."

"I always envisioned rum drinks."

"Stuff will kill you. This will keep you alive." He poured. The Greek saluted. "To new loves."

Fred nodded, not entirely convinced. The wine was dry as pencil lead and light-bodied. Maybe it had herbs in it. He couldn't imagine drinking a lot of it, which might have been the point.

"Um," Fred said, trying to encircle the Greek's good humor like a cowboy might a steer in heat, "I don't know where this thing is going with this woman, but until I do, I'm sticking to my plan, and that means living here."

"No problem, Romeo. In fact, I'm leaving the apartment to you."

"What?" Fred nearly dropped his glass right on the keyboard. His ears filled with buzz. He was left wondering where the sense of relief was, the one which would have flowed over him if he'd heard the same words months ago. "What do you mean?"

"I'm getting nowhere on the deed front. I've bought lawyers. I've bought translators. I've bought local community leaders. I've palmed cash over to the clerks. I put out a lot of what we took in. Then we went to the islands. We were on these little sundrenched pieces of rock with one church and one market on Wednesday and a thousand grapevines and a thousand olive trees and a thousand fish. Do you know how different that is from Los Angeles? How different it is from here? And it's cheap living, I mean it's almost like they don't believe in money. You wouldn't even know their economy was collapsing until you went to cash a traveler's check. And then you're a king. We spent less in two weeks than I did in two hours trying to wrestle this place from the smirks in suits at the Directorate of Foundations."

"Why the Directorate of Foundations?"

"Euphemism. Greeks were a religion, so their property was 'managed' as part of the country's religious and cultural heritage once they were 'gone.' But I'm not going back there, not for a while."

"What are you going to do instead?" Fred envisioned the vast apartment. It would just be him and the floor-to-ceiling doors of pine, always open. Him alone with the cabinet full of brass whirling dervishes, caught in their reveries and completely uninterested in his schemes. He tried to imagine as much sex with Ayşe as he could. It would hardly fill the place.

"Write."

"Essays?"

"To start. You yourself said you only wanted to be at this two years."

"Then what?" Fred didn't like having his terms dictated back to him.

"Spy novels."

"You're joking."

"You reminded me, the other day, how much I like them. How we're sort of involved in one now. And it reminded me of this guy, Eric Ambler."

"Sounds like a fake name. Richard Muller, Johnny Wanderer. I wouldn't trust him, whatever his angle."

"Wrote spy novels. Kicked around LA trying to pitch scripts in his twilight years. Loved this part of the world, would always come into my granddad's place to talk about the old times. He wrote a lot, published a little. He was just full of ideas. I remember the two of them, out on the concrete patio in Reseda, sucking down aniseed liquor and Ambler spinning these winding stories about the mists that creep from the Balkan woods and the undeniable Aegean sun that hides murder in plain sight. Anyway, I figure I can take some of his old ideas, stuff he wrote or told to my granddad, use it to make my own books." The Greek strode back into the room that was once Virginia's studio.

"Make your own books?" Fred called after him.

"Yeah." The Greek cracked a battered paperback he'd probably stolen from some beachside hotel. The cover was a silhouette of a man tossing something, or looking for something, over the edge of a waterside cliff by night. "Listen to this: *But it was useless to try to explain him in terms of Good and Evil. They were no more than baroque abstractions. Good Business and Bad Business were the elements of the new theology. Dimitrios was not evil. He was logical and consistent; as logical and consistent in the European jungle as the poison gas called Lewisite and the shattered bodies of children killed in the bombardment of an open town. The logic of Michelangelo's David, Beethoven's quartets, and Einstein's physics had been replaced by that of the Stock Exchange Year Book and Hitler's Mein Kampf.*" He refolded the dog ear and closed the book. "Wouldn't be too hard to modernize that. Update it with a little personal experience."

"You're going to plagiarize him."

"No, you see, I love to write. That's what I figured out, writing all those stupid essays. I think it was the two hundredth that convinced me. At first I hated it; each word was like a brick I'd have to pick up and move into place. But it got easier and easier until I could just see through the words to the whole edifice. You like that word, edifice? Anyway, a spy novel is just an essay on schemes with a lot of sex thrown in. Bottom line: I love to write, and I love my family. This isn't working out for us, but I see something that could. So that's the direction I want to go."

Had those months in the Cage brainwashed the Greek into believing he loved to write? The most galling part was Fred suspected the Greek would be good at it. He had no hang-ups. "But what about what we've got going on now?"

"I'll do the two years. We'll mostly finish out the fall here, go back next break and buy a place. Then I'll do it remotely, from where the money will go farther. I mean, it's hateful work, but I can mostly do it without thinking now. And truth is, I'm getting bites on the few houses in LA I kept out of foreclosure. I feel like the market may turn around, at least long enough for me to get out. And you got to think of this from your perspective, too. You've got something new going on. You really want us around when you make that booty call?"

Fred filled the glasses again. Autumn light was streaming in through the west-facing kitchen windows. This was the time on Sundays when Virginia would lay out on the couch with one of her books. It wouldn't be five minutes before her eyes closed.

"Well," Fred said, "I don't know. You're just going to give up on this place?"

"You know, it was just Columbus Day. Back home that meant a bunch of Indians showing up to the parade with placards about Plymouth Rock landing on them. They'd try to get the Mexicans in on it—after all, their land had been stolen too, albeit after they'd stolen it from the Indians. Anyway, the Mexicans didn't want anything to do with it. They didn't want their kids growing up thinking they were victims. And I guess I don't want my kid thinking that either. Not when he can grow up simple and strong."

Fred just sat there. His laptop felt like a millstone, like the stupid obelisk that sat in a ditch near the Holy Wisdom. The one that once marked the zero mile to calculate all distances in the empire.

"You know people live well past a hundred on the islands. If I'm lucky, I'll be around to see the big earthquake this place has coming. Everyone says there'll be one in thirty years. Maybe then we all who'd lost our places can get back in on the ground floor. Till then, you and I should take what we can and get out."

The Greek scooped up his tumbler and downed his medicine with suspicious vigor. Taking the bottle, he swaggered back toward the room that was once Virginia's studio, leaving Fred to wonder if there was anything to what the Greek had said. He let his anxiety play out. *So the Greek leaves. So it's all been for nothing.* It was like he'd been struggling, clawing against the City and its history, sacrificing, and suddenly he was out in a frictionless space. It was like he was on a ship. He imagined the apartment as such, its soaring doorways sails pulling out over the rolling hillsides of the City. He could take it wherever he wanted. He could sail it all the way to rural Illinois, where he could tell Virginia that he had defeated the Greek and she could come back. He could sail it out to the suburbs and pillage the rich man's daughter again. He could do both while filling his treasure chest with banknotes he plucked from library books. No one would know. The apartment was a pirate ship, and he, like those European renegados tired of wilting under the eye of God, had turned Turk.

He shoved his laptop on the bookshelf. From his archaic CD wallet, which had been filed there, he pulled out the disk with the yellow banana on it and seated it inside the boom box Virginia had insisted on buying, used, so they could listen to Fleetwood Mac. He pushed the FF button to seven, listening to the little motor-driven laser make its adjustments. As Lou Reed's anxious strum crackled on, Fred kicked himself. He was totally out of aniseed liquor. He had some whiskey squirreled away as usual, but that didn't seem appropriate for this private celebration. He paused the track just as it declared, ever so calmly, "I don't know, just where I'm going."

He set out for the closest little shop, one of those people called Monopoly because they sold things the state once had a monopoly on, booze and cigarettes. Two alley cats were preparing to fuck on the landing, entirely consumed with one another. Normally Fred would break them up, spare himself the yowling. But today he thought, life is short.

The monopoly shop was a hundred meters up a side street he never took. He normally avoided shops of its ilk because their markups were high compared to a chain grocery. The air was sweet. Fall was one of the better seasons in the City. The summer smog had succumbed to a few rainstorms, and it wasn't cold enough for people to start burning coal. He scampered up the steep cobblestones, his money already in hand. When he reached the through street where the shop was, he was surprised to see one of the majestically rundown bow-front townhouses had been given a fresh coat of paint. Someone had also replaced all the shutters and the street-level lamps. Someone had turned the clock back, sparing no expense.

It was a hotel. It hadn't opened yet, he gathered, trying to understand the covered woman who ran the monopoly shop. Virginia had called the covered woman's husband Charlie Brown because he always wore the same orange sweater. Perhaps because he couldn't afford another. He was one of those men who pushed a flatbed cart through the neighborhood, looking to pick up or trade for bits of the place's hollowed-out glory. Fred would see him go by with a marble basin, or a tea table, or a half a carpet, and be amazed there were still such things hidden among the antique façades.

"Hotel good for business," Fred said, or at least thought he said, gripping his overpriced bottle of Goldmine in its paper bag. The woman rolled up her sleeve and pinched her forearm hard like she was trying to peel a layer of skin off.

"Those people do not see us" was what Fred thought she said.

His Turkish failing him, Fred just said "Bad" and "Thank you" before setting off home.

EIGHT.

THE END OF THE park had been a long time coming. Like most people, Fred had ignored the five or so communists standing outside the Watering Square metro decrying the conspiracy. It didn't help that their claims were perfectly Orwellian. The government, along with a team of developers, was going to use a historical preservation law to circumvent the protections granted to the City's few public spaces. They were going to rebuild the Ottoman-era barracks that had stood on the Watering Square Park a hundred years ago. It had been a three-story fortress placed in the city's heart to remind the foreigners and the minorities who did business in its shadow that the Turks were running the show. Some abutments from its foundation still defined the edges of the park. But this building wasn't going to serve as a barracks; there already was a high-rise full of soldiers a few blocks down. It was going to be a mall. It was too bizarre, even for the City.

Neither Fred nor the millions who got out of the metro at the Watering Square had ever given the little park itself much thought. Everyone poured from the underground right onto Independence Avenue, where young and old strolled and window-shopped while eating rings of a sesame-coated bread that was sort of half bagel, half pretzel. The park was the opposite direction, leading nowhere in particular. It was a couple hundred closely packed trees shading some of the City's most hardcore drunks. There was an ugly modernist fountain in the middle and two tea gardens at caddy-corners. Fred and Virginia had gone once to read, but it quickly felt like they were the only ones not having an affair or buying drugs. It was as close to a forgotten corner as you could get while being only a hundred yards from the City's busiest walking street.

But then the bulldozers showed up. There was roadwork going on near the Watering Square, so people didn't notice until the first tree was uprooted. The communists showed up, along with their art school classmates. The story was they stood in front of the earth-moving equipment, Tiananmen style. The workers eventually threw up their hands and went home. The protesters were about forty in number, and since it was a warm autumn evening they gathered camping supplies and set up for a night of drum circles and hacky sack against the man. Hardly anyone noticed.

At the behest of whatever general or minister was funding the project, the riot cops showed sometime after two a.m. After all those hot and boring summer days watching protest after protest in front of the green gates of the Old Royal High School, they must have been excited to finally operate their equipment. And operate it they did, on the dozing activists. Everyone was driven out of the park in a murky cloud of tear gas. At least one got a broken jaw for his troubles. The cops erected a quick perimeter fence, and that was how Fred found it in the morning.

He was on his way to the Starch. Orders for midterm papers had come in and it was the most business they'd ever done. Each day Fred was hauling home twenty-plus paperbacks neatly stowed away in his satchel, his gym bag, and his "essay" bag. The Greek, liberation on his mind, almost had an anxiety attack. Fred, on the other hand, couldn't help but see the floodgates swinging open. He was starting to wonder if it wasn't worth setting this operation up as a real business. If he could teach the Greek to write passably illiterate essays, he could probably teach anyone. Perversely, he even thought about hiring his former students. Better for all concerned. He could pay by the paper and have the work spread among different writers, lessening the chance that some style element be identified and targeted. If he could trust them, maybe he could even have them bring the books in from the library. It was tempting to envision the whole scheme operating without him. He didn't want to end up like Paula. Last he'd heard, she'd moved in with her now aged parents in Oklahoma, the same house she'd run away from all those years ago. But why shouldn't he succeed? And while things were good, he might as well get something nice for Ayşe. Something he envisioned swinging between her static breasts as he had her from behind.

The Starch: those two blocks of Paris grafted onto the City in the dying days of the Ottomans. It was almost a Potemkin contrast to the neighborhoods around it, including High Field. Whereas most of the City's core was an organic maze of narrow alleys overhung with bow-front townhouses spread across hillsides, the Starch was a rigid grid of Art Deco apartments cut by a single arbored boulevard. The City's bourgeois laureate, Mr. Cotton, filled novel after novel waxing over the scent of those linden trees. The effects of the countless dermatological products could be seen across the faces of gently aging matriarchs idling over French wine at the sidewalk cafés.

Fred hated the place. It stunk of international luxury, stores that proudly proclaimed branches in Beverly Hills and Sao Paolo. It reminded him of the students of the Castle, though they, along with the City's super wealthy, had long abandoned neighborhoods like the Starch for closed developments like Strait City, where people couldn't just wander in. Virginia had liked walking to the Starch because it was one of the few unimpeded walks. She'd window shop the boutiques and then, if she judged Fred wasn't too annoyed with being there, suggest they sit at one of the cafés near the little baroque jewel-box mosque and have a glass of rosé. This was nice, he'd have to admit, but he still felt put upon and let her know it. If he'd had it to do over, he might have kept his feelings to himself.

He felt his way around the barricaded park. He saw the occasional cops asleep in the soft autumn light, heads in padded helmets, backs cradled in riot shields on the grass. He had to cut around the employee entrance of the Ceylan InterContinental Hotel, perched at the northeast corner of the park. Finally he found his way to Republic Avenue and followed it past the military museum into the Starch. He went straight for a jewelry boutique Virginia had liked on Place of Encouragement Street. She'd liked the rings.

The work was too understated for Ayşe, too clean and modern. But he did find a large gold pendant with some hammer work and a small sapphire set off to one side. The woman was almost embarrassed when he selected it. "It's one of my early pieces, before I'd learned to do things on a smaller, more elegant scale."

Fred thought she'd continue to say the piece had sentimental value, but instead she gave him what must have been a good price. It was still more than he was used to spending, but he'd come prepared, and peeled the bills onto the counter like a pro. He was done so quickly he indulged the perverse impulse of going to the café on the square and ordering a rosé, even though it was not quite 11 a.m. He was a criminal returning to the scene of the crime. But it didn't take long for him to feel that the wine was bad and expensive, and he brought the median age of the patio down by twenty years. He slugged it back and laid down another bill.

Coming back around the park, he noticed that the barriers were still up. But the riot cops were no longer snoozing. They were forming ranks on the cobblestones where the park emptied out into the Watering Square. Fred stood behind them and looked where they looked. About a hundred yards away, at the mouth of Independence Avenue, there was a swell of people. Distantly he could make out some placards among the crowd. The yellow on red hammer and gear, the green tree and red star on yellow horizon, the chipper red and blue stripes with a cartoon sun above.

To get to High Field, he'd have to cross in front of the massing cops. Fred felt he might as well wait until they marched up to the crowd and asserted their presence. There were scenes like this every May Day, he'd heard. They mostly ended with a lot of screaming young lefties putting their weight against the cops' riot shields and then, their convictions asserted, going back to the beer bars to celebrate. Fred could slip behind them and enter the back alleys that lead to the apartment.

In the meantime, the little red nostalgic tram was rounding the statue in the middle of the square. The tram was one of those things the ministers had brought back to give a theme park twist to the neighborhood's dilapidation. It drew tourists, not just foreign ones, but people from around the city. They leaned out the windows of the single wood-lined car and photographed the crowds milling in front of the sagging arcades. They'd get out at the other end, have an ice cream and ride back.

In the past, protests for causes as varied as justice for a murdered journalist to steeper bread subsidies had allowed the tram to pass unhindered. Sure, a protester or two might jump aboard, call out a slogan. But what happened in front of Fred hadn't happened before. The crowd swallowed the tram; they must have been too thick for the driver to proceed. Then like a moment out of a thousand zombie films, a mass of hands pulled the tourists from the windows, pulled the wood trim from the tram, pulled the little bug-eye lights off the tram's front like Thomas the Tank Engine had tooted into *Mortal Kombat*. Protesters later interviewed would say the tram represented the same thing the barracks-cum-mall did: an idealized vision of the neighborhood's past that was really just a way for the rich to assert their ownership.

The entire square had been blotted out instantly, like the angry sky had swatted the ground. Fred couldn't keep his eyes open, but his ears were filled with the popping of tear gas launchers, answered by the chipping and clattering of hurled pavement stones. Before he knew it, Fred was tearing up. He ran in a direction he thought would take him to High Field but, more importantly, away from what seemed like the center of the action. Like most Americans, he'd never been tear gassed before. He'd always imagined it as being attacked by a strong onion. But if he could have stuck his hand down his throat and ripped out his lungs to stop the feeling, he would have.

He crashed down a hill, joined by a scattering of other protesters. They formed a loose unit, dashing through alleys with the gas nipping at their heels. He didn't even realize until he'd made the last left turn that they were headed into a building's courtyard. Someone shoved what felt like a giant soda bottle into his hand. He swigged it, coughing uncontrollably. He was righted, his head tilted back. The contents of the bottle spilled all over his face. Relief wasn't immediate. He was guided to a folding chair, where he sat slowly appreciating every passing moment it was easier to see and breathe.

Someone asked him something in Turkish, maybe not Turkish but like it, the same thing a few times. After he didn't respond, the same person said, "Are you a tourist or something?"

"No," Fred said, "I live here."

The man said something to another one of the protesters. They both laughed. He turned to Fred and said, "You may have stayed here before, but now that you've been gassed you can say you truly live here. Gassed sticking a finger in the assholes of those who thought they were too good for this City, who moved out to the endless gated suburbs and now want it back. Gassed standing up to the people who invited us here to work in the factories and then bomb our brothers back home because they teach our sons our language, isn't it?"

"Yes," said Fred. He was suddenly a bit nervous. His eyes clear of the gas, he could see the man he was talking to was sporting the kind of scraggly beard made synonymous with extremism by the US media.

"You know who we are?" The man leered a bit.

"Yes," Fred said, looking at the flag patch stitched to the man's olive-green army shirt: a red star for the workers on a golden background for the hills of Kurdistan. "You're the ones responsible for all the terrible pot in the City."

The man remained fearsome for a moment, then laughed. "You do live here. Well, I'm glad you are on the right side. Have you recovered?"

Fred nodded.

"Do you know where you are?"

Fred thought for a moment, retracing his steps. "Are we in that funny little pocket of apartments on the Silver Water hillside? The ones the main roads all seem to lead to, then veer away from at the last minute? I always wondered how to get here—seemed like there must be a lot of apartments with great views on the Strait. I figured they must be available since their windows were darkened at night." And then he shut up.

The man gestured over to another two, who bound Fred's wrists and ankles together with long cable ties. They did it with the ease of a pair of brothers preparing to launch a kite. One tipped him onto the back of the other, who locked his elbows into Fred's, and they proceeded to haul him up into the buildings like a rolled carpet.

Fred had been right. The Strait views were amazing. Whatever chaos was unfolding up at the Watering Square had done nothing to alter the honeybee dance of the ferryboats crossing the mouth of the Strait. He watched them for what seemed like forever, sometimes imagining he was on board and heading for a fish dinner in Asia, one where he'd get hammered and tell everybody about the hilarious time he was kidnapped by Kurdish militants. He tried to hold on to this calming thought as sweat soaked the sides of his oxford shirt. As drops wicked along the seams and gathered in pools atop his pants, the men talked behind his back. He thought they were discussing his fate until they abruptly stopped and turned on the television. They flipped channels, slowly at first, then with increasing speed, until finally settling on the now familiar sounds of a soccer match: rapid-fire announcing over the white noise of crowd din. The men seemed to be watching intently, though for all Fred knew one could get up during halftime and put a bullet in his head. He was pretty sure these were guys who blew up police stations consistently, every month on the month with the whole government's monopoly on force directed toward them and their families. They were like the IRA without any gloss of Brad Pitt romanticism. They could do him, dump him in the Strait, and who would miss him? Probably only the kids who were counting on him to write their papers. The thought brought a tear of pure self-pity to his eye, one he couldn't blink clear.

"Do you like football?" someone called over to him in English. They conferred a bit more in their native tongue. Someone else added, "Soccer?"

"Yes," Fred said, swallowing the sob that had been collecting in his chest. He was like a third-grader's soda bottle terrarium: his sweat had cooked off his stomach and precipitated in his lungs. And he knew next to nothing about soccer. Someone walked over and with surprising politeness turned his folding chair so he could face the TV.

Mercifully, the game was between two of the three unavoidable clubs. All three were based in the City, and everyone in the whole country rooted for one or the other or the other. On the field were the red and yellow side that took its name from the Old Royal High School and the black and white side from the Cradle Stone neighborhood. The red and yellow were the Lions, the aristocrats of Turkish soccer, who had once beaten Manchester United to the tune of their fans chanting "Welcome to the Hell." Big-time European stars cycled through every few years, cashing bloated contracts before retiring or redeeming themselves in the eyes of more powerful clubs. They were the generals' team, and every kid at the Castle owned a red and yellow scarf. The black and white were the Eagles. They claimed a dockside, working-class edge, complete with a notoriously violent hooligan crew called "Marketplace." Fred watched the two teams duke it out in the midfield. He may not have known much about soccer, but he knew enough to know this was a boring game. Still five or so militant-looking dudes sat on a ragged sofa with their elbows on their knees, watching with every ounce of their attention. Just outside his field of vision, a group of men huddled over a large table, an architect's light intent on whatever was occurring on its surface. Were they studying a map? Or building a bomb? Fred probably wasn't meant to know, though it was clearly more exciting than what was happening on the TV.

After twenty minutes of uninspired play, an Eagles midfielder lost possession to a Lions winger, who booted the ball to their predatory, if lazy forward. With a few tenuous touches, he put the ball in the Eagles' net. The Kurds on the couch exploded, exchanging high fives.

"I sort of thought you guys would be Eagles fans" Fred ventured, in English.

The guy he'd first talked to, down in the courtyard, left the table and went over to the couch, where Fred could see him better. "Why'd you think that?"

"Eagles are more left wing." Even in this compromised position, Fred was proud of his pun.

"The Eagles are losers. Who wants to be with the losers? Besides, the Lions have our colors: gold for the hills of Kurdistan, and red for the blood we spill for them."

"But I thought the Eagles were the generals' team. Aren't you all against the generals?"

The others on the couch demanded a translation, and when they got it they glowered at Fred. He should have been worried he was digging himself deeper, but really, was there anywhere for him to go?

"What do you know about the generals?" the Kurdish guy asked.

"I teach their kids." Fred was careful. "Up at the Castle. Let me tell you, you have nothing to worry about with the next generation. Dumb as a box of rocks, the whole lot of them."

The Kurd translated. Fred hoped the idiom would hold and they wouldn't think he was comparing them to a jewel box. "What about the girls?" he was finally asked.

"Peacocks."

The word, translated, sent the couch into hysterics. After what Fred imagined were some lewd bird jokes, the couch went back to the game, which had returned to its earlier plodding pace. The Kurd who spoke the best English, however, remained interested in Fred.

"If they are so stupid and full of feathers, why do you teach them?"

"Money," was Fred's reply.

"Money of the generals." The Kurd got thoughtful, caressing his scraggly Fidel. "Money of the generals is why we are here. A hundred years ago, the generals come to us and say, you're so poor out in the east. But you are Turks, you should come to the City. We'll give you jobs, we'll give you the houses of the non-Turks. We'll give you the whole place, since we don't like it anymore and we are all moving to the Capitol. What shit. We say we are not Turks, then they come with guns to tell us we are. We don't want to move to their ghost City, they come with guns and say we must. And as for their money, what good will it do your broken back. We figured this out. Now all we want is not to be Turk. What is Turk but someone who eats the cows he did not raise? We are Noah's children, isn't it? The first people from him after he landed his boat on Ararat Mountain. Who would want to be Turk if they can be that?"

"No one," Fred said.

"You want to be Turk?"

"No," Fred answered like it was an absurd question, hoping his face wasn't flushed.

"Then why are you here?"

"Money."

"This is a poor place, there is more money where you are from. I have seen the show of Robin Leach."

"There is more money for what I do here."

"Teaching idiots."

"Teaching them to write."

"Well, teach the landless Turk this: Damascus is sweet, but one's own lands are sweeter. Teach it to yourself, since you are not from here either." The Kurd winked at him and went back to watching soccer.

The game ended, and as the sun set the Kurds let the TV bleed into the next match, which from its utter ineptitude must have been between teams in the second division. Whenever players from opposite teams contacted one another, both would end up rolling on the field. It was one of those displays that would reassure any American of the exceptional nature of their particular brand of football. The Kurds rotated between the couch and the table while the sun passed far over the ridge, until just the light and the TV illuminated the room.

"Don't you guys want to see if there's any news about the Watering Square?" Fred asked, wondering if being forced to watch unentertaining sports was a sort of torture. He asked a few more times, trying not to sound too insistent or desperate. Finally his friend, the one who spoke the best English, grabbed the clicker. He cycled the channels. Each was showing a wildlife documentary, one more absurd than the next. First it was penguins, then fruit bats, hippos, then marsupials. The Kurd lingered on one that seemed to be about lions, but switched it after a few minutes focused on the cubs. Eventually he came back around to the deathly soccer match and put down the remote.

"Things must be going well," the Kurd said. "If the police finished their job, it would be all over the news. Something ugly must have happened."

"Don't you want to see what's going on?"

"When it is fully dark. The ways back are too exposed while there is light."

"I'd like to see too."

"Because you are a tourist."

"Because this is my neighborhood. I saw what happened to the gypsies. I saw what they've done to Vine Clad Mosque." He almost added, I saw what happened to the artists' lofts of Providence Rhode Island.

"And now you want to see what happens to the Watering Square?"

"I want to stop it."

"Really? Well then, I have a van you can borrow. Don't worry about returning it." The Kurd translated for his compatriots, and they all laughed. For his brief flirtation with idealism, Fred got a hot face.

He'd lost track of time, one scoreless game bleeding into another, when his friend strolled over from the pool of light around the table. Pulling a knife from his boot, he cut the cable tie around Fred's legs like a frigatebird snatching a fish from another bird who'd snatched it from just below the ocean's surface.

"We're going." He had put on full fatigues complete with red star shoulder patches. Clearly they weren't worried about blending in. "You're coming with us. As you asked, isn't it."

Fred tried to stand, but with his wrists still bound and his legs stiff, he just managed to squirm. His friend grabbed the cable tie around his wrists and yanked him up. This hurt. A lot. His friend said, "You should piss. Easier if you do it sitting down. Then my guy doesn't have to do the shake shake for you." He smiled.

Fred was led to the bathroom. Through the accumulated grime, Fred could tell it had once been lavish, with crown moldings and a large silver-backed mirror. Now shot through with black faults. *If you just cleaned this place up*, he thought. And then, *Does thinking this make me the enemy?*

On the street, the Kurds moved with military precision. You'd think they had rifles, which might have been the point. They kept Fred cozily amidst them, jostling him to indicate which jagged alley or narrow staircase they planned to take next. The one thing each leg of their route had in common was relative darkness, those little wedges between buildings seemingly left there for the explicit purpose of abducting young girls for the harem. When Fred's eyes began to sting, he knew they were getting close. He tried listening past the Kurds' boots on the paving stones, for the whoops of riot or the cries of protesters driven before shields and truncheons. There were neither as they ascended the hillside to the square.

At the crest, five soccer-jerseyed men milled around a barricade of overturned dumpsters. Across the top of their barrier, the men had lined bottles: some appeared to be full of beer, others full of gasoline. At least that would explain why some were swigged while others trailed bands of cloth. The men threw some questions the Kurds' way and satisfied with their responses, rolled one dumpster aside.

The square was dark, but packed. Claimed. Among the trees and abandoned earthmoving equipment, students and old lefties milled anxiously, paper respirators hanging from their necks. One source of light was the Starbucks at the base of the Marble Sea Hotel. The remnants of the glass façade, shattered across the pavement, shimmered like a pool of water. Inside protesters were neatly lining up for free coffees. Cartons of cigarettes and crates of bottled water circulated among the crowds. Another source of light was a ways down Independence Avenue, past what appeared to be a massive and teeming barricade built around the denuded tram. It was the light of fires. Fred figured the front lines were there: the cops, the thugs, the anarchists. It was probably where the Kurds would go too, and he with his bound wrists. Maybe they thought he'd make a good news story: foreigner, jaw-shattered, facing down fascist police. It would be his noblest contribution to the City, even if it wasn't by his choosing.

The Kurds seemed to be discussing strategy. They'd left Fred off to the side, but made it clear they were wary of him. He watched the Square's occupants as they chatted and smoked. This was shaping up to be more than the weekly placard-waving event. These people weren't going anywhere, and more seemed to be streaming in through side streets. From a nearby alley, he couldn't help but notice a pack of young women in Charlie's Angels jumpsuits and construction helmets. They were all smiles, like they'd finally made it through the stadium parking lot as the opening act was taking the stage. And right in their midst, there he was. The cartoonist.

Fred called out to him. His friend, right there next to him, already had his boot knife out. "Who's that?"

"The guy who draws The Wolfman."

"How do you know him?"

The cartoonist seemed to acknowledge Fred, but wasn't heading his way. The girls seemed to be drawn to the dead center of the park, like it was there they would find the beacon of cool which had sum-moned all these people to this once-rejected grove of trees. They'd disappear soon enough, leaving Fred to his fate.

"Football," Fred said, "American Football. The Pittsburgh Steel-ers. They are sort of America's Black Eagles."

"You think he'll do a strip about tonight?"

Fred nodded, and without ceremony the Kurd cut him loose, the knife moving again with the precision of a sushi chef. Or a murderer.

"Make sure he knows there were some handsome Kurds here tonight. We're always looking for support from his readership, you know what I mean." His friend elbowed Fred in the ribs a little too hard. Then he seemed to explain the situation to the others. It took Fred probably too long to get the lead out, but when he finally did he managed to intercept the cartoonist without jogging. The cartoonist's hug was ordinary, but Fred shook in his arms. The cartoonist seemed not to notice. "You did right to leave your woman at home. This park is so full of crispy girls it's like being inside a bag of chips."

Fred muttered his ascent. He was taking in the scene, but also plotting a route home that would cut as wide a berth as possible from whatever action was unfolding on Independence Avenue.

"So, did you score some dope?" the cartoonist asked. He must have seen Fred with the Kurds.

Fred shook his head.

"That's okay, those guys won't sell to just anyone. They're mostly in wholesale. I've got you covered." With that, the cartoonist revealed a joint of impressive length and girth, bound together with several papers like a swaddled infant. Just how Fred wanted to feel at this moment. "And after tough losses to the Ravens and the Texans, the Black and Gold are on their way back to the Super Bowl for sure."

"Isn't it a little early to tell?" Fred said, like he was talking about his own escape.

"It's never too early to dream of gridiron glory. At least that's what they told me in America." The cartoonist did some bodybuilder moves in his hoodie to oohs and aahs, slightly mocking, from the girls around him. The Wolfman was in his element. They found a less crowded patch of earth near the park's central fountain and all plopped down like picnickers. The cartoonist lit the joint with great ceremony and handed it to Fred, saying, "This is great, huh?"

NINE.

FRED MADE IT HOME just in time for the protests to follow him there. The previous night's rioters had been driven by the cops into High Field. Nearly every doorway had the mark of sheltering the opposition: lemon rinds, boxes of antacid tablets, empty or shattered bottles. There was a spent tear gas canister in the building's entryway that choked Fred up when he arrived. Everywhere was graffiti. Fred imagined bandanaed kids leaving their mark before falling back under police pressure. Most of it was directly political—fringe communist slogans from the Bread and House Party or calls for liberation from Fred's new friends at the Peace and Democracy Party, the political arm of the revolutionary Kurds. But there were some choice sentiments, sprayed out elegantly in English for the benefit of the international press. Fred was actually proud of a few.

WELCOME TO THE FIRST TRADITIONAL GAS FESTIVAL.

YOU THINK TEAR GAS WILL SCARE THE PEOPLE WHO LIGHT A MATCH TO CHECK WHETHER A GAS OVEN IS WORKING?

YOU DID NOT NEED TO USE PEPPER SPRAY TO MAKE US WEEP, WE ARE EMOTIONAL PEOPLE.

WE'RE NOT GOING THE WAY OF THE GYPSIES. WE'RE NOT GOING THE WAY OF THE GREEKS.

Fred spent the day holed up, watching things play out on the internet. The government had upgraded their response. Now, instead of a nostalgic tram shuttling up and down Independence Avenue, there were "Social-Event Intervention Vehicles," armored semi tractors with turret-mounted water cannon. They'd trundle along the cobblestones accompanied by a half-dozen betel-black riot cops. When they'd come to an alley where a handful of college students or communists had gathered, they would inundate it with water and gas. At the same time, other alleys would spill out their provocateurs to unleash another batch of slogans and broken windows.

Independence Avenue finally looked like the rest of nineteenth-century Europe, blown out and smoldering. And it wasn't the indiscriminate destruction wrought by a World War; it had the personal touch of a country working out its contradictions in real time. The rioters went after the chain stores and the banks, torching the latter while leaving the manikins in the looted former in lewd positions. Then they would flee the cops through the arcades, which the cops treated with no particular nostalgia. In the end, the developers wouldn't need to rebuild the barracks to host a new shopping mall. Plenty of storefront space was suddenly available.

The Greek emerged from the Cage, having just about worked his way through the batch of midterm papers. He was wan, like all the sun he'd gotten on the islands had been used to power his laptop.

"Well, after that I feel like joining them," he said.

"Really." Fred was watching more "unofficial news" clips on his laptop. The footage was of the pepper spraying of a young woman up on the Avenue, not a third of a mile from where he was sitting. She was wearing a red sundress and you had to feel that the cops would keep spraying her until the poison tore the clothes off her. "I thought you'd be in favor of the barracks. It's going to put property values in High Field through the roof."

The Greek snorted. "With all the noise of breaking glass and unity chants, you might not have noticed, but there hasn't been a single jackhammer at work in this neighborhood. This is the kind of thing that sells units in gated communities."

"Maybe." Fred was thinking about the tables, about the gypsies. It made him a little sick, his cynical instinct that the protesters were doing the developers' job for them.

They watched another clip, this time a wall of protesters colliding with one of the "Social-Event" vehicles. The thing was spraying like crazy but couldn't get an angle on the protesters, who clung to its sides and hammered it with paving stones. Quickly enough, another two of the things pulled up with a bevy of cops and the whole scene disappeared into a puff of smoke and water. The next clip was of the prime minister wrapping up a screed.

"You want to know what he's saying?" the Greek asked.

"Terrorists, looters, infidels, etc.," Fred muttered, but pulled up a blog that was covering events as they unfolded in English. It gave a rundown of the prime minister's remarks, most of which were simply veiled fuck yous to the groups Fred mentioned: the terrorists, communists, and students who were so diligently destroying the park and neighborhood they claimed to be protecting. But then things took an interesting turn. The prime minister claimed that the precedent allowing him to build the barracks-cum-mall was in fact the Castle. The generals, in order to circumvent the law preserving green space, had claimed there had been a castle overlooking the Black Sea and they were simply rebuilding it, but as a university. What was good for the generals was good for the ministers.

Fred didn't know whether to be nervous or to revel in how tightly woven the City's web was.

The Castle closed as the protests continued into the week. The official reason was a mealy-mouthed something between transportation difficulties and giving the apolitical students a chance to have a voice in their city's future. Really it was clear the generals didn't want the place to become another focal point for protest, an analogy to the park-consuming barracks. They'd put the Castle on the City's final hill for a reason, and it was not because they liked their kids to breathe the nice fresh air. The last thing they wanted was a crowd of hippies, communists, Kurds, and kids from the state universities camped out in front of the gates. Worse, having those factors throwing themselves in front of the comings and goings of new model year Audis. The optics would be bad, the possible confrontations much worse. Better to leave the place quiet, safe.

Fred waited forty-eight hours before he decided to rejoin the protests, this time on his own accord. His decision was in part because there was a lull. A cop had put a twelve-year-old kid in the hospital, hit him with a gas canister. The outcry in the Western press led to a pull back. A fresh influx of protesters joyfully marched right into the center of the park where a hard core had weathered the past days. They set up drum circles and pamphleting tables and even did a rendition of "Do you hear the people sing?" from *Les Mis* for the BBC. Fred watched all this like the Redskins fan he was, anxiously awaiting the moment where it all turns bad. It was only a matter of time before the eyes of the world media turned elsewhere, leaving the City to sort out its own, as it had with the Greeks, Jews, and Armenians before. The City which had once been the world's center was now sufficiently at the edges of its justice. Fred contemplated calling Ayşe, but for whatever reason was afraid of what she might say about the protests. Or what he might say. They were, in some sense, against her. Maybe more against her family, but Fred was still wary of letting principles come between her legs. Hardly worth getting into when the whole event could be buttoned up in a matter of hours. There hadn't been a second protest in the Water Tower after the police broke up the first. Now there were Ottoman-style townhouses ready for ribbon cutting, the gypsies off in some forgotten housing project, their dancing bears dead in the ground.

His first instinct was to try and write another spec script, maybe one that would touch on the protests. But looking over his previous attempts, he had to wonder if anyone in the United States would care. People there understood the Middle East, because they depended on it for gas, and they were afraid of it. And they understood Europe, since most of them were extracted from or oppressed by Europeans. But Turkey was a different thing. Trying to explain it was like biting into an onion: you could describe the experience as layered, but really it's just acrid and hard. Fred considered helping the Greek with his load of essays. He slunk over to the Cage to observe. The Greek wore studio monitor headphones, and from the way he moved Fred imagined they were playing the drumbeat of a slave galley. The Greek pecked out a few words, then consulted looseleafs he had scattered on the desk. Then he rattled out what must have been several sentences, a paragraph with machine gun speed, punching the enter key like a bullfighter. Maybe Fred understood the principles of the essay scheme, but the Greek knew the practice. Tonight wasn't the night to start learning.

So Fred went back to his laptop. Bouncing around, he couldn't help punching in the address for Virginia's site. There was a link there to a review of a show she had in Chicago. The reviewer started out invoking Ozymandias, an easy comparison for canvases that silhouetted "Oriental" shadows over Midwestern space. But then his critical distance seemed to fall away and he began to talk about the loss he felt, the emptiness as if he had known these buildings in a distant dream he now realized would never come to pass. It made Fred feel a little ill. It was a feeling he knew he could solve with the bottle of aniseed liqueur. But instead he rose from the couch and headed for the door.

The streets were ghostly and strewn with trash. He took his back route to the Watering Square, in case the cops and their Social-Event vehicles had returned to the Avenue. Ordinarily lively fruit stands and sundry shops were boarded up. A few had been rewarded for their care with spray-painted slogans Fred couldn't decipher. He realized, most of the way there, that he wasn't really dressed for this thing to go south. He was wearing a light professorial sweater over a T-shirt and a pair of cheap loafer-like shoes he bought because he hated to wear socks. He could have been going out for an evening cruise on the Strait. All the same, he kept going. He didn't have a soccer jersey and gas mask lying around the house.

When he made it out of the maze of alleys, he figured the park was compromised. There were klieg lights in every corner, driving all shadows from the place. He was about to turn back when he heard the faint tones of "Burn One Down." *Fine*, he thought, *at least one hippy still lives*. Still he decided not to go through the main entrance, up the wide marble stairs that led to the once and future barracks' doors. Instead he went for a side staircase between the shuttered offices of the national airline and the "modern WC," which was neither. It was quite literally a shit hole. The stairs left him in a small, scrubby grove. Through the branches, he could make out clusters of people, some sitting, some with blankets on their shoulders and playing guitars. It all seemed like it might have been playing out on some West Coast beach. Fred normally ran in the other direction from this kind of sentimentality. But in a part of the world where so many different populations had been purged, exchanged, forcibly assimilated, here was a small place where everyone was just who they were.

That was when he felt a hand clap his shoulder. He didn't recognize this particular guy from the other day, but from the paramilitary getup he figured the worst. The man grunted something. Fred didn't open his mouth. The guy could have been asking for a password or merely saying hi. It didn't matter, since he was in the business of keeping those who didn't belong out, and Fred clearly didn't belong. He was going to take his cardiganed self back down the stairs, but the man was already in his face, talking at him like he might understand. It was the second time in two days Fred truly understood, in his stomach, that there were thousands of ways to die in the City. That the Strait really was the empty center filled with corpses just under its surface. He would no doubt end in one of the garbage dumps, where only the trash without any redemptive qualities remained. He thought about the pickers working around his body, fishing out the beer bottles and scrap metal and corrugated cardboard from beneath him.

"It's okay," and then a string of syllables he now recognized as Kurdish. The paramilitary backed off. "I just told him you were a foreigner here to buy pot."

It was his friend from the other day. He was still sporting his full set of fatigues with the red star in the gold sky emblazoned on the chest. On a normal day, you would be picked up off the street by the cops for wearing that, just as sure as wearing an Osama bin Laden T-shirt would get you taken off the streets of Times Square. "I would say you were here to support the cause, but he'd probably want to know which cause it was you were here to support." The man left this in the air like a question.

"I just think the City should belong to its people," Fred said.

"Which people?"

"These people," Fred was aware he was stepping into the void.

The Kurd scoffed. "These people, whose hearts break for a few trees? How can the City belong to them, when its heart is poured concrete?"

Fred muttered a bit. The Kurd was watching a distant drum circle, the little ember of a roach slowly making its way around. "Did you come back to take part in that?" he asked.

"No, I guess I just wanted to see what was happening." Fred caught himself. He really did sound like a tourist. A cautious observer of the life and struggles of the other. There was a Susan Sontag quote about this, it being the modern condition. At least for Americans.

"Now you've seen. Why don't you tell me what you think is happening?"

Fred took his time looking around. It was a picture-perfect protest. In the center of the park, near the ugly fountain, circles of good-looking young people sat on their placards. Fred imagined they were talking about the City's bright future that they were in the process of securing. On the periphery were the varied political factions, some underneath their banners, probably considering how they would court, cajole, or capture the future that was being dreamed up on the lawn. Among the trees that ringed the park, Fred imagined, were the forces of political violence: soccer thugs, bikers, separatists. All invested in the cause not because it represented a particular vision, but because it was a crack in the established order, the one which had keep them on its peripheries.

"It's the City's future," Fred hazarded.

"Let me tell you something about the City and its future, since you say you live here. You know the story of its conquest."

"It was a ruin."

"The conqueror knew as much. He told his followers that it was a city in name alone, and that within the walls all they would find were unweeded vineyards. And when they did take the City, that is what they found. And they did not stay. Why live in an abandoned rabbit warren when you were masters of the horizons? When you already had all of Rome that mattered? So who did the conqueror give the City to?"

Fred shrugged, but knew the answer.

"Slaves. Slaves in the army, slaves in the marketplace, slaves with the sultan's ear. Slaves and the renegade castoffs of the West. Some of the most powerful slaves in the world. But slaves and renegades the same. And the time always comes for people like that, when they've built up something worth having. Happened to the Janissaries, to the Sultanate of Women, the black eunuchs, the pirates, the Greek tradesmen, the Armenian builders, the Jewish bankers. The gypsies, who were so sure no one would ever notice them hiding in the shadows of the walls. Just the same, the time will come for all those you see here."

Fred shook his head.

"You are a tutor to the powerful. I remember. You said they were stupid, that they were cheats. The master is always stupid, because he can be. The slave is always crafty, because he must be. Eventually the slave must rebel. If he is successful, he becomes the stupid master. If he fails, he dies and there are new slaves. It is always this way."

This sounded to Fred like many a discredited historiographical ideology, though he didn't think the Kurd would appreciate it put in those terms. Instead he said, "I'm taking a break from the City's past tonight. So should you. Everyone else here seems to be."

The Kurd scoffed. "The past will be there in the morning."

Fred let him have the last word, apparently in exchange for letting him go. He waved, and his friend gave a curt goodbye. Proceeding into the humming milieu of protesters, who chatted and made out and smoked and argued, Fred felt like he might run into everyone he'd known in the City. There was April and Ata standing tall among the bikers, Ata with their kid on his leather-padded shoulders. There was Bulkington, the football-loving contractor who'd died in a plane crash outside of Erbil. There was Eddie, teaching the Turks-only prostitutes about what it meant to be a nation. There was the Greek and his family, exchanging housing horror stories with the Kurds. There were all his cheating students preparing to reprise "One Day More" from *Les Mis*. There was Ayşe, in a red one-piece: she was the lifeguard for the ugly fountain. And there was Virginia, looking like Courtney Love after a good trip to the Salvation Army, taking it all in as usual. It all seemed possible; it was just a matter of time. He took a seat among some affable-looking student types and smoked their pot while telling them lies about his plan to motorcycle the Silk Road.

He didn't remember coming home. Going to the teashop to clear his head, he picked up a copy of the English-language newspaper. The headline was PARK CLEARED. The cops had gone in heavy during the predawn, just after the lights had been shut off. There were no sure numbers for the injured: most everyone who had been in the park's center had been corralled into requisitioned buses and taken to a holding and processing area, a stadium in the distant suburbs. Once the park was cleared, the government sent in the crews who maintained the highway medians to replant the greenery. The paper had pictures of them, their high-visibility vests catching the dawn. The prime minister declared that protesters destroyed things, while the real champions of the City's environment were going to plant five hundred and sixty-one tulips, one for each year since the conquest.

TEN.

Fred was in a black mood when he received Ayşe's text message. The Greek was going forward with his move to the islands. Requests for end-of-term papers were already coming in, flying in the face of an unseasonably warm November. But as far as Fred could tell, the Greek wasn't doing anything about them. The paperbacks lined their shelf and were starting to form a stacked layer above. His plan to recruit former students to take over the work wasn't getting anywhere. The students didn't need money. Not a single one. And this before he even suggested the nature of the work. The obvious solution was to find clever students at public universities interested in a little side money. But he couldn't count on them being as morally bankrupt as the Castle kids. Public university students might object to helping their future bosses cheat their way to a degree. He couldn't blame them.

To top it off, he'd spent the past few workdays "training" Kiki to ID Paula papers. The trouble was, he and the Greek had driven Paula out of business, so there weren't a lot of recent examples to bring to Kiki's attention. And to make matters worse, Charlie, the fastidiously gay Irishman always on the edge of getting fired, had picked up on one of the Greek's "tells." The Greek loved the "however" construction, and against Fred's strict advice he always did it perfectly: lead-ing with a semicolon, following with a comma. There just weren't that many students at the Castle who knew proper punctuation, and among those there were probably even fewer that cared. The Irish-man had been collecting example essays through the summer and now had dumped a critical mass on Fred and Kiki. This could po-tentially be very bad for business. If a bunch of the Greek's papers were sent to the disciplinary council, it would shatter the impression of security they'd created and the high premiums they charged for it. So Fred was stuck mealy-mouthing the notion that the fastidious Irishman had actually put such undue emphasis on grammar and punctuation that his students were terrified into using the semicolon. The guy insisted that students refer to the current season as "autumn" and would take points off if they called it "fall." Kiki seemed to buy it, but the possibility that some other teacher would come forward with the same inexplicable phenomenon was giving Fred indigestion.

He was again trying to gear himself up to take on essays him-self. He figured he'd work on his own assignment first, since only he would evaluate whether the fakes were convincingly terrible. He al-ways ended the semester with the same prompt: *Can political violence ever be justified?* He was almost eager to write about it, but found himself getting caught in the same contradictions he enjoyed ensnar-ing his students with.

Just as he thought he'd figured something out, Ayşe called. He considered letting it go to voicemail, knowing she wasn't the kind of woman to call twice. But in the end, he answered. He needed some-thing to look forward to.

"So you survived your first 'social event,'" she said. "I was really afraid it was going to turn out like the late seventies, when the Grey

Wolves brought machine guns to May Day and killed forty communists in broad daylight. Happened right in the Watering Square. Whenever I wanted to go see a movie in your neighborhood, my parents would talk about that incident like it was the bogeyman."

"What do they think about it now?"

"Their opinion hasn't changed, but a friend of mine wanted to check out what happened. I told him about you, that you can show us around."

"I don't know," Fred lied. "I didn't go up to the square while things were happening. School was canceled. I was really just at home."

"It's okay, we'll all go together. Then maybe the three of us can have dinner somewhere in your neighborhood. Then he'll go home."

"And you."

"We'll see. I'm too old to have a secret boyfriend. When shall we come?"

"Saturday." The Greek was headed to the islands to do a final overnight inspection of the house he'd bought. Soon Fred would have the apartment to himself. The thought, which should have filled him with relief, jolted him hard like he had been asleep at the wheel and finally hit a jersey barrier.

"See you Saturday, then," she said with the verbal equivalent of a flip of her hair.

Meeting them at the metro entrance in the Watering Square, Fred felt exposed. He felt at any moment the Kurd would show up. Or that the Kurd was watching from some distant corner, sipping from a tulip-shaped tea glass. Or that some agent of the Kurd would report that the foreigner was actually on the other side, allied with the wealthy, the ones who raise their glasses to the extinction of the Eastern languages. The slavers. It would not, then, be a distant conclusion to think Fred had been a spy. That he would reveal the secret location of the Kurds' headquarters. Then where would they watch soccer? He bought a newspaper and shielded himself with it.

Ayşe and her friend did not emerge from the metro. They stepped out of a cab in front of the luxury Marble Sea Hotel, all its shattered glass restored. Fred should have figured. They both looked businesslike, Ayşe in a skirt and jacket combo, the man in a sport coat and slacks. Fred found it cringe-worthy, and might have fled the scene were it not for Ayşe's dress shirt, which had essentially given up trying to hold in her breasts. The two proceeded toward him, crossing paving stones that had just recently been put back in the ground. The government had done such a good job returning the square to normalcy Fred almost wanted to pry up a couple stones in memoriam. Ayşe's friend seemed to be contemplating the paving as well, his eyes down as they approached.

Ayşe gave Fred a conservative pair of pecks, one on each cheek. She introduced her friend as Ahmet. He gave Fred a weak sort of handshake. Even though he was wearing a polo shirt, Ahmet had an air of obsequiousness about him. Or maybe it was because of the polo shirt.

"So you know each other from the hotel business?" Fred ventured.

"No," Ayşe corrected. "Ahmet is more of a family friend." Fred suppressed a groan. He hadn't dressed for an interview, though they clearly had.

They mounted the steps and entered the park. It was, as the government had promised, pristine. Ahmet seemed to be taking notes with his eyes. Ayşe walked between him and Fred, her pumps clicking on the flagstones. Fred wondered what he should say. Was he really some kind of guide? And what could he relate, considering he'd lied about visiting the park during the protests? He felt fresh out of stories. Fortunately, after a quick turn around the park, Ahmet said something to Ayşe in Turkish.

"Okay, he's all done."

Fred was relieved, but worried he was flunking the family test. "Well," he said, "I'm happy to talk about what it was like to be in this neighborhood during the protests, but honestly after the first day or so all of the action was just up here. I teared up once or twice, but it could just be my sensitive nature."

Ahmet nodded. Fred sort of wished he'd say something that confirmed he knew English. Ayşe laughed a little but it was clear this wasn't going to break the veil of awkwardness that had settled on them.

"So should we head toward dinner?" Fred asked. He'd picked The House Cafe, a place as bland and international as its Anglicised name. He and Virginia had mocked it mercilessly as a place that solely catered to exhausted tourists and a class of locals who thought it was sophisticated to eat penne with pesto sauce. The place was expensive enough for what it was, but it wouldn't be a check too heavy for Fred to pick up himself. If they were left alone, he could take Ayşe to one of the hotel rooftop bars. Cap the evening off in suitable style.

"Can you give us a tour of your neighborhood first?" Ayşe asked. The question threw Fred for a loop. He was already weighing which rooftop bar would provide the most direct route back to the apartment. Unfortunately, most of the nice ones were on the far side of Independence Avenue, and he was nervous about taking Ayşe by a burned-out storefront. The last thing he wanted her to be was skittish.

"Yes, that would be most agreeable." Ahmet pronounced the words in a labored fashion. "I am very interested in the history of this part of the City."

"Sure," Fred agreed. "You want to see what's left of the churches and synagogues. The old taverns?"

"I want to see everything from the minorities."

Ayşe took Fred's arm at the elbow.

There wasn't much in the way of dinner conversation. Ayşe picked at a Lite California Salad with avocado and quinoa. Ahmet, who had recently traveled to Italy only to storm out of a trattoria because they would not serve him Sambuca with water and ice alongside his dinner, contentedly ate penne pasta and sipped aniseed liqueur. Fred had the twenty-dollar burger. It was good, with real bacon and Swiss cheese. The restaurant bustled around them, though on their way there they had passed countless piles lemon wedges, squeezed and discarded. When Ayşe asked about them, Fred was tempted to make a joke about someone setting up a lemonade stand. "Helps relieve the effects of tear gas," he'd said without going into detail.

The neighborhood tour seemed to have gone well. Ahmet was quite the shutterbug, taking pictures of random buildings with the same alacrity as the more notable churches and taverns Fred had gone out of his way to feature. He was also very curious about which buildings were owned by foreigners, which had been restored, etc. Fred almost felt Ahmet was pushing for a tour of Fred's apartment much more than he was the Holy Trinity church, from which Turks had been banned since the mid-century pogroms. Fred had gotten them access to by feigning touristic ignorance. The priests had refused to clean the church or the surrounding buildings after the pogroms, so the whole edifice was scorched black inside and out. Fred was afraid Ayşe and Ahmet might take offense at this indictment, but they seemed to ignore it in favor of lighting candles in front of the icons. They said it was considered good luck.

"But you must have liked something about Italy." Fred tried to reignite the conversation Ahmet had extinguished. "Did you go to Venice?"

"Who needs Venice when you have the City? They have a grand canal through their town, we have a Strait that connects the Black Sea to the White. Their church is a copy of the church we demolished to make way for the grand mosque of the conqueror. They are sinking into the mud, but our City was there at the beginning of the world and it will be there at the end. We are alive and they are dead." He tried killing some of his pasta with his fork for emphasis. Ayşe giggled, thankfully.

"I'd still like to go," she said. "It's romantic. It's got none of the ugliness you find here."

"Well, we all know who's to blame for that. And how to fix it," Ahmet said cryptically. Fred pressed him, but Ahmet fell back to mopping up pesto with the too-soft French bread. Ayşe didn't have anything to add. She'd opted for white wine tonight and only had a glass. Fred on the other hand was twitchily sipping up anise liqueur. He and Ahmet had agreed to split a small bottle, but the waiter had only been refilling Fred's glass. At this rate, he could end up drinking too much to make a night with Ayşe. Then again, the way things were going, his only consolation might be to get drunk.

"So you know," Ayşe said, "Ahmet graduated from the Castle. He was one of the first students there, more than ten years ago. You had a good time there, right?"

Ahmet nodded. "If you can believe it, I got quite tan in my years there. I lost it, though. Office work. Ayşe told me you teach English there."

"Writing, actually." Fred tried to picture Ahmet coming to his office for an MIC. The wan face with the flared nostrils. The reluctance to talk. He'd've pegged Ahmet for a cheater, back in the bad old days before he knew precisely who was cheating.

"Do you enjoy working there?"

"It's a very scenic campus."

"And the students?"

"Some of the best in the country, I'm told. But I don't think they very much like my class."

Ahmet smiled knowingly. "No, it wasn't my favorite when I was there. It's not just difficult to work outside your own language, it is demeaning. You know, at first, all the schools of the Turks were in French. That was while we still had the Empire, but Napoleon had taken Egypt from us. Then the Germans beat the French and all the schools switched over to German. The Americans beat the Germans; now all the schools are in English. The good ones, isn't it?"

"Well, when the Chinese beat us, I guess I'll be out of a job. And your poor kids will have to learn Mandarin." Fred resisted taking a drink. Ayşe laughed a little, but Ahmet shook his head.

"Someday we will teach our children in our own language. The language of the last emperor of Rome."

Fred again held back a crack, this one about the fate of Latin, but he let the moment pass. Ahmet, probably the son of some general, had been spoon-fed this nationalist shit since he'd been weaned from his mother's milk. It was funny that he should be interested in the fate of the Greeks, Jews, and Armenians, since it was the generals who so thoroughly tried to erase them from the City. But perhaps that was what allowed them to be objects of curiosity rather than a threat. Fred imagined Ahmet had no fascination or affection for the surviving Kurdish minority.

"Anyone want dessert?" Fred asked. But no one wanted the evening to go on longer than it had. Fred paid the bill without looking at it, in part out of flourish and in part to avoid the twinge of guilt he'd have for dropping well over a hundred bucks on what could be kindly described as mall food on white tablecloths.

"There's a taxi stand around the corner," Fred said to Ahmet, sort of hoping this might propel Ayşe into sending him back to his benighted suburb. They were speaking Turkish together for the first time. It was a formal exchange, from what Fred could tell through body language. Neither of them stole a glance at him, which made him think it was not some kind of post-game analysis. In fact, Ahmet seemed animated for the first time that evening. He ended the conversation pointing at his watch. Ayşe turned to Fred.

"I'm afraid I can't stay," she said. Taking back the two kisses she'd given him when they'd met, she whispered, "I'll make it up to you. My father leaves on business tomorrow morning." Ahmet shook Fred's hand, and the two of them proceeded to the taxi stand.

It occurred to Fred that it might be best for him to call it a night. Be fresh for whatever the next day brought. But being alone with his thoughts in the apartment was much less appealing than being alone among the old drunks at one of the neighborhood taverns. He was only a few short of drunk himself anyway.

————

He awoke with the back of his teeth coated. There was a steady anise flavor rising from his gut that confirmed the source of his ill feeling. His arm was thrown around the bed's second pillow and he wondered whom he had dreamt it was. The faint sounds of the accordionist reassured him that the day had not completely passed him by.

"Come over, we can have a picnic," Ayşe's text read. The thought of food had no draw for him. Even sex had only a faint allure. He'd started drinking water, but rather than clear him up he felt like it was reactivating the booze in his stomach. He'd made the coffee as strong as he dared, and now weighed the acid that would fill his gut against its promise of energy. He'd also found some remnants of a cheese pastry that he must have bought on the way home. Its grease had gone hard. Still he ate it, and it helped his overall state. Next weekend would probably be better, he thought as he wrote, "As long as you are on the menu."

Sunday traffic was light, and his hair was still damp as the cab pulled up to the security perimeter of Strait City. He'd remembered to bring along the pendant, which might serve to distract from his being the worse for wear. The cabbie rolled down the window next to Fred and the guard approached. He got a bit panicky at this. He didn't know Ayşe's last name. So he said, "Ayşe, Little Raven." He said this a few times, making sure to emphasis the comma. The guard was confused and called over another guard. Fred said it a few more times. One went in and dialed a phone, which reminded Fred that he could call Ayşe to sort this all out. It wasn't necessary. "Ayşe Aksoy," one said to the other. "Ayşe Aksoy," the other repeated. They gave directions to the cab driver before opening the gates.

It was strange to be back driving through Strait City, maybe because some of the initial oddness had worn off. In the late autumn light, Fred noticed a film of dirt that dispersed the gleam of the glass and steel high-rises. The signs directing cars around the various traffic circles had begun to rust at the bolts. And both the Holy Wisdom and the Six Minarets Mosque had lost cone tops from one spire each. Fred could take all this in because the traffic within the compound was stop and go.

When he finally made it to the Little Raven house, his hangover had reached its nadir. While he didn't feel sick anymore, he just felt drained. In the mood to watch six hours of television, eat pizza, and go to bed early. Virginia was a champion at helping him wade through this feeling. She'd help him find that reserve of decency and light when necessary, and when not she'd put in the order for two pizzas. Even the tight jeans and checkered-tablecloth blouse Ayşe wore to greet the cab didn't stir him as it should have.

"Your picnic is served," she said, pressing her big lips to his. Arms around him, she took his hand and led him inside.

That the sex was bad was not her fault. She had set out to fuck him like he imagined a sorority girl would: putting his hands on her curves, panting, taking him in her mouth, taking off her shirt but not her bustier. As they cycled through positions, Fred felt the eyes of the full cast poster of *Beverly Hills 90210* upon him. He kept telling himself, "You are getting exactly what you want." Every part of Ayşe bounced but her breasts, a surreal effect of the implants. For a while he thought he could pretend he was taking so long because he wanted to please her. But finally he just told himself, "You are in another country." Something clicked, and he came out of nowhere with a sort of clipped yelp. Ayşe looked relieved, but not in the way any man would hope. She dismounted. He got up and went to the bathroom to toss the condom in the toilet. When he got back, she was sitting up in the bed smoking.

"You know, when I was in Coral Gables, I dated a string of bartenders. Not because of the free drinks. I can pay, I'm sure you know. I dated them because a lot of them were trying to do something else, trying to act or paint or do stand-up comedy. That one I never got. But it felt good to make them feel good. Not that they weren't jerks who knew how to get a woman. But they weren't who they wanted to be, and I liked that. I wasn't what I wanted to be."

Fred was going to say something, but he stood there naked, feeling round-shouldered and thick in the middle as she lit another cigarette.

"Are you who you want to be? Doing what you want to do?"

Fred mustered a yes, one he could tell wasn't convincing.

"Okay." She stubbed out her butt. "Because I am, now." She folded her arms, her stacks of golden bangles like armor. Fred didn't know whether to climb back into bed or put on his tangled clothes, so he just stood there as Shannen Doherty, Jason Priestley, Jennie Garth, Ian Ziering, Gabrielle Carteris, Luke Perry, Brian Austin Green, Tori Spelling, and Ayşe Aksoy studied him with indifference.

ELEVEN.

IT WAS DECEMBER. ORDERS for end-of-semester papers were piling up. The Greek had given lip service to the idea of doing them all, but he had gotten the keys to his new house. His wife and child were already there, along with a first shipment of their things. The Greek was coming back, but only to "tie up loose ends." Fred found himself with expanses of time on his hands. Though he'd left Ayşe's that day with the taste of her cigarettes in his mouth, she hadn't called him since. And despite often recalling their times together in pornographic detail, he hadn't called either. He had nothing to say. He kept trying to fill some of the essay orders after a couple drinks. He'd start out okay, following the pattern he'd laid out for the Greek. But after a paragraph he couldn't bring himself to write more on the inane topics. Was television bad for you? Does welfare help, or make people lazy? Should colleges prepare their students for real life work? (Fred knew this one—the only way to get a good grade was to argue no.) Is abortion morally justified? (The right answer was yes.) Is political violence ever acceptable? He and Virginia had developed that one as a kind of private joke. Most of the students would say yes and point to their fathers' suppression of the Kurds. But of course, if it was acceptable, then so was the Kurds' armed resistance. He tried writing on that topic again and ended up getting nowhere, which made him laugh a little, and cry a little.

The Greek finally showed up, sparing Fred from helping himself to another whiskey. He wasn't holding back, figuring he would travel somewhere over the winter break that he could resupply his non-aniseed liquor cabinet. The Greek was ashen. Fred secretly hoped something had gone awry with his purchase of the house. Maybe there was some obscure law about using money from a bank here to buy a place in Greece. It wouldn't surprise Fred.

"I've just come from the Directorate of Foundations. You'll never believe it," The Greek declared.

"They wouldn't give you the deed back?"

"No, I would have seen that coming. You know what they told me? They told me for the equivalent of $200, they'd validate the deed and the place would be mine."

"You're kidding."

"No. It's some new law, just passed the legislature. Some kind of olive branch to help them enter the European Union. It's funny, because they said that the window was very short, and it only works for a couple neighborhoods around here."

"Shit. So are you going to do it?"

"Don't know. Would I have you for a tenant?"

Fred thought about it for a minute. "I'm just not sure how long I'm going to stay anymore. But what about the rest of your plan? A couple places here could give you a pretty steady income even if you weren't flipping them."

"The idea crossed my mind. It's a long cab ride from there to here." The Greek sat. "You drinking whiskey?"

Fred nodded.

"What's the occasion?"

"You know we work through Christmas?"

"Makes sense," the Greek said. "It's not a holiday here."

Fred shrugged. With this news, he'd never be able to focus on the hypotheticals of political violence. "I'm going to take a walk. But I'm excited for you."

Fred set out for the old city. His light jacket wasn't quite warm enough, a sure sign that he wouldn't run into the cruise ship crowds. He crossed Independence Avenue and walked down to the Straitside Road. It wasn't the fastest route, but the grayness off the water and the turn-of-the-century industrial docks fit his mood. Where the New Market Road hit the Straitside Road was the mosque built by the pirate Ali the Sword. Cervantes, captured by the pirate at the battle of Lepanto, worked as a slave building the mosque. At least that was what was said, marking it as the place that Cervantes met the mythical Cide Hamete Benengeli, whose work *Don Quixote* he translated into Spanish. Ali the Sword was an Italian turned Turk, known as the Sword not because he was brave but because he could cut through enemy ships and make his escape. Appropriately, the mosque had all the trappings of the grand dome-and-spire imperial style common in the old city, but the interior was small and dark.

He came to the landing of the old inlet bridge. Across the water, the Sublime Tower of the Cannonball Palace peeked out from a patch of autumnal trees. If he were to crop out the Strait with its bustle of ferryboats, he could be looking at a small town in Connecticut in October. The fishermen along the span moved from manning their rods to warming themselves at coal braziers like yo-yos. For a scene of a thousand people, hundreds of thousands more implied in the maze-like marketplaces of the old city, it was calm. Even the gulls seemed absent.

The earthquake would be brief, its epicenter out in the north of the Marble Sea. Right in front of where Fred was standing, the tunnels beneath the Black Town tram stop would collapse. The ornate bank headquarters built during the Ottoman decline would fall like dominos into the pit, finally burying the underground gun shops that had bothered Virginia on their walks. The bridge would likely survive. Maybe fishermen and those sitting on the pontoons drinking beer would be thrown into the inlet's water, blued and vibrating sympathetically with the land around it. Up the banks, the cheap new developments in the Milky district, the Paper House district, and the Treasury district would sluice off their hillsides and into the shallow tip of the inlet. A modern, comprehensible disaster. Something that could happen in Seattle. But on the ancient peninsula, the quake would be history in reverse. The vast Grand Palace compound, over which the Six Minaret Mosque was so callously built, would shake off that overblown edifice with all its precious tiles. The countless cisterns, many known only to the great heroin cartels of the seventies, would collapse, depriving the skyline of its palisade of minarets. Perhaps the only great building that would survive would be the Holy Wisdom, either by the grace of the archangel Michael who served as the church's personal protector, or by virtue of the sacred daub mixed by Mohammed himself and sent from Mecca to patch the church after it was damaged in a sixth-century earthquake. Or it would simply remain because it had, weathering countless events, including the sixteenth-century "lesser judgment day." Either way, Fred imagined the city turning back fifteen hundred years in fifteen seconds. No doubt he would die. Probably not from injury, but by being a friendless foreigner with no water and miles of densely and desperately populated city between him and his consulate. The Americans had moved way up the Strait after the various hostage crises in neighboring countries. The prospect of the earthquake made the tips of Fred's fingers tingle.

He crossed the bridge into the chaotic marketplace. He cut left as quickly as he could to dodge the cheesemongers, the spice sellers, and the exotic animal bazaar. He was taking the fastest route to the Holy Wisdom, one he and Virginia mostly avoided because it followed a road perennially congested with box trucks hauling an infinite variety of textiles and tchotchkes. He wove through their idling exhaust. It was a steep road, such that the trees around the Holy Wisdom shielded it from view until you were almost right in front of it. It was a massive, hulking building. More a place to hide the darkness of a divine secret than one to let in the light of God.

He had only been inside once. He and Virginia had swallowed their pride and bought a package tour soon after their arrival. In six brisk hours, they saw all the sites of the ancient city, from the harem of the sultans (the guide was eager to talk about how much music and art the girls practiced, and less about how they filled the rest of their time) to the historic market (the guide was eager to introduce the tour to his cousin, who had a carpet stall, just for a hot glass of tea and a lesson in how to choose a carpet). After, they swore they would never do any of it again. But there was one piece of unfinished business, Fred felt, for him at the Holy Wisdom. The Weeping Column. It was a column in the northwest corner of the building, where some or other early martyr was interred. The column had a hole in it, where you could feel the dampness of the martyr's tears. It was said that if you kept your thumb in the hole and managed to turn your hand in a full circle, the martyr would grant you one wish. Fred and Virginia watched a couple tourists fail at it and opted to take in each and every stern depiction of Christ rendered out of chips of glass rather than wait in line.

There was no line today, but Fred did not approach the column immediately. Instead he walked to the empty middle of the building, beneath the dome's apex. At the four corners where the dome met the walls of the building, there were mosaics of four seraphim. Only one was uncovered, the rest plastered over in keeping with the Islamic prohibition against images. And also perhaps because it was said that anyone who laid eyes on one of the burning cohort would be reduced to ashes. They were the angels who stood between man and the garden and between God and the other angels. They were kin to the watchers, who in the book of Enoch fell, having lusted after human women.

This one, just a face peering out of his fiery wings, looked concerned. It was the face of someone who knew something bad was about to happen because they had seen it happen so many times before.

Finally Fred approached the column. He'd been thinking about how he was going to perform the circle. Even if he started with his wrist fully pronated, elbow in the air, he wasn't sure if he could complete a true circle and keep his shoulder in its socket. Perhaps this was why the Holy Wisdom didn't have a reputation among charm seekers on the level of the Polish Black Madonna or the Hill at Tepeyac. But he was going to give it a try, because he had a wish.

With his elbow in the air, his back nearly to the column, he stuck his thumb in the cold, damp hole. He felt the seraphim watching. He snapped his body around, feeling his fingers sweep a diameter out along the column. But just as he passed three hundred degrees, he could go no farther. He stood there for a long moment, bent over like the column had him in a wrestling hold. He willed, to his greatest ability, his hand to continue following its circular path. But he had no luck, literally.

The Greek was still in the apartment when he got back. He was sitting at the kitchen table, which he never did. At least never when Fred wasn't already there. He looked much more like a person who'd lived with his wife and kid in a single bedroom for months only, emerging at night, than one who'd just moved to a Greek island.

"What did you tell them?" The chair wasn't holding the Greek anymore. He was up in Fred's face.

"Who?" was all Fred could manage. It was funny. He wished he were again holding the Jack Daniel's bottle he'd refused Virginia the chance to crack over the Greek's head at their first meeting. In the end, it would have been money well spent.

"They bought up all the deeds."

"Who?"

"The goddamned Turks is who. Said they were Armenians, to hear my uncle tell it."

The Greek had called LA to ask about the deeds. He said he wasn't sure if he even wanted to go through with it. But it was hard, maybe impossible, to pass up the possibility entirely. So he phoned up an uncle he knew had one. There'd been a "collector" of Ottoman memorabilia. An Armenian, some distant relation of the bubble-assed family who were famous for being famous, had put out ads in local papers. He would pay top dollar for anything, but was most interested in documents. Was going to set up some kind of library in his mansion in the Glendale foothills. The Greek's uncle had gotten $500 for his deed. Others had let theirs go for less. Everyone his uncle knew had gotten on the bandwagon, times being what they were. And besides, wouldn't these things be better kept in a library, for posterity? So everyone knew what wrongs had been done to them all those years ago in the City?

"Shit," Fred said.

"Yeah. So I'm thinking, no coincidences in this place, right? Whoever had enough power to enact a law to validate the deeds could easily have tracked them down and bought them up. The Directorate of Foundations has records of all the minority owners of buildings here from back when the minorities were taxed at a higher rate. Wouldn't take much more than an internet search to see where they ended up after the pogroms. But what I want to know is who's behind it, and where they got the idea."

"I know someone," Fred said, though he already had an inkling of what Eddie might tell him.

"Well, get him on the horn. They already tried to steal this City once—I'll be damned if they do it again."

Eddie said he was just walking out of a meeting.

"With who?"

"Ayhan Aksoy. Seems he's turning his attentions from building Legoland versions of the City to downtown revitalization. Looks like I'm going to be working a lot more in your neighborhood. In fact, I'll be there tomorrow to scope out his new properties. You want to get lunch? There's a great new place. First of many. You're even going to get a Thai restaurant, if you can believe it."

Fred had nothing to say, so he just hung up the phone.

"What did he say?" The Greek had been at his shoulder the whole time.

Instead of responding, Fred pulled up Ayşe's number and punched call. He didn't know what exactly he was going to say. When it went straight to voicemail, he was just going to say "Bitch," but the word died in his mouth. Was it even her fault? The otherwise unemployed daughter of a real estate developer? He'd given her the tour, bragged about expats buying up places cheap, using Eddie to fix them up. She probably just mentioned it over dinner. Fred could picture it, between the bites of broccoli or mac and cheese or whatever absurdly Western meal they would eat together. Ayşe trying to reach out and engage with a man who probably expected her out of his house a decade ago. "You'll never guess where I spent the evening. You'll never guess how much it's changed. All the young people, hip, with money."

"Who were you calling?"

"Typhoid Mary" was all Fred could muster. He thought about the ads he'd seen in Providence just before he and Virginia moved: LUXURY LOFT LIVING: UNITS START AT ONLY $200,000. He'd been living there for free, too.

"So it is your fault." Fred half expected the Greek to punch him after he explained Ayşe and everything. But instead he slumped into a chair. "This City," he said. "If you don't conquer it, it conquers you."

When Fred sat next to the Greek, he truly felt as if he were among the numberless Bulgars, Avars, Arabs, Vikings, heretics, and companions to the Prophet who'd tried to have the City for themselves and ended up dead far from home. But unlike all those who had come before him, he at least had a bottle of whiskey.

———

They'd emptied it, gone out and bought another at great expense. Neither of them could stomach the idea drinking aniseed liquor.

"At least you are done with this place," Fred said, letting his drunk slide ever closer to self-pity. "I don't know what I'm going to do."

"Live out your days telling anyone who'll listen how much better this neighborhood was before it got a Thai restaurant. That, or establish a paper-writing empire."

"That's not who I am," Fred said.

"Had me fool." The Greek poured himself three fingers. "Fooled, I mean."

"There's got to be something we can do to stop them."

The Greek laughed. "I'm going to make sure that if I ever write a character who says something like that, they get killed within five pages. We gotta stop them, Captain America. We gotta stop them, Batman. No, we're going the way of the square protesters, the gypsies, and all those who came before, my wretched progenitors included."

"Wretched progenitors?"

The Greek cracked a drunken smile. "I have to thank you for that thesaurus. Changed my life."

"I have to ask you," Fred slurred, "how do you do it? Write these essays. I keep trying. I mean, I should be great at it, answering my own goddamn question."

"You have to pack the middle with inside jokes. The students may not write, but the teachers don't read either."

Fred should have felt embarrassed, but instead he balled out laughing.

"Yeah." The Greek chuckled a bit himself. "I especially liked the political violence prompt. I'd write something like, the solution to the Kurdish problem is to put the textile factories on the back of trucks, or lorries if I was writing for that Irish guy, and ship them out to the desolate east. Then I'd bomb the ones who had moved to the City. Bombing them out east just forces them to move in with their cousin Ali, here to look for work. When there is none, you've got mad dudes with nothing but time. Then a police station gets blown up. Why not give them some encouragement to do the opposite, switch the carrot and the stick."

"The generals like blowing up the ones in the east. Just like the British liked chasing down foxes."

"Probably true, but not much of an argumentative thesis." The Greek took a healthy swig. "Anyway, it doesn't matter now. I've got a tiny house on an island where people live to be a hundred on local wine and olives. I've got a whole repertoire of spy novels to rewrite."

"And you have this place," Fred tossed in, more out of self-pity than anything.

"Fuck this place." The Greek drained his glass.

It was a bad idea, but it didn't seem to matter.

"What about the guy who thinks he owns it?" the Greek slurred. The sun was up. He'd already packed what was left of his stuff, just tossing it in pell-mell.

"Yeah, I don't know. He's probably dead."

"In another country," the Greek added with still-drunk poignancy.

"But what do you think? You're the owner. It was your family's."

"They left it behind. They're doing fine. Los Angeles is paradise, or haven't you heard. As for me, I've got the other half of my life. More than half, if I catch up on that island diet."

"Okay," Fred said. "Then I think I'll do it."

"Fine. My money is out by Friday. I'd advise you to do the same. Anyone puts it together, you'll be a straight-up terrorist. Last time I checked, they get it worse than American students trying to smuggle out hash."

They didn't really know how to say goodbye, standing in that same hallway they'd never said hello to one another in. Both men were drained and drawn, they'd hit themselves with the bottle. They finally shook hands, and the Greek made his way out. As he left, he said, "What you are talking about doing, it's a better end than what I'd wanted for the place. I just worry you are too stupid to pull it off. But you have my blessing, and the blessing of all of my kin who made this place their home."

And so Fred was finally alone in the apartment. The Greek had, for some reason, felt compelled to put Virginia's stuff back as it had been in her studio, the room he'd claimed without any particular regard when he'd first moved in. There was the easel and the paints box sitting squarely in the center of the otherwise empty room, turned favorably toward the window. On it was the canvas Virginia had been working on, before everything. Fred had entirely forgotten it, just as he'd forgotten the cat. When they first moved to the apartment, there had been a building cat, a thuggish tabby who managed to lay claim to the stairwell and lobby. Other cats might have ventured in, but he drove them off. That he had entered their lives was pure chance. On their first trip to the grocery, they'd picked up a bottle of what they believed to be milk. Instead it was a popular local drink, a mix of yogurt, water, and salt. Totally undrinkable. But the cat lapped it. It would lap up a whole saucer in a desperate second. Then it would hack a bit, probably because of the salt.

At first the saucer remained on the doorstep. But in those early days, when no one knew they were there, Virginia was happy to have the cat come in. Fred was allergic. He tolerated the cat in the apartment, Virginia nicknamed him Romeo. Then the day came that the cat didn't return. No other cat took his place, but he did not return. Virginia was beginning to paint the foreign contours of their neighborhood, doing one canvas for each window. "And I'm going to put a little orange cat in each," she'd said, "just for me." On the canvas, just a tiny flash between a cascade of grey bow-fronts, the flame of Romeo's tail. Fred took it as a sign.

Fred had no problem finding his way back to the building in Silver Water, but he figured he couldn't just walk in. So he set himself up in a darkened doorway, hoping his friend would be coming or going before he got too cold. He wished he smoked. Thankfully, it wasn't too long before a van pulled up to the courtyard's entrance and a number of paranoid figures in olive drab emerged. His friend was among them. In the low light, Fred could appreciate that he wasn't a particularly handsome man, that behind his Castro beard he had a round and anonymous face. Without having fully thought things through, Fred stepped out from the doorway's shadow and said, "Hey, did you see you guys in The Wolfman? He said he drew you duking it out with the cops."

There was a stunned silence. Fred braced himself. He didn't know if the cartoonist had followed through with his stoned request. Then his friend said, "You couldn't tell it was us. We were off in the back while the Wolfman was chatting up some chick with boobs and a construction hat, isn't it?"

"Well, you can't blame him, can you. But look, I don't mean to interrupt, but I have a proposition for you."

———

Over tea, Fred outlined the plan. It was simple really. He was going to give them the paper scheme, along with the apartment to run it. He'd help them through the stack of final essays from this semester, and then he'd leave it in their hands. They'd have to figure out how to get the books from the Castle library, but beating the main gate guards and the librarians should be a piece of cake compared with bombing a police station. As he explained the rest to them, he saw himself as heir to all the slaves who'd shaped the City, from the black eunuchs, to the Viking guard, to the "new troops" composed of abducted Christian boys, to the harem girls, to the Greeks of the Lighthouse District, to the Kurdish revolutionaries. And now the English teachers. But really, when he'd finally finished laying it out, was he doing anything more than writing a childish love note to two women who'd moved on?

"But our English is not good," his friend said.

"Which is why this is perfect. The one of the hardest things is to write convincingly poorly. It will come naturally to you at first."

"I'm not sure." The Kurd wavered. "This is not how we make our revolution."

"Think of it this way. Did you, or your friends here, go to college?"

"No. That would have been impossible."

"Well, writing these essays, that's like going to college. What you learn about logic. You'll learn to tell people about your cause better. Trust me, you'll be writing about it a lot. And guess who is paying you to go to college? The children of your enemy, who are all too happy to give you both their money and their education. I don't see how you can pass this up. And if you don't like it, you can quit any time. All it means is a bunch of Castle kids will fail their writing course again."

His friend consulted with the others. The van was in the building courtyard, and it seemed to cast a shadow on them, even though it was they who loomed above it. Finally he said, "Okay, some of us will try."

Fred hardly slept in the weeks leading up the end of the semester. He didn't drink either, though he was much tempted reading over the Kurds' first attempts. It was like he was back to really teaching at the Castle, though he really wanted to teach now. And mercifully, his students really wanted to learn. At first he'd have them all work on the same essay, spread around the apartment like they were taking a makeup exam. Then he'd hold a seminar where they'd all read each other's attempts and he'd help them critique themselves and their peers. They were working to the last minute, the tea robbing their mouths of every drop of spit, but they filled all the orders to Fred's satisfaction.

When one of the Kurds ran the last of them to the Pirate's bookshops, Fred took a minute to look around the apartment. It was Christmas Eve, which made it no different than any other Wednesday night. The whole place was under a veil of cigarette smoke, like the coal fog outside had found a way to creep in. He gazed out one of the windows at the light layer of snow that had settled on Throat-Cutter Lane. Everything about the City was so ill-suited to winter: the tea gardens, the fish houses, the alleyways full of beer bars. They closed down so thoroughly you'd think there were only fourteen people living in the City, instead of fourteen million. The apartment had mostly been converted into a war room, with sample papers, outlines, and early drafts tacked up on the walls. Full ashtrays were smoldering on every surface. The sink was a bouquet of empty tulip tea glasses.

Only one part of the living room remained as a kind of shrine to the fact that people had once lived there. There, crammed together, were Virginia's instillations, the carpet he'd splurged on. The stacks of books on local history. The liquor cabinet. All Virginia's art supplies. Fred sat down on the couch with his laptop, which he'd lent to one of the Kurds. He bought himself a ticket back to America for the day after the semester ended, just before New Year's. It was probably twice what it ought to have been, since it was inside that holiday week, but he could give a fuck. He'd go to the bank the next day and transfer what he'd saved to a US account. Tell the guy he was going to buy a home in the country where he belonged.

There were two suitcases stored beneath the bed. One was massive, army deployment size. When they'd moved to the City, they'd packed it with all their aspirational clothing. The nice dresses, the oxford shirts. Their thrift-store threads went back to the thrift store. They were going to be real people, adults, with jobs and a home. The other was a carry-on, a cheap one they'd bought here for local trips. On their weekend in Bulgaria, Fred pulled the rolling handle right off the bag. Not even Ata could fix it. He decided to take that one. He filled it in a purely sentimental way: the now too-tight leather jacket he'd had since college, his "Poison's Greatest Hits Motorcycle Club" T-shirt, the Turkish bathrobe Ayşe had worn after their only night together, the one he'd thought she'd be wearing all the time. Then he put in all his socks and underwear that didn't have holes, and all his shirts that didn't have sweat stains. This didn't even fill the bag. He went and got Virginia's painting. He removed the staples that held it to the stretcher and rolled it into the corner of his bag.

His friend came by, wondering if he wanted to spend Boxing Day with them watching the English soccer matches. It was the one day a year they allowed themselves to break discipline and drink beer. They'd like it if he'd celebrate with them. But then he took note of the suitcase. He faced Fred, and with square shoulders and something of a true soldier's demeanor, he formally thanked him for everything he'd done for the City.

The taxi driver who took him to the airport was perfect to the type: tea-cured skin, cigarette dangling, permanent squint. Fred found himself making small talk in pigeon Turkish, mostly so the driver would know not to try and rip him off en route. He wasn't going to end his time in the City negotiating the indignities of a luggage fee. As they crossed the pontoon bridge, he saw the Holy Wisdom among the ancient hills, hulking and grey and cold in the sun, and did not give a damn about it.

The driver, as if compelled, said, "Istanbul, beautiful."

AUTHOR'S NOTE:

As a work of fiction, this book takes a number of liberties in depicting life in Istanbul in the early twenty-teens. The most egregious is the novel's timeline, which compresses and shuffles events beginning with the 2008 demolition of the Sulukule neighborhood through the summer 2013 Taksim Gezi Park uprising, with the 2011 Roboski massacre and Super Bowl thrown in between for good measure. I would like to apologize for this misrepresentation, along with the impossible walk described in the second chapter. The sites mentioned there represent a kind of personal geography plucked from the neighborhoods of Çukurcuma, Cihangir, and Tarlabaşı. It is also, as ever, worth noting that the characters in this book are fictional. Any resemblance to actual persons, living or dead, is purely coincidental.

The intellectual underpinnings of the book are the writings of the historians Amy Mills, particularly *Streets of Memory: Landscape, Tolerance, and National Identity in Istanbul*; Jason Goodwin, particularly *Lords of the Horizons: A History of the Ottoman Empire;* and Richard Bulliet's lectures on medieval Persia and the modern Middle East. Also the work of anarchist writer Hakim Bey, particularly *Pirate Utopias*, and Rafil Kroll-Zaidi's striking piece "Byzantium: Their ears were uncircumcised..." from the May 2012 issue of *Harpers*. The

Taksim protest graffiti mentioned was originally selected and translated by Elif Şafak for *The Guardian*. For better or for worse, it is also impossible to separate my thinking about the city from the work of the great Orhan Pamuk.

I'd like to thank Shya Scanlon and Alex Young for their help with earlier drafts of the book, and Nathan Deuel, Kelly McEvers, Anthony Swofford, and TC Boyle for their early support. Also Pamela Grove and Gerald Nelson for use of the Clifton, where much of the early work on the book happened, and the University of Southern California, which has funded me through the later stages. Thank you to everyone at Dzanc, especially Guy Intoci, who championed this book off a cold submission, and Michelle Dotter, who whipped it into shape. Thank you to my family: Jean, Dave, Don, Wendy, Jesse, and Chris. Thank you to my parents Carmen and Jos, who passed me the wanderlust gene. Thank you to Nora Lange, my partner in all things, with whom I wrote this, under the orange tree in the backyard. And to all my friends in Istanbul then and now, the immortal words of Pir Sultan Abdal as sung by Selda.